LINEAGES *and* LIES

LINEAGES *and* LIES

A Nick Herald Genealogical Mystery

Jimmy Fox

Writers Advantage
New York Lincoln Shanghai

Lineages and Lies
A Nick Herald Genealogical Mystery

All Rights Reserved © 2002 by Jimmy Fox

No part of this book may be reproduced or transmitted in any form or by any means, graphic, electronic, or mechanical, including photocopying, recording, taping, or by any information storage retrieval system, without the written permission of the publisher.

Writers Advantage
an imprint of iUniverse, Inc.

For information address:
iUniverse
2021 Pine Lake Road, Suite 100
Lincoln, NE 68512
www.iuniverse.com

This book is a work of fiction, and everything in it proceeds from the author's imagination.

ISBN: 0-595-25899-9 (Pbk)
ISBN: 0-595-65417-7 (Cloth)

Printed in the United States of America

Si ce n'est pas vrai, ça devrait l'être.
[If it isn't true, it ought to be.]

—JACQUES VULPINE
19th-century New Orleans
historian and bon-vivant

Chapter 1

Nick Herald stared at the back of the elevator operator's gold-braided scarlet tricorn cap. The man kept to himself.

Not a bad idea, Nick thought. He'd probably do the same, after an evening of ferrying cops up to a murder scene. New Orleans cops with lots of questions.

Nick watched the palsied arrow jitter past numerals on the gleaming brass plaque above the doors as the elevator made a slow, vibrating, moaning ascent. A hidden bell dinged arthritically, imprecisely, to mark the passage of each floor.

Concentrating on details that normally would have amused him did nothing to slow his racing heartbeat. His friend was dead, and Nick had too many reasons not to suspect natural causes.

The Grande Marchioness was one of New Orleans' oldest, priciest, and most eccentrically charming hotels—a gracious courtesan in the sleazy, endearing period farce that is the French Quarter. Nick had always liked the establishment. Other guests had certainly died here over the years—of pleasure, more than likely—but after tonight, after this death, he wasn't sure he could have the same fondness for the quaint landmark ever again.

The eggplant-skinned elevator operator in his elaborate uniform said without turning, "Tenth floor, sir." Then he slid back the shiny brass gate, opened the outer doors, and waited for his passenger to come out of his reverie.

But Nick stood motionless in the ornate elevator.

Was it too late to turn back? Twelve hours ago he'd been an unassuming genealogist trying to make reasonably honest but paltry bucks; now he wondered if he might be a few steps from those terms of culpability DAs sprinkle into felony indictments.

"Tenth floor," the operator repeated, with a lateral glance of impatience. "Sir?"

"Yeah, thanks," said Nick, shaking his head a little, brushing his graying brown hair off his forehead, as if doing so might allow him to see things more clearly.

His musing brown eyes now registered the runway of floral arabesque carpet that stretched out grandly before him. He stepped from the elevator and started walking, trying to pin down just why he was so sure his friend Bluemantle had been murdered.

Scowling husbands stood sentinel in their robes outside the majestic paneled doors of their rooms; wives peeked around their spouses at the noisy investigation down the hall.

"What's going on, officer?" a bald-headed man with a field marshal's waxed and twirled mustache demanded of Nick.

"Are you with the hotel, young man? I want to complain!" barked another husband, who looked like a bad-tempered, obese pug on its hind legs.

Nick owed these tourists nothing. He owed the dead man in the room down the hall much more.

Two attractive young women in skirts and blazers, no doubt MBAs from the upper reaches of the hotel's organizational chart, conferred together in the hallway below a sconce dripping with crystal. Their pinstripes bent into unaccustomed acute angles of indecision. Both women paused to give Nick the once-over; they seemed not too displeased with what they saw, before liability angst reclaimed their full attention.

Nick stiffened his posture and puffed out his chest a bit, hoping to add some phantom bulk to his thinness. *Vain even in a crisis.* Sometimes he disgusted himself.

Maybe they'd been in his English classes. He couldn't place them. Like a half-remembered dream, the reality of his former life as an academic was fading.

Near the hotel women, two paramedics squatted outside Woodrow Bluemantle's room, packing gear in orange boxes. They took their time.

A uniformed NOPD cop emerged from the room but was called back in; paraphernalia on his belt clacked as he pivoted. When he re-emerged, he ushered Gillian Vair not too gently by the elbow toward Nick. She'd been crying but had just pulled herself together after a shock, Nick judged. Tears still glistened on her camellia-petal cheeks.

Maybe the cop was just holding her up. *The rough bastard!* Nick tried to control the protective tension spreading through his body like a virus.

She wore silk—a bold-print tunic over baggy coral pants and sandals. Clothes for a fun evening. She was the same delicately beautiful blonde he'd met earlier that day at the genealogical seminar downstairs, except that now her raiment of poise quivered like the shantung caressing her to such great advantage.

Despite her agitation she looked gorgeous, glamorous, the kind of woman who turned heads in restaurants and inspired drunks in bars to say crude things.

At least he'd been wrong about being stood up. He was glad he'd donned a tie, even if it was fifteen years old. *Isn't wide back in?*

They were to have met downstairs. What was she doing up here? Nick put the disturbing question aside for later.

Gillian's face morphed instantly from anxiety to relief, as if she'd just seen her lover after a long absence. "Nick, I tried to find you," she said, her voice unsteady, a touch desperate. "He's…he's dead!"

"Come on, miss," the big cop grumbled.

His nametag told Nick he was New Orleans Irish; his beefy torso suggested he knew every lunch special in town. Gillian seemed as vulnerable as an origami hummingbird against the light-blue bulk of the cop's uniform shirt.

"Hey!" Nick said, maybe a bit too forcefully. "Go easy, will you?"

His protest worked. The cop's firm grip gave way to a gentle hand on Gillian's fragile spine.

As they passed Nick, the cop pointed at him and nodded his head to another uniformed cop, a woman the color of chamois, who now stood at the door of Bluemantle's room. She nodded in reply.

Cop sign language, Nick assumed. He should have kept his mouth shut. His cockiness began to chill with his sweat. You cross a New Orleans cop and you're liable to end up in the hospital—if you're lucky.

A hotel functionary ran in front of Gillian and the big cop and unlocked a door to a room. Nick started to follow.

"You want to give me your name?" a woman's voice said behind him. A command masquerading as a question.

He turned to see the female cop, her big shoulders testifying to frequent hard exercise, her cocoa forearms reminding Nick of sinewy crape myrtle limbs. She was about his height—5' 10"—tall enough to be adequately intimidating.

What an epic tale must be coded in her Louisiana genes! A veritable living map of ancient folkways: African, Southeastern Indian, French, Spanish, probably Portuguese, too, by the looks of her surname. As a professional genealogist, he was fascinated; as a possible murder suspect, he was too uptight for chitchat.

Nick gave her his name and the address of his apartment, which was not far away, on Dauphine. She wrote down the information in her notebook.

"Were you acquainted with the deceased?" she asked.

"Who's dead?" he replied, even though he knew.

She chose not to answer. "Would you come with me? A detective will want to talk to you. Please don't touch anything and step only where I direct you."

She turned occasionally, studying him, as they walked into the entryway of the suite and veered left to follow a strip of yellow crime-scene tape on the floor. "POLICE LINE DO NOT CROSS," it warned repeatedly, as if in a vain attempt to circumscribe with mere words the infinitude of crime. The narrow tape snaked along the edge of the main room and led to the dressing and bathroom area. Many shoes had tramped this route already; a few more wouldn't make much difference, Nick figured.

Across the suite, two plainclothes cops pointed flashlights into a dainty trash can painted with pastoral scenes. They straightened up as the female cop parked Nick and walked over to them. After a muted conversation, she came back and asked Nick to follow her again.

"We need you to ID the deceased, if you can," she said.

Nick had never been in a police line-up, but he thought this was how it must feel. Three sets of eyes watched him intently. Were they searching for signs of guilt, waiting for a blurted confession? Nick realized the two men must be detectives. The pressure was almost enough to make him believe he'd actually done…whatever they wanted him to admit.

The magnificence of the room momentarily distracted him. In more prosperous days of scholarly grants and anthology royalties, he might have stayed in a suite like this. Really first class: high ceilings, chandeliers, antiques, oil paintings, fresh flowers, French windows with extravagant layers of curtains. Bluemantle had been living like a high roller. Nice work for a dipso has-been genealogist.

The cleaning staff had waged a losing battle with Woodrow Bluemantle's legendary boorish habits during the past week or so of his stay. A suitcase that might have been a relic of Mississippi steamboat days disgorged his scruffy belongings. On desks, bureaus, and nightstands were a dozen or two of the mini-bar bottles—empty. The huge bed looked like Lake Pontchartrain during a hurricane.

Magazines, typed pages, reams of photocopies, and books lay scattered about on the carpet. An old portable typewriter sat on a desk. A pen had leaked on a cushion of an exquisite damask sofa. Nick suspected the mess wasn't all Bluemantle's doing. Someone had been looking for something.

The corpse lay face up on the marble floor of the outrageously luxurious bathroom. Like a beached ship a nearly empty bottle of expensive brandy occupied a corner. Beside the body, a straight razor swam in a sickening wash of blood and amber liquid.

Nick and his guide stared for a moment at the horrible scene. "My papa used to use one of those to shave with," the female cop said abstractedly. "To kill hogs, too."

Bluemantle had been a traditionalist in trivial matters like shaving, an iconoclast in important ones like genealogy.

Nick felt himself go pale. He tried to swallow the snails of nausea crawling up his throat. True, he delved into human mortality every day, but only on paper. Death up close, with no intervening centuries and footnotes—especially the death of a friend—affected him with an unanticipated dread and sorrow.

"Do you know the deceased as"—she leafed a few pages back in her notebook—"Mr. Woodrow D. Bluemantle?"

"*Dr.* Woodrow D. Bluemantle," Nick said.

Recovering a bit, he forced himself to pay attention, to bring the dead past to life, as he did for his genealogical clients. What had happened in his friend's last moments?

Bluemantle had been shaving; that much was obvious. His face was still covered in lather withered and stained pink in a few places where the blood from his crushed skull had been soaked up. Sprucing up for their evening together, the three of them? Probably he'd been drunk; that evidence seemed to be all over the hotel room and the grisly bathroom floor. Being soused was Bluemantle's natural state, anyway.

Had he lost his balance, tripped over the dangling belt of the no-longer-white hotel terry-cloth robe he was wearing? Nick studied the sharp edge of the marble encasing the bathtub; there was a lot of blood there, some hair and scalp, too. Much of Bluemantle's left fourth finger was missing, cut off at the middle knuckle. Maybe that's what the detectives were searching for in the trashcan.

Bluemantle's eyes and mouth weren't quite closed. He seemed to be merely half-asleep, dreaming about a point of great genealogical import. Perhaps the "very interesting new things" he'd mentioned to Nick, earlier in the day.

The female cop and Nick left the suite, followed closely by one of the detectives. He was a white man about thirty years old, wearing an ugly beige polyester suit, a badge on his belt, and a pistol under his coat. Passing them, he diplomatically drew aside one of the hotel executives. He spoke in a low, calm voice to her; she adamantly shook her head.

To Nick, the detective looked like a senior in high school, but he undoubtedly pulled a lot of weight.

Another plainclothes detective was knocking on a door down the hall. The bumptious guests had become timid.

Suddenly, the hotel woman held up her hands and declared, "We've done all we can, Detective Bartly! I'm sorry."

Bartly turned, rolling his eyes in the universal gesture of a teenager making fun of a grownup who doesn't get it.

"We're trying to find another room to use," the female cop explained to Nick, public servant to taxpayer. "Appreciate your patience. Please wait here." She left him outside the suite, talked to Detective Bartly for a minute, and then crouched with the paramedics.

A chest-high strip of yellow tape barred the doorway now; Nick hadn't seen who put it up. Bartly ducked under it. Nick followed him as far as the tape would allow. Looking through the foyer and into the room, Nick saw him take a few steps on the carpet and stop. The detective's hands jangled change in his pants pockets as he regarded the crime scene his partner now diagrammed. Bartly seemed to be a human camera, and each nose-drawn breath was an exposure. He had a curly mop of sandy hair and wore thick round rimless glasses, tinted slightly green.

Not exactly NOPD standard issue, something of a misplaced, undernourished hippie, Nick was thinking.

"Where's the crime-lab unit, Ty?" Bartly asked, walking over to his partner, a stocky young black man in shirtsleeves and latex gloves, a very large pistol holstered upside down under his left arm.

"Too many murders," said Ty. "They're dropping like flies tonight."

"Too many of *our* guys under the magnifying glass," Bartly replied. "That's why we're shorthanded. Put in another call."

The two men continued to speak; Nick couldn't decipher the meaning, but he was almost positive he heard his name mentioned once or twice. Bartly pointed to various areas of the room that needed attention. Then he turned and locked eyes with Nick.

Nick instinctively took a half step backward as the detective walked toward him. *Hey, not me, pal! I didn't kill him.*

"Dave Bartly, Detective, Homicide, New Orleans Police Department." He didn't offer his hand. "What's it look like in there to you?" He tilted his head toward the suite behind him.

"A dead man," Nick said, arching a thick eyebrow, his self-confidence creeping back. He could do sign language, too: *Look, treat me like a fool and we'll get nowhere.*

A slight grin tickled the edges of Bartly's mouth. Nick knew he was dealing with a fellow smart-ass.

Bartly ducked under the tape. "What I mean is, do you think it was an accident or foul play?"

"That's your job, Dave."

"Would you mind coming down the hall so I can ask you a few questions?"

"Yeah, as a matter of fact I do," Nick answered, genuinely peeved now, fed up with the whole apparently disorganized circus. "I've been led around like a dog on a leash long enough."

"Maybe you'd like a more formal chat," Bartly suggested, testiness breaking through his politeness, "at headquarters." Then, in a less aggressive tone, "I promise, no bright lights or rubber hoses."

"Let's get it over with, then."

Bartly had commandeered a small service room at the end of the hall. Janitorial supplies filled metal shelving units. A card table and three chairs crowded together against one wall. Nick noticed above the table a calendar featuring a dramatic Resurrection and pious quotations in Spanish. Mingled smells of cleaning fluids, cigarettes, and spicy meals reached his nose.

They sat on the rickety chairs.

"So, let's start with how you're involved in this thing," Bartly said casually, as he opened his notebook and found the next empty space. "You seemed pretty curious back there."

"You're begging the question, aren't you, Dave?"

"I don't follow," said the detective.

"I'm not 'involved in this thing.'"

"What's your line of work, Mr. Herald?"

Police talk tacked elusively for a purpose, Nick realized: the sudden changes of direction were unnerving. "I'm a genealogist."

Bartly nodded, diverted by a thought. "In a way, we're both in the business of death, aren't we, Mr. Herald?"

"The blood is usually dry long before I investigate," Nick said, recognizing some imaginative depth in his questioner.

"I see what you mean. This one is ugly and very suspicious. Funny meeting a genealogist, like this. I've always been interested in learning about my own family," Bartly said, almost apologetically. "You know, where we came from, whether we have anybody famous—or maybe infamous—way back." Detective Bartly seemed pleased by his neat turn of phrase. "I guess you get that a lot, that sort of vague curiosity about family history."

Nick wondered if this was another devious investigative maneuver. Under normal circumstances, he would have been happy to mention that Welsh research could yield Bartly results. *No free advice for someone trying to hang a murder rap on me.* The evening was beginning to feel distinctly like a '40s noir crime film; unfortunately, it was distressingly real.

"Been at genealogy long?" Bartly asked conversationally.

"Long enough to know I'm not going to retire rich," Nick answered. "Like you New Orleans cops with your cocaine deals. I once taught English literature at Freret University."

"Oh, yeah…I thought your name sounded familiar."

Bartly looked at Nick with a show of new interest, but Nick was almost certain he was being finessed: Bartly must have known who he was at least since his conversation with Gillian.

"Something about plagiarism, right?" the detective remarked. "Made the papers and the TV." He seemed to be waiting for Nick to elaborate, but getting no response, he cast another lure. "Always wondered what really happened with that."

That makes two of us. Nick had fought the charge and lost; colleagues he had considered allies heeded insinuations instead of facts. Former friends nursing old grudges turned on him overnight. An old wound. He didn't intend to bare his scar to a stranger he hoped never to see again.

"I graduated from LSU, Criminal Justice," Bartly said, apparently somewhat off the track again. "So, Mr. Herald, I'll make this as short as I can. The deceased, Dr. Bluemantle, was a genealogist, too. There was a meeting here, right? You in on that meeting?"

"Just a spectator."

"What were you doing up on the tenth floor tonight, Mr. Herald?"

"I had an appointment with Dr. Bluemantle, in the bar. I knew him professionally." Enough of the truth not to be an outright lie. "We were going to talk shop, discuss research strategies. He was late; I came up. Is that a crime?"

Bartly took a deep breath, then released it slowly, as if practicing a meditation ritual designed to counter hostile vibes. "Okay, Mr. Herald. I know you're not happy to be here. Bear with me. You're acquainted with Ms. Gillian Vair. Want to tell me about that?"

"Not much to tell. I saw her for the first time today, at the Society of the *Allégorie*—"

"Come again?"

"The Society of the Descendants of the Passengers of the *Allégorie*. It's a group of people who share some familial link with the passengers and crew of a ship that sailed into New Orleans during the French colonial period."

"Oh. And you're a member?"

"No."

"But Ms. Vair is?"

"I don't know. Possibly. I just met her this morning." Nick massaged his forehead. "Look, I've already told you, I'm a genealogist. I go to things like that for fun."

Bartly pressed on: "But you know Ms. Vair?"

"Yes, I've said that already, too. We had a dinner date."

"And your appointment with Dr. Bluemantle? Sounds like a schedule conflict to me. You sure you got your story straight?"

"It's not my *story!*" Nick shouted. His hands were shaking; he put them in his lap, below the table. He cleared his throat and then continued in his normal voice: "It's how things actually happened. What's so strange about three people planning to have a drink and then go out to dinner?"

Nick realized anew his reason for avoiding the police whenever possible—aside from guilt over the venial sins he occasionally committed for convenience, fun, or profit. Talking to a cop was like getting stuck in flypaper.

It would be easier to tell Bartly everything. More or less.

Chapter 2

Droning April rain had drenched the perpetually soggy Crescent City since daybreak that Friday morning. It was just after ten, and Nick sat in the audience in one of the rococo meeting rooms of the Grande Marchioness Hotel. The program booklet for the seminar told him that the tall man wearing the sparkling Ray Bans at the lectern was Preston Nowell, Captain-Director of the Society of the Descendants of the Passengers of the *Allégorie*.

Nick had come here mainly hoping to snare a few clients from this crowd of family-history enthusiasts who could afford four-hundred-dollar hotel rooms. It had been a lean winter for him. He owed too many creditors, his one employee was badgering him for back wages, and his corduroy sport coat, khakis, and Russell chukkas looked too slovenly even for the ex-academic that he was.

But also he was here to talk with Woodrow Bluemantle, mentor and friend, who sat, apparently snoozing, behind the draped presentation table. Seven years ago, Bluemantle had taken a liking to Nick, then a dispirited, disgraced former professor of English trying to break into a new field, genealogy. It was an improbable friendship, the older man needing a disciple, the younger a tutor, though neither would have said so—the kind of impulsive and profligate friendship that blossoms and fades in a single season. Even if briefly, Nick and Bluemantle thrived in each other's company, discovering that they shared a faith in humanism, a hatred of hypocrisy, a penchant for perversity, and a passion for genealogical truth.

Bluemantle was not an easy man to know, as friend or enemy, and at last their mutual interests could not withstand their stormy individualities. Yet, Nick had always felt, the friendship had been worth the trouble, and worth a rainy April morning in an uncomfortable chair to revisit. In mischievous moments, he hoped that when he himself reached sixty, twenty years hence, he would be at least half the cantankerous renegade Woodrow Bluemantle was now.

Nick returned his attention to Preston Nowell, who was speaking with practiced ease. He sounded affable and learned, and he looked distinguished in his double-breasted blazer, the badges and ribbons of the society forming an impressive mane for his stag-like neck.

"We of the Society are justly proud of our descent from these intrepid pioneers of the ninth of October, 1731," Nowell said. "New Style, of course, for all of you thorough researchers out there."

"What does he mean, 'new style'?" whispered the young woman three empty seats to Nick's left.

She must have come in late, while he was daydreaming; he shouldn't have missed such a stunner. Was it true what he'd read recently in an article about the gradual waning of men's testosterone levels?

"I'll tell you later, over a drink," he whispered back, resolved to prove "male menopause" a myth. She smiled. They returned their attention to Preston Nowell at the lectern.

"And not only important in the history of New Orleans and Louisiana. Some of these names, indeed, can be traced back even further, to the momentous events and personages that have shaped Western Civilization…to the field of Crécy, to the Battle of Hastings, to the Domesday Book, even to the great Charlemagne himself. Our lineage has helped to make this city and this country leaders among their peers."

"Field of what?" the young woman asked. She was taking copious notes.

Nick's day was definitely looking up. What a pleasant change from the blue-haired women and their nodding husbands in the rows ahead of him. Retail genealogy usually attracts older folks like these, whose days have begun to collect moss. The children are grown, probably the spouse is dead. They seek new impetus from the lives of ancestors they believe were more adventuresome. But it's often a one-shot enthusiasm: after the initial thrill, they realize that their ancestors' lives were similarly undistinguished and disappointing, at least in a tabloid historical sense. The real joy of serious genealogy turns out to be more of an effort—physical, intellectual, and spiritual—than they thought.

This young woman...*Hmm, very nice.* Twenty-five, twenty-seven max, he guessed she was. Fashionably waifish but not compulsively thin, moderate-blonde hair cut loose, straight, and casual. Cognac eyes that had a delightful way of catching oblique light. She wore a cream jacket and pants, the coat having lots of pockets that lent her the look of a journalist on a desert assignment. Perfume...something expensive and subtle. Class, lots of class. Bites her left index fingernail while she writes. No wedding ring, but half a dozen other whimsical ones. He recognized at least one by Mignon Faget, the famous New Orleans jewelry designer.

Nick leaned toward her across the empty chairs. "Hundred Years' War, English victory, 1346, Edward III, Philip VI, the Black Prince. Sound familiar?"

"Oh, yes, of course. I'd forgotten," she said unconvincingly, her Waterman between her lips. "Thanks."

A woman with a lilac perm swiveled on them like a tank turret.

"Do y'all *mind*?" she said. "My husband and I have come all the way from Birmin-ham to hear the next speakuh. I would thank y'all to carry your convah*sash*un somewhere *else* so people can get their money's worth." Her husband slumbered on peacefully beside her, getting *his* money's worth.

Nick and his historically challenged neighbor made long faces at each other in a charade of contrition. *A good sense of humor, and a beauty, too! We're going to get along fine....*

At that moment, a heckler bounded up from the second row. Nick, enchanted as he was by his new friend, didn't register the first few shouted invectives. But now he heard how furious the young man was.

"You son-of-a-bitch! You're nothing but a con man. This whole thing is a bunch of *bullshit*! All you people, don't you see? It's bullshit! You're being lied to, cheated, just like my grandmother and all of her people before her!" The man faced the crowd now. He'd lost the thread of his tirade.

He was a balding, kinky-haired fellow, short and stuffed incompletely into his clothes; his stomach threatened to explode through the gaps in his shirt, his fat arms stretched the seams of his coat sleeves, and his bloated neck strained the crazy knot of his splotched tie. Sweating copiously, he swept the crowd with his gaze, his face flushed crimson with anger. Mad eyes paused on Nick.

"It's got to stop!" he shouted, more incensed than ever. "Somebody's got to stop it!"

He knocked over the two women sitting in front of him and, like an all-pro linebacker blitzing, he leaped the long, low table supporting Nowell's lectern, upsetting water pitchers and glasses and lavish flower arrangements and complimentary pencils and notepads. The next moment he had Preston Nowell in a headlock, delivering rapid-fire punches with his free fist.

Nick scrambled out of his chair and down the row, past the blonde, and ran toward the front of the room, arriving just in time to be grazed by the heckler, who was, oddly, airborne. Nowell had already broken from the man's grip and thrown him away like a sack of garbage.

Two burly security men rushed into the room and hustled the dazed man away.

"Thank you, sir," Nowell said, producing a comb for his mussed, receding light-brown hair. After cleaning his glasses with a tissue, he read Nick's nametag. "Mr. Herald. Again, many thanks."

"You didn't seem to need much help."

"Well, I keep rather fit." He seemed shaken, angry, out of breath, his mind only partly engaged in the conversation. "*Gentlemanly sports*, as they used to be called. I was also in the military, some years ago." The next moment he'd collected himself. "Are you interested in joining our group?"

"I'm a professional genealogist," Nick said. "Just trying to upgrade my knowledge."

"Oh, I see. Excuse me a moment. Ladies and gentleman, there's no reason we cannot continue. Please, be seated." And then to Nick, "Mr. Herald, I do appreciate what you've done. Perhaps you'd like to visit the Society library. You would be most welcome."

"Thanks," Nick said. "I've meant to for some time. Did you know that guy?"

"Most definitely, I regret to say. He has become fixated in an unhealthy way on genealogy."

"That can happen," Nick agreed, commiserating to be polite.

"In fact, he has anointed himself with specious grandiose lineages." Nowell sighed, straightening his tie and coat. "A comic-book character from his own diseased imagination. An unfortunate case.... You will excuse me, Mr. Herald. I would like to continue the program. Remember my invitation. It is genuine."

Nick returned to his seat.

Nowell cleared his throat several times for order. "Ladies and gentleman, I've been accused of giving boring presentations, but this reaches a new height of criticism." Chortles and titters. The unease was passing. "Please, if the program becomes too tedious, a simple word or two will suffice." Louder laughter. The tension seemed gone.

"And so, without further ado, I take the greatest pleasure in introducing the speaker you've all come to hear. Some of you have read his many thought-provoking books, or seen him on television. Perhaps you've become acquainted with him through his videotaped tutorials. Others will have the thrill of hearing him for the first time. Please join me in welcoming Dr. Woodrow D. Bluemantle, renowned genealogist and now Honorary Scribe of the Society of the Descendants of the *Allégorie*."

Nick glanced at the program booklet, as the decorous applause filled the room.

Woodrow Demosthenes Bluemantle, Ph.D., CG, CALS

Author of *Handbook on the Guise Manuscripts of Kentucky; Bibliography of Early Louisiana Purchase Sources; Pitfalls of*

King Philip's War Genealogical Research; Charlatanism in Our Midst; Salt Lake City Shakedown; More Money for Mormons; Ethnic Hustle: Genealogy for the Masses; numerous articles which have appeared in *The American Genealogist, National Genealogical Society Quarterly,* and other magazines; former syndicated columnist; former Assistant Compiler, Library of Congress; past Invited Lecturer, College of Arms Foundation; past visiting scholar, Bagwyn College and Samford University; former Fellow of the Am. Society of Genealogists; member of, and former advisor to, many lineage and patriotic societies. He is a Certified Genealogist and a Certified American Lineage Specialist.

They left out his shoe size, Nick thought. *Bluemantle must be a big catch for the Society.*

He was familiar with a few of these works by Bluemantle, and a handful not mentioned. None of them would make a good read on the beach; not exactly lucrative barnburners. A bit too recondite for the common taste. Nevertheless, most of his works bristled with a refreshing combative genius. Bluemantle had joyously trashed many undeserved reputations and sloppy theories, slaughtered many a sacred cow. He relished confrontation and wielded a wicked pen. Genealogists of lesser mettle around the country hated and feared him; no one knew where he would pounce next. Judging from the program, it seemed to Nick that there had been nothing very recent in the way of accomplishments from Woodrow D. Bluemantle.

Nick had heard the rumors at recent conferences. Bluemantle's years of insulting his peers, defiling marriages, and violating female students and clients had caught up with him. He'd been hounded out of Salt Lake City, his base for the past four or five years. He was receiving the collective cold shoulder. Now, he would never join the ranks of the Olympians of professional genealogy, transforming himself into a profit factory through writing and speaking, as he seemed poised once to do.

And here he was, neck-deep in retail genealogy, something Nick knew he despised. An irony bordering on the pathetic.

Now at the microphone, Bluemantle didn't seem ready. The applause had long since stopped. An awkward silence hung in the air. He donned his Franklin glasses, shuffled his papers, mumbled to himself, and smoothed back his unruly long gray hair several times, his hand finally pausing at the back of his neck as if to pull himself physically into his task. He surveyed the audience, slight confusion, slight irritation twitching across his aquiline face, still striking even though the last few years had manifestly not been kind to him. Women used to swoon for Woodrow Bluemantle. Nick was pretty sure he was tight.

But not too tight to make a great presentation. Nick heard echoes of the legendary venom, but also much of the old sharpness of mind, of the unconventionality and freshness which once had distinguished his approach to genealogical scholarship, which once had made even his bitterest enemies envious.

As a former teacher, Nick recognized the often misunderstood element that makes great teachers: joyous arrogance. Egoism so supreme that all self-consciousness and doubt fall away, leaving a pure, exhilarating conduit for the outpourings of a substantial intellect. Though they may despise his ideas, students never forget such a teacher. They might detest him personally, and in all likelihood he will be a monster outside the classroom. Yet, they will cut other classes, not his; for he has accomplished what teachers rarely do: he has awakened in them undying curiosity and the critical spirit. He has opened a door.

In a bit under half an hour Bluemantle surveyed seventeenth- through nineteenth-century Atlantic civilization; delved into the complexities of vital records in the American colonies under a rapid succession of European national flags; speculated on the personal histories of the passengers of the *Allégorie*; and explained the royal and commercial settlement projects. It was all no doubt too complex for the thirty or so novices who filled the lovely little room of the Grande Marchioness Hotel.

Preston Nowell, perfect master of ceremonies, took back the lectern and magnanimously led the clapping, a big grin of gratitude and pride on his boyish face. Nick wondered if he'd played basketball in high school, as he should have. Debate team, student-council president, history club…Nick had him pegged: highly focused at a young age, a miniature adult. As a youngster in Southern California, Nick had known the type—and had avoided them like the plague.

"Splendid!" Nowell said. "Really splendid, wasn't it, ladies and gentlemen? Thank you, Dr. Bluemantle!"

From his chair Bluemantle forced a smile that reminded Nick of the snarling grimace of some mythical beast on a coat of arms.

"I'm sure many in the audience will want to meet Dr. Bluemantle personally. He'll be standing by for autographs or advice, after a short interval of rest following his exertions, just behind you in our refreshment area. Thank you again, Dr. Bluemantle, for that enlightening presentation."

Bluemantle stood again to applause, gave a curt, insincere bow, and hurried to the rear of the room.

"Allow me now to say a few words about the Society of the *Allégorie*, as we refer to it in shortened form," Nowell continued. "Following in the wonderful tradition of these United States, *we* have endeavored to make candidacy in the Society as democratic as possible. There are quite a few lineage societies that actually discourage new membership. The candidate is subject to artificial rules, which serve only to give complete control to members jealous of their status. We believe, on the contrary, that these are outmoded, elitist practices, just what those brave souls on the *Allégorie* came to this new land to escape.

"We unconditionally welcome descendants of *all* relations of the brave group of colonists, whether lineal or collateral; brothers, sisters, cousins, in-laws, step-relatives, adopted children—each shares in the honor, each confers the rights of membership to you. This is what the passengers and crew of the *Allégorie* would have wanted, don't you agree? Families were so very important to them. Families that stayed together, families sharing in hardship as well as triumph."

The audience approved of these noble sentiments. No one dozed anymore.

"Well, ladies and gentlemen, we're here to lead you to exciting discoveries your own descendants will thank you for making. To help you find out if you're one of us, so to speak, the Society has prepared this outstanding do-it-yourself starter kit. It's only $235.75—a real bargain, I might add, for anyone with a general interest in tracing one's ancestry. Dr. Bluemantle has lent his expertise to the project, and you'll find his powerful insights into the wonderful world of genealogy."

Pens already hovered excitedly over checkbooks, credit cards danced in manicured hands.

"Of course, if you'd prefer to start with professional assistance, we can arrange that too, for a very reasonable fee. Our Society library, a landmark right here in New Orleans, is a superb repository of genealogical and biographical information. And with your starter kit, you are entitled to a special three-month period of access, at no extra charge.

"Now, allow me to guide you through the many, many useful elements of the starter kit..."

Nick decided to forgo the rest of Nowell's infomercial. The Society of the *Allégorie* and Nowell would monopolize any business Nick had hoped to land. He couldn't compete with such boiler-room tactics, however sugarcoated. A conversation with Bluemantle seemed a much more interesting option.

"What about that drink? You promised," the young woman said, pouting in a most alluring way as Nick exited the row.

"Because you're such a willing student, let's say dinner, too. I'm Nick Herald."

"Gillian Vair."

The soft *g* of her given name was pleasing to his ear. They shook hands.

The woman in front of them turned her head slightly to let them know she was bothered.

"Meet you here, the hotel bar, seven o'clock," Nick said. He waved a silent adieu as the lilac-permed woman reached threateningly for her umbrella.

◻

At the back of the room, Bluemantle watched his drink being made. "More! More! Go on…agh!" he complained acridly. "Here, I'll do it."

He snatched the bottle of brandy from the hesitant hands of the young man behind the mobile bar; he poured a gusher of it into his Milk Punch—now more punch than milk. Nick ordered a Mimosa.

"Nothing like a little bubbly on a rainy morning," Nick said. "Might even bring a smile to your face, Woody."

Bluemantle perfunctorily shook hands with Nick. "You've come to gloat, have you? Oh, how the great ones have fallen! Precisely why I didn't call you."

With mixed success, the Society had groomed him like a prize dog. His new suit was slightly big on him; he seemed to have lost some weight lately. He needed a shave—a small act of dissent, Nick supposed. But his bleary, flinty eyes still blazed with Rasputin energy, and his indomitable face, overhung by gray crags of eyebrows, was an icon of vengeance Michelangelo would have wanted to paint.

"Come on, you know better than that," Nick said. "Remember when we met in New York, at the gathering of the Flagon and Trencher? I was the one down in the dumps. You cheered me up with bawdy anecdotes of your life in genealogy. I'm just trying to return the favor. Your presentation was excellent, by the way."

"Ah, yes, the Descendants of Colonial Tavern Keepers," Bluemantle said, recalling happier times. "That was indeed a good meeting, made better by your presence, Nick. A damn jolly society. And ditto for the Descendants of the Illegitimate Sons and Daughters of the Kings of Britain. Never met a more enjoyable bunch of bastards! Genealogy as it should be: a celebration of life in all its lusty energy, its folly and its transcendence—not this insipid grasping for filthy lucre and vicarious status."

Bluemantle emptied his glass and burped. Nick couldn't miss his Society ring, a flamboyant piece of jewelry portraying the fabled ship sailing on a sea of emerald and framed by banners bearing the society's motto: *En Foi, Invincible!*, and at the bottom, *In Faith, Invincible!*

"You're working for the Society full-time, now, I understand," Nick said.

"*Ehnvehnsibleu*, indeed!" Bluemantle snarled mockingly, caustically, butchering the pronunciation of part of the Society's French motto.

"Utah got too crowded for you, huh?" Nick asked, still trying to get his old friend into a better mood.

Bluemantle's lips curled, as if he'd swallowed something disgusting.

"Don't move to Salt Lake City, Nick. A black hole, sucking in genealogy, homogenizing it, commercializing it."

Salt Lake City, where the Mormons had built the Wall Street of genealogy in the wilderness. From a tenet of their faith—that each church member was responsible for identifying ancestors and conducting rites for their salvation—the Mormons had changed the nature of genealogy in a matter of decades. Nick actually thought the Latter-day Saints were performing a priceless public service, rescuing and microfilming irreplaceable records, promoting awareness of family history with an admirable non-sectarian attitude. But he knew Bluemantle and his grudge against the genealogical establishment were inseparable. This was not a case of religious prejudice.

"I'll admit it's not easy to make a living here as a certified genealogist," Nick said. "In New Orleans, family history is half illusion, half vainglory, and nobody wants the real story. But you can believe I've never considered moving to Utah."

Bluemantle slammed his glass down. "Wise boy! Bartender, another, the way I like it," he demanded. "No Mardi Gras out there. No Bourbon Street depravity, so sad and disgusting it's fascinating. No world-class jazz, blues, and…what is it, Xylo-something? With the washboard and accordion?"

"Zydeco, you mean?"

"That's it! No soul-satisfying cuisine and the mindset to enjoy it. No Galatoire's, Antoine's, Commander's Palace, or Bayona. No heritage of moral rot, histrionic fatalism, and insane lust that has made this glorious city a continuous wonder simply because it hasn't been wiped from the face of the earth by God!"

Bluemantle had lost none of his fire and brimstone.

"Take my advice, Nick: get out of this tainted business now, before you become an old, bitter, impoverished intellectual whore like me. Before betrayal begins to seem the height of justice."

Nick detected some dark meaning within the torrent of words.

"I read your article," Bluemantle added, between sips. "The one on establishing the identity of colonial clerks through chirography. Quite good, except for some lingering postmodernist nonsense from your academic days. Yes, overall, rather a satisfactory performance. There are only a few things with which I would quibble."

"Tonight's your chance. Why not join me and a lovely woman for dinner? You can take me to task all you like."

"No," he sighed. "I'm a little tired." A lecherous gleam enlivened his eyes. "You say she's pretty?"

"The blonde in the seventh row."

"Ah, yes, I noticed her earlier. Quite enchanting. Quite. Your work in *that* area I cannot criticize. Anytime after seven, then." He grabbed Nick's coat sleeve, pulling him down the few inches to his face. "There are very interesting new things I must tell you, one gadfly to another. Shocking things…about—about lineages and lies. All is not Bristol fashion, shipshape." He was slurring. "But we must be discreet for now, content ourselves with puns and evasion: gadflies sometimes get squashed."

You're being discreet, all right, Woody; so discreet you're making no sense.

Nowell was fielding questions from the audience.

"This is not for *them*," Bluemantle said, a little too loudly, gesturing toward the audience. Several women shushed him. "They haven't a clue, never will. Professionals with specialized knowledge—*honest* professionals and scholars—we, yes, we are the ones, the only ones who should be doing the noble work of genealogy. This is anarchy, promulgation of confusion! If it weren't for my arthritis, I'd throw this damn ring into the river! Can't get the blasted thing off."

He tugged briefly at the ring, spilling some of his drink. Then, his eyes gazing into another time and place, he said, "Oh, my young friend, tonight I will spin you exciting tales, of the good old days when the fertile plains of genealogy were unfenced by these uninspired farmers. When the bold rider of history could marvel at sunrises over mountain ranges of unknown facts, forests of unguarded sources, canyons of unthought hypotheses, countless flocks of unindexed wonders. Ah, for those days of rapturous discovery.... Tonight, tonight, we toast the glories and ironies of this great masque of life! My new boss, P. T. Barnum up there, will foot the bill. Call me from the bar when it's time. I have work to do. I'm writing my memoirs, did I tell you?" He took two steps, but came back. "Thank you, Nick. You *have* cheered me up."

Then he stalked with drunken dignity out of the room.

Bennie, the bartender in the Chevalier Room at the Grande Marchioness, was a friend of Nick's. Otherwise, Nick wouldn't hang out with any frequency at such a ritzy place.

Here in the Chevalier Room, Nick rated special privileges. A few years back he'd discovered, in the course of some unrelated research, that one of Bennie's lineal ancestors was a colonial tavern keeper who had served Spanish Louisiana's Governor Galvez meat and drink, and then had served *with* the governor in successful raids against the British in West Florida. This discovery earned Bennie, after Nick completed the appropriate affidavits and applications, membership in the Flagon and Trencher and in the Sons of the American Revolution.

Nick relished a bit of stagecraft. He liked to bring his best clients to this bar, especially if they were the bibulous sort, to deliver his completed work in the elegant setting of antiques and crystal.

Bennie understood that when Nick showed up with a client, he and his excellent waitresses were to help Nick lose the battle for the check, while allowing him to retain a little face. They possessed a multitude of tricks for such occasions.

It was fitting that Nowell would have selected one of the best hotels in the city. The Grande Marchioness was the kind of place that runs a small ad in the *New Yorker* and *Town & Country*, and is booked solid for years. What better way, Nick thought, to attract potential members of a certain age and income than to gild the lily, lend their lineage a glamorous patina of Old World luxury, appeal to their snobbish instinct to stand out in the American mobocracy? Nick was beginning to appreciate Nowell's marketing savvy; the Society was a demographically targeted growth industry.

Facing the hotel's marble-encrusted entrance hall, at a table beside an interior wall of mullioned windows, Nick sat with his second Negroni, heavy on the Campari and lemon. Seven o'clock came and went. No Gillian Vair. Bennie had told him a woman had called three times before his arrival; no name, no number, no message. Nick decided he'd been stood up, and ordered another drink, content to intensify the buzz he was already enjoying. He looked around for a phone; he might as well call Bluemantle. It could still be an interesting evening, listening to his friend's tirade.

Bennie had just set his new glass down when two paramedics jogged through the entrance hall. A few moments later, two uniformed cops followed, radios squawking underneath their wet ponchos.

Demonstrating the traditional omniscience of bartenders, Bennie told Nick one of the guests had suffered a fit, died in his bathroom; word was, he hit his head big-time awful.

"Say, you mighta knowed him. One a dem whatchmacallem, like you." Bennie spoke with the mellifluous New Orleans accent of the Irish Channel and other working-class enclaves of the Big Easy: quasi-Brooklynese stirred by a swizzle stick of French, Spanish, Italian, and Caribbean, with a dollop of Southern drawl like so much cane syrup to slow things down. "Wit dis lineage society bunch."

Nick stood up quickly and reached for his wallet. "How much do I owe you, Bennie?"

"Nuttin', man. On de house. Come back and see us."

"Bless your ancestors, my friend."

Chapter 3

"That's it?" Detective Dave Bartly asked skeptically, when Nick had finished his explanation of the events leading him to the crime scene.

"Yeah, that's it. More or less." Nick had also volunteered his whereabouts for the afternoon: he'd worked at his office, alone, where he took two verifiable calls from clients; then he'd been at the downtown public library from roughly 5:15 to 6:15. This was his Friday to teach adult reading class.

It had taken the better part of an hour to give his account.

"Look," Nick said, not appreciating Bartly's veiled tone, "I've been more than cooperative!"

"We just want the truth."

"So what do you think that was, chopped liver?" Nick snapped. "Why are you picking on me? Talk to the heckler. Now there's a real suspect, if I ever saw one."

Bartly pinched the bridge of his nose, as if struggling with a difficult essay question on a test. Then, once again, he jingled the change in his pocket. *The meditation routine again. This guy's definitely done acid before, and enjoyed it, cop or no cop*, Nick thought;

that mesmerized dissociation with the moment was a dead give-away of past trips into other realms of consciousness.

Nick was beginning, if not to like him, at least to respect his tenacity and weirdness.

"Mr. Herald, there's no need to lose your temper. I assure you, we're talking to many other people. This is nothing personal."

"Well, it sure feels like it," Nick said, somewhat mollified.

"We don't know who or what's important just yet. For example, do you know why Ms. Vair was up here? She found the body and called the front desk."

"You'd better ask her that."

"Okay." The detective jotted a few words down. "From what I gather, Dr. Bluemantle had a few enemies. Would that be a fair statement?"

You don't have enough pages in that notebook, buddy. Nick simply shrugged an ambiguous reply.

Bartly pressed on. "You say he was wearing some kind of a ring when you last saw the victim alive? With a crest or a logo or something on it?"

Nick handed him the seminar program booklet, on which the Society's insignia was prominently displayed.

"Keep it," Nick said.

"Thanks a lot. I imagine that ring was valuable. Maybe we have a robbery here that turned violent."

"People get killed in New Orleans for a lot less," Nick said, by way of unfair indictment of NOPD for failing to read the minds of criminals before they struck.

"There's one other thing: a room service guy reported seeing a woman in the hall about the time Dr. Bluemantle met his Maker."

"Gillian, right?" Nick couldn't help thinking of that bizarre meeting between Bluemantle, with a list of grievances, and God.

"Description doesn't match her," Bartly replied. "White female, short brown hair, thirties probably, nice looking, large breasts….Not my words," he hastened to add. "This is a horny young waiter giving us the details. We're checking the women signed up for the seminar, but I understand they're all a lot older than our mystery lady."

"Battle-axes, every one. Can't help you with that, either, Dave. The hall was full of cops when I got there. No stacked brunette. But I'll certainly keep looking."

"If I were single, I would, too." He wrote in his notebook, paused, and gazed at his cheap ballpoint for a moment. "I was just wondering…you being the expert and all—mind if I give you a call on this case, if I have a genealogical question? Which seems pretty likely. We'll put it on the meter, of course…Professor." He grinned.

Nick decided Bartly was being deferential, not sarcastic. It was nice to hear the title again.

"Definitely. Call me," Nick said. "But I'm not billing for my help; maybe next time." He felt an obligation to his friend to find the murderer; Bluemantle would have done no less for Nick.

"Fair enough, Professor. I'll probably be in touch. So, I guess that's all," Bartly said. They stood up. "Before you go, can I see some identification? Standard procedure. Driver's license—if you don't mind."

"Will this do?" Nick took a traffic ticket from his wallet. Another damn left turn on St. Charles Avenue the day before. "New Orleans: the City of No Left Turns. Just look at that, Dave." Nick was still angry over being ticketed, though it was certainly not his first such infraction. "This is what NOPD is worried about, while genealogists are keeling over at the Grande Marchioness!"

Bartly studied the ticket and jotted some further notes. He handed it back to Nick.

"Genealogist," said the detective. "Singular, so far, and I hope it stays that way. But I get your hyperbole."

"You didn't skip English classes at LSU, I'm pleased to see."

"I'll take care of this for you," Bartly said, obviously tickled to be verbally jousting with a man of letters. "You'll be getting your license in a day or two. You can go now. And the department wishes to thank you for your assistance."

He offered his hand this time.

回

Gillian Vair took a long drag from her cigarette and then sipped her margarita. She savored each sip from the shallow glass, as if the milky green liquid and the encrusted salt around the wide rim were an antidote to a slow-acting poison sapping her strength.

They had come to this tiny French Quarter bistro after their separate sessions with the detective. Eleven o'clock was approaching.

She smoked almost reflexively, as one would blink or breathe.

"I quit…about a dozen times," she explained to Nick after a minor coughing fit, her lungs protesting the latest insult to recuperation. "When I get too nervous, I just can't help it."

"Murders do that to me, too," Nick said jocosely, eyeing her over a flute of fine champagne, which was serving to lift his spirits considerably. "Fortunately, my pacifier is comparatively benign. If I were a physician instead of a lowly Ph.D., I'd advise you to give up the cancer sticks and steer clear of murders."

A welter of emotions surged across Gillian's beautiful face. *Resentment? Anger? Guilt?* Nick could only guess, and he wasn't wild about doing so, for he didn't want to discover some ugly truth about her. That would tend to put a damper on the young flame of their romance.

She wanted to say something but stopped herself; a long, nervous drag bottled up her words.

Her reaction was out of all proportion to a comment intended merely to amuse. Nick couldn't help wondering why. *And did I intend merely to amuse?*

After more deep drags and sustained sips, Gillian regained a semblance of composure, and with it the charm he'd seen and admired that morning. Their relationship forged in the trauma of Bluemantle's death and the unnerving investigation that followed, they were quickly becoming more and more attracted to each other—or so it seemed to Nick. His hand sought hers across the tablecloth.

New Orleans is a passionate city, where an impatient goddess of sensual desperation holds court. Love and hate move with startling speed here, below the slow-motion illusion of ease and comfort. All is transitory, evanescent, a magnolia petal turning brown, even the city's legends, which are born and die anew in different bodies with each telling. Disease, floods, hurricanes, wars, duels, and overnight regime changes have helped to shape the character of New Orleanians into a fickle, childlike, selfish, melodramatic, beautiful thing.

Nick found his dinner companion to be interesting, intelligent, and refined, even if neurotic and mysterious. Often he forgot she had a cigarette trembling in her slender fingers. It seemed she was trying to conceal it through some sleight of hand. Very little smoke escaped from the cigarette or her mouth, and just the filter was left when she rubbed one out in the ashtray. She held it out of reach of the waiter—she'd bummed two from him already—as if she were afraid he was going to steal it. Not that she was being considerate of Nick or anyone else by trying to smoke unobtrusively: that was the last thing on her mind just now, her veiled expression told him. She wanted every last soothing curl of smoke. She needed it to subdue some inner riot.

"So, what did the detective ask you?" Nick asked nonchalantly, hoping to get the answers to Bartly's questions without having to ask them, whatever they had been.

"If I had anything to do with Dr. Bluemantle's death," she said. "He didn't come right out and say he'd been…murdered. But that's the impression I got. That he had been—that he *thought* he had been, at least. The detective guy, I mean."

"Bartly," Nick added helpfully.

"Yes. Bartly. He told me not to leave town. They may need to interview me again. 'Interview'—that's what he called it!…can we talk about something else, please?"

"Sure," Nick said, happy to change the subject. Murder wasn't exactly a romantic topic; and he was sick of thinking about Bluemantle, lying dead in the bathroom of his hotel room. Literally sick. The magnificent champagne and food and setting almost let him believe that Bluemantle's death was someone else's nightmare, and that Gillian was a wish granted by a particularly accomplished jinni…and yet, he still wanted to know what she might know.

"I love this place," he said. "The owners, a man-and-wife chef team, hate publicity. Food writers don't get in, I'm told. They'd rather have a few regular customers who understand the restaurant's unique qualities than a busload of bickering tourists on a tight schedule. You won't get rushed here, no matter what time it is. And the food—that's the real clincher. I'll put this place up against any one-Michelin-star, magazine-touted restaurant in France. The one-stars are always innovating, working their tails off; the threes have crested and become corporations intent on squeezing every last euro from their brand names."

Nick offered his companion the last of the delicious sampling of the day's appetizers.

She nibbled a few items and agreed with his high assessment.

"I'd rather be a genealogist than a restaurateur," she said. "Even in a restaurant like this, as wonderful as it is. Genealogy sounds so—I don't know—so different, so fascinating, so intellectual. Such a powerful weapon."

Weapon? Odd way to put it. "There's a lot of drudgery in both professions," Nick said between bites, trying not to let Gillian's infatuation with genealogists go to his head. "But I don't have to worry about the inventory going bad, that's true. Genealogical facts have an infinite shelf life."

Watching her, listening to her, he wondered if she could have killed Bluemantle. The old guy wasn't a martial arts expert, that was for sure; nevertheless, he was bigger and he had a dangerous temper. She could have surprised him in his room, hit him over the head, pushed him down. And what of the missing finger?

He surreptitiously studied Gillian as she tore a piece of bread from a crusty New Orleans loaf and spread butter on it. Were those delicate hands of hers capable of such a knife-wielding atrocity? What did she have to gain? Was the secret of Bluemantle's undignified demise concealed there, within those luminous eyes of hers watching the candle, behind that opaque, but very, very pretty face?

"That look you're giving me is full of question marks," she said, startling him out of his reverie. "You're curious about why I was in Dr. Bluemantle's room, aren't you?"

"Partly. I'm staring mostly because you're nice to stare at. If you want to tell me or not, it's okay."

Her smile showed him she appreciated the grace period.

"Well, I'm really, really interested in genealogy," she said, by way of beginning to explain her presence at the crime scene. "I'm interested in a lot of things, which is why I've been in college so long." She laughed in that sad way of hers at the admission, which Nick didn't find fault with in the least; he himself preferred knowing a little about many things, rather than a lot about one subject. "My father used to call me a professional student."

"Oh, I'm sorry. When did he die?"

"He didn't—hasn't, yet. He's…sick. Depression they said at first, then a few years ago they decided it was Alzheimer's, or something physical like that, one of those awful wasting diseases of the mind. I don't think they really know. Seems like every day the doctors have a new label to hang on him, but no new cures. He's in a nursing home, out in Metairie. Usually he recognizes me, other times he's almost a stranger."

Metairie is a city-sized but unincorporated proto-white-flight suburb bordering New Orleans on the northwest and hugging

Lake Pontchartrain. It may lack the Old World enchantment of big sister New Orleans, but Metairie compensates for that shortcoming with raw American energy that has fueled many new fortunes, and with a proudly independent identity, which at its best is friendly and fun, and at its worst occasionally takes the form of a virulent strain of racism.

A good place for nutty people, Nick reflected.

"It's a lovely institution," Gillian said, "if you have to be in one, I guess. And my mother…well, Mother isn't exactly a Ma Joad. You know, from *Grapes of Wrath*."

"I think I understand," said Nick "You won't find her volunteering as a candy striper at a hospital."

Gillian nodded enthusiastically, gratefully. "Exactly, exactly! Mother divorced him about fifteen years ago. I was just a kid. She remarried immediately, a much younger man. That didn't last long; the next one didn't, either. We lived all over the country, whatever resort was 'in' at the time. She got a lot of Daddy's money, what wasn't in some trusts set up for me and my brother.

"But when I got older, I wanted to be there for Daddy. Mother didn't like that idea. Wow, did she ever raise hell! Said he was getting the best care, and I would only upset him, that I should live my own life, that kind of crap. We don't talk much now. Anyway, I got in Freret University, God knows how, my high school grades were so awful. Since then, I've been skipping from course to course and major to major. I've even made it up to a green belt in karate." She playfully curled her hands into lethal-looking tomahawks. "But I think eventually I'd like to be a writer, use these fingers for something less violent. I've written a few poems."

A writer—a poet, no less! Nick silently castigated himself: he seemed to have an unerring knack for romancing women who were more screwed up than he was. He desperately wished at that moment that he'd never attended the damn seminar; what a load of trouble it had brought. Yet…he would endure a lot of discomfort to enjoy the company of a lovely woman.

"You mentioned a brother. Where is he?"

"He died. A skiing accident in Colorado, almost two years ago. He—" She took a deep drag and then forced herself to continue. "He ran into a tree. What a prosaic way to go. I idolized him. He was six years older, a successful attorney in Atlanta. Wife, three kids."

"I shouldn't have pried."

"No, no, that's all right. I need to learn to deal with it. And besides, you're nice to talk to," she said, her eyes lingering on his to show she'd deliberately echoed his earlier compliment. "For a while, I was a basket case. Had to be hospitalized. Does depression run in families, you think?"

"That's a tough one," Nick answered, without answering. "If we're not there yet, we soon will be. Science already can predict physical traits from DNA. Even genealogy is being invaded by genetics. Not a happy development for professional genealogists like me. Who'll need our painstaking research when one swab inside the cheek pegs your chromosomes to family lines across human history? If it's all chemical, it's anybody's guess when we'll be able to say this one will drink too much, that one will be a serial killer, this one will be a good mother, the way we can predict sickle cell anemia. Maybe environment and experience override genes in behavior, maybe there are too many variables to ever predict unerringly if someone will commit suicide, for instance. Maybe we shouldn't know: the uncertainty could be a vital part of being human. And what happens when we start meddling? Can we ever stop?...I'm beginning to sound like Mary Shelley." *And Bluemantle.*

"Well, I think we should know," Gillian said in response to Nick's inebriated bombast. "I think you *have* to know, you *have* to find out the truth. Even if it's unpleasant." She was taking this more seriously than Nick had meant it.

She watched twisting strands of smoke ascending for a few moments, and then resumed her story: "Anyway, Jules—he was my brother—Jules was really into genealogy. As a lawyer he knew where to look, anyway, for a lot of that stuff. He was going to write a book. The last time I talked to him, he said there was something...well, never mind, that's all ancient history now."

They switched to a superb Oregon Pinot Noir, which the waiter had presented with a minimum of fuss, though, in Nick's mind, it deserved a symphony orchestra to proclaim its wondrous qualities. He ordered another bottle. *Credit-card limit be damned!*

"I wish I'd known you were a genealogist—I mean a real one," she said. "Not just a dilettante, like me. Maybe I wouldn't have asked Dr. Bluemantle for advice and then gone up to his room and found him like that. Did you know him well?"

"We were old friends," Nick said. "He taught me a lot of what I think I know. As a matter of fact, I was hoping he'd go out to dinner with us. He'd promised to pay." They both laughed. "You feel like telling me briefly what happened? I know you've been grilled once already, and you're not even on the menu."

"Oh, I'm not?" she asked, a mischievous invitation in her eyes.

Some Pinot Noir went down the wrong pipe. "Yes, well…maybe together we could discover something meaningful that would help Detective Bartly."

"I don't mind now. You've put me at ease. Consider it my way of expressing condolences for your loss." She drank some wine with unstudied poise. "I talked with Dr. Bluemantle before the seminar, and he told me to see him afterward. But he left so suddenly. I thought it would be okay if I stopped by, since he'd already agreed to talk with me. I called from my apartment about four. He was alive and well and…somewhat suggestive. But that didn't bother me, really. I can usually take care of myself. When I got there, his room door was open. I knocked until my knuckles hurt, and finally went in."

The cunning devil—he'd made a play for her in my absence.

"What time was this?" Nick asked.

"Six-thirty exactly. I didn't want to be late meeting you downstairs. That's when I found him. I tried to reach you at the bar. I didn't really know what to do. After I got myself together a little, I told the hotel operator to call the police."

So she was the woman who'd called three times.

"Did you see an attractive brunette woman in the hall?"

"I don't think so. It's all sort of a blank after I saw the body. Who is she? A suspect?"

"I'm afraid the murderer could be anybody in the hotel this afternoon. We're all suspects, Gillian." That stunned her visibly and sent her to her cigarette for a tremulous drag. "What were you going to ask Dr. Bluemantle? Maybe I can help."

Suddenly animated, she exclaimed, "Oh! I completely forgot. Maybe you can." She rooted around in her capacious purse. "Ummm, these 1790 census schedules, I mean the ones that weren't burned in the War of 1812…where did I put that list of questions? Here it is." She took a deep breath, as if about to dive underwater. "Well, my great-great-grandmother's first cousin, twice removed…"

The entrees arrived just in time, and Nick was spared another endless genealogical recitation that even he would not be able to follow without a pedigree chart.

◧

The few words they murmured to each other in the dimness, later in bed at Nick's Vieux Carré apartment, had nothing to do with ancestral barons and bastards, proprietors and philanderers.

Chapter 4

Wayne Therman walked unsteadily to his car. It was late. Downtown New Orleans was dark and desolate. A very dangerous place to be.

He'd spent much of Monday afternoon in the downtown branch of the New Orleans Public Library. The armed security guard had rudely run him off at closing time. The creep! He had it in for him, just like all other pawns of the System; he'd hassled Wayne for weeks, ever since he'd begun his research at the library. Each time he set off the metal detector the guard made him nearly strip. It pissed him off. There were people who literally *lived* in the library, in their envelopes of funk; yet the guard picked on Wayne.

But today, guerrilla fighter for justice that he was, Wayne Therman had given him his best mad-dog kung-fu stare. The young black man was clearly abashed.

The library remained open only from eleven to four because of a chronic shortage of funds in the Murder Capital of America. The mayor always promised more crime-fighting money, but somehow most of the dollars other departments had to do without didn't make it to the insatiable police department. And the mayor kept winning. Politics, New Orleans style.

With such a short window of access, Wayne had made scant progress penetrating the walls of genealogical untruth that had been erected to thwart him.

After the Friday incident at the Grande Marchioness Hotel, the police kept him till almost seven o'clock in a Central Lockup holding cell, even though the magnanimous Preston Nowell refused to press charges. Wayne still hated him, maybe more than ever for this display of clemency. Ultimately, Wayne received no more than an assistant DA's nasty threat of lifelong incarceration in Angola State Penitentiary if he caused any more trouble. But Wayne wasn't afraid of the law; the whole government was illegitimate. What was this, his third time in jail for "harassment"? *Oh, that's a good one,* he thought: Wayne harassing Captain-Director Preston Nowell!

He recalled the confrontations with pride: there was that time at the Society library, then a few months later at Nowell's boat out on the lake, and today at the seminar…oh, yeah, what about the time he tackled him when he was coming out of Emeril's. All right! That was his favorite.

Good thing he had a job and an employer that understood his need for lots of personal time. The administrator at the nursing home where he worked had smoothed things over with the Gestapo each time.

Wayne was fighting a holy war against the Evil One, the Poisoner of the Past. There were no rules in a revolution. He was doing it for the world, for the future.

He'd just scored some more marijuana, and he was feeling even more omnipotent than usual, which explains why he was so unconcerned during this perilous stroll through the valley of the shadow of death that was downtown New Orleans at night. The stuff had been obscenely expensive, but it was good, damn good. The doctors didn't know shit about psychopharmacology; one of them, by coincidence, had her office just down the street at the Medical Center. Wayne, as a "caregiver" at the nursing home, considered himself an expert. These idiotic HMO doctors kept telling him to stay off grass and the other underground drugs he liked, because of the unpredictable interactions with the mood controllers he had been taking since his teenage years. Only good thing about this HMO bullshit was the emphasis of medication over counseling. He had always hated those analysis sessions! Wayne knew that it was only when he *was* toking on his finger-sized brass pipe that he was anything like normal.

He made quotation marks in the air: "'Normal.' Who the fuck wants to be 'normal'?" he said aloud, and laughed his nasal grunting guffaw. "*Sheep* are normal."

He had conveniently erased from his memory the fact that all of his outbursts happened after missing a dose or two of his antidepressants. Each time he had been either too stoned on some really good shit or too preoccupied in his various investigations to follow the prescribed regimen.

It was all a conspiracy, anyway. For a while he had believed it was an unholy alliance of Jewish bankers in the Swiss Alps, the UN, the Trilateral Commission, al Qaeda, environmentalists, and the Masons, with assorted Foreign Powers thrown in. But since he no longer received free newsletters from the wacko-fringe group which propounded that theory, he had done some deep thinking and come to new conclusions. Preston Nowell and his infernal Society were the real leaders of the conspiracy!

Wayne was on to them. He had pursued them through all of his incarnations: Wayne the veteran (he'd served a four-month hitch in the Army before being booted out as a mental case); Wayne the muckraking journalist (there was a phase of letter-writing to the *Times-Picayune*); Wayne the scientist and philosopher (he'd hung around the University of New Orleans campus for a year); Wayne the private investigator (peeping Tom). And now, Wayne the genealogist.

The only member of his family who would have anything to do with him was his grandmother who lived in Kenner, a city of Indian-settlement and plantation roots that had become a densely commercial setting for Louis Armstrong Airport. He loved his grandmother dearly. She had been shafted, he believed. And it was partly his fault, he realized, in rare lucid moments. She had poured thousands from her meager savings into the pockets of Nowell and his Society, convinced by a few of Nowell's seminars that her family had come over on that ship, the *Allégorie*.

What had she gotten in return? At first, when her checks flowed regularly to the Society, the news had been encouraging. But then, when she started to question the cost, she got a cock-and-bull story about her, and his, ancestors being peasants, felons, and madmen, and *not* heroes, pioneers, and patriots who had sailed into New Orleans on the famous ship. That's when Wayne rode in on his white horse.

He was certain that he sprang from illustrious loins. Just as he was certain that Nowell was trying to steal his ancestry!

But he had the goods on the guy, now—if he could only figure it out. Old Monty at the nursing home had redeemed himself by providing Wayne with the key to the whole mystery, the ugly cover-up. As well he should have, for it was Old Monty in the first place who'd turned Wayne and his grandmother on to the Society. Well, not exactly. Old Monty didn't say much that made any sense, but Wayne *had* noticed his ring. The only trouble was, Wayne didn't know what the old fart had meant the other day when he scribbled:

ALLÉGORIE = TRUE FAITH.

Wayne's efforts to decipher the cryptic message so far had been unsuccessful. It was the city's fault, for squandering the funds that should have gone to the library, that no doubt went into the bank accounts of the mayor's cronies. If he only had more time for research! Nowell was probably somehow to blame for that, too. The infamy of these people cried out for justice!

Wayne had spent the last six hours in the bar of a run-down Chinese restaurant near the Medical Center, drinking beer chased with shots of tequila, and losing every dollar he had on video poker. Now he headed for his car, parked behind the tall Holiday Inn on Loyola Avenue.

The building had once housed the Howard Johnson's that became infamous on a cold January day in 1973. Wayne vaguely remembered news coverage of the sniper incident that ended on the roof of the old Ho-Jo with the shooter blasted by gunfire from a Marine helicopter. The dude—and maybe another guy who got away—had killed nine people and wounded ten.

That wasn't Wayne's style, though he understood where the dude had been coming from. Rage, blinding rage against unseen enemies all around you. But in the long run, a sharp intellect is much more powerful than a rifle, Wayne had come to believe. Besides, he couldn't afford a decent assault weapon.

He tripped over a curb but regained his balance.

The Superdome rose to his right, surreally huge like a giant egg ready to hatch vicious spawn. He'd heard rumors at gun shows, read bizarre tales on websites, that aliens had brazenly set up a transporting center inside. That was a load of crap, in his opinion.

The real story was that the government and the phone companies were conducting microwave experiments on dissidents; drove them mad, turned them into junkies. He knew it for a fact: they had kidnapped him while he slept several years ago and tried it on him. But he had resisted. That explained his nightmares, of course.

Wayne turned his back on the Dome as he walked from Loyola Avenue to Gravier Street. The sidewalks and parking lots threw weird shadows and giant echoes at him. There was hardly any traffic. It didn't even seem like New Orleans, more like a set from *The Outer Limits*. The streets seemed bigger than during the day. He fantasized that he was the sole survivor in a post-apocalyptic world.

He walked along an arcade sheltering offices, a diner, and shop entrances. Above, a tall, slumbering building cloaked the sidewalk in deeper shadow. Aggregate planters held brown and withered yew and oleander.

Suddenly he felt an odd, hot pain in the left side of his chest. The words "heart attack" popped into his mind, but when he glanced down, he realized that something else had happened.

Wow, man, look at that! A beautiful shaft of silver light, coming from the shadows of an arch, in front of that travel agency. Goes right through my coat, and—damnit!—right through my bag of dope and Old Monty's note. Right through my ribs, and my heart, and my back...

Wayne understood fleetingly, in those few seconds before he died, that a white glove held the other end of the shaft of light connecting him to the darkness.

Chapter 5

The frosted glass in the oft-shellacked wooden door read:

New Orleans Genealogical Services Worldwide, Inc.
J. N. Herald, Certified Genealogist, Ph.D.

About as accurate as calling a lemonade stand General Motors.

Nick's office filled two rooms on the fourth floor of a sparsely occupied building in an undistinguished section of the Central Business District. It was close enough to Canal to hear the streetcars' unmistakable roar, to the Quarter to hear snatches of jazz and drunken, bawdy cheers, and to the river to see ocean-going vessels riding high, dwarfing buildings in the line of sight. Otherwise, no outstanding characteristics much recommended it. The area called to Nick's mind post-Cold War East Germany more than guidebook New Orleans.

His business wasn't incorporated and was far from being worldwide. Nick had no qualms about the slight misstatements he used in the course of his business. His experiences had taught him to be no more ethical than he had to be. No one else was.

From his doomed fight to save his academic reputation he'd learned that the living bend the present to their needs. From years of sifting through censuses, conveyances, and wills he'd learned that the dead deceived no longer: the certainties of their lives had solidified into diamonds of truth, buried and silent. Nick's passion for the meaning of words strung together in poems and narratives had given way to a passion for helping give voice to the unimpeachable testimony, the poignant beauty, the tragedy, and the glory slumbering in the recorded events of the lives he studied. Woodrow Bluemantle's death hid such secrets; Nick was determined to unearth them.

He sat behind his messy desk, his head propped on his hands, his fingers woven into his brown hair. A long gray strand fell on the piece of junk mail he had lost interest in a half-hour before.

> Dear MR. HERALD: The history of your family name, available *now* to you at a discount during our special *50th Anniversary Sale*! Yes, now you can learn about your ancestors of the famous HERALD line. Where they came from, what great deeds they performed...even what the HERALD coat of arms looks like and signifies! Wouldn't your neighbors be impressed by an authentic full-color shield bearing the HERALD coat of arms? Our research specialists search our extensive archives....

They would even put his "coat of arms" on a credit card. There were more and more of these frauds landing in mailboxes these days, beguiling the naïve into thinking that genealogy could be purchased like a box of cereal. Would the saps who fell for this ever learn—or want to—that armorial bearings were granted to specific individuals and could be passed on only to certain descendants in strictly defined ways? Possession of a surname guaranteed nothing. Nick shook his head. What devious, unethical scams—

Lucrative scams, he had to admit. Why shouldn't he have his own genealogical swindle? Just a small one that didn't really hurt anybody?

In ghostly rebuttal, he heard the chastising words of his murdered friend, Bluemantle:

> *What about your responsibility to the past? To me?! You know very well that your grandfather dropped the ethnic consonants in your Old World family surname to make it easier for his descendants in an anti-Semitic world. You were Herzwald before you were Herald. An irony, there, isn't it Nick: that you bear the name of the ancient guardians of the past, heralds, yet you are so willing to violate that trust, join the purveyors of pseudo-genealogy? What do you believe in, my friend, if not the truth? It is your mission, one that chose you.*
>
> *Never compromise, never surrender. There is no substitute for systematic individual research, for conclusions based on the best possible evidence.*
>
> *In genealogy, as in murder. Doubt, above all! Lineages and lies, Nick; all is not yet Bristol-fashion, shipshape.*

The final words had haunted him throughout that resplendent Wednesday morning and afternoon. But he had not been inactive.

"Hello?! Hello?!" a female voice demanded. "Anyone home in that head of yours, boss?" Hawty Latimer, Nick's assistant, was accustomed to his speculative fugues, when a genealogical puzzle could keep him distracted like this for hours.

"Have you found it?" he asked in reply.

"Not yet," she admitted, sitting in her wheelchair in front of the monitor of the office computer, where she had been working quietly and diligently. "Still searching." Hawty's tone conveyed her frustration: she hated to be stymied, in any undertaking.

There were days when no more words needed to be spoken between them. They worked well together and implicitly understood each other. Nick wasn't the kind to tell her how much he valued her. Just as well. She wasn't the kind to take such praise graciously.

Hawty scooted her battery-powered wheelchair over to the wall of bookshelves opposite the windows in the narrow main room; she used her telescoping grabber adeptly to reach the volumes she needed.

She was a dual-degree candidate at Freret University—English and computer sciences; she also taught freshman introductory literature classes. An overachiever bound for fame in any discipline she would finally choose. She had become fascinated with genealogy, to Nick's good fortune; and he felt like a proud parent watching her knowledge and enthusiasm grow.

Her "chariot," as she called her souped-up wheelchair, was a veritable rolling laboratory of cutting-edge digital communication and mechanical miniaturization. The contraption was the pet project of the computer-sciences division at Freret, and each week it gained some new, astonishing capability.

Technophobe that he was, Nick couldn't help admiring the ingenuity of it.

As a child, Hawty had suffered some devastating illness that left her with chronic, polio-like weakness in her legs and hips. He didn't like to ask her about it, but he seemed to remember that it was either a reaction to a swine flu shot or an attack by one of the spinal viral maladies that prey on children.

Hawty was brilliant, hard working, and as tough and sassy as growing up poor and black in North Louisiana can make a person. Her given name was Harrieta; she preferred Hawty, and five minutes with her showed why "haughty" was an adjective that sometimes applied. She could be headstrong and downright rude, a tough customer, if she didn't like or respect you. He had Professors Una Kern and Dion Rambus to thank for her—and for much else.

"Why Bristol?" Hawty asked, now again at the brawny computer she'd convinced Nick to buy on credit a few months earlier. At the moment, the workstation was querying Salt Lake City, Washington, D.C., Houston, and New York City for vital records—birth, death, and marriage information—to fill out the family trees of several clients. Hawty was also searching for a particular reference source Nick wanted: *Ship Departures & Passenger Lists from the Port of Bristol to America, 1700-76.*

"Just a hunch," he replied.

"Oh, it's just a hunch? Why am I not surprised?" she wisecracked.

Una and Dion had been his best friends in the English department at Freret. For a time, Una had been even more. They'd both stoutly defended Nick when the charge was broached that, in a published article on Keats, he'd stolen ideas from a long-dead scholar. He didn't do it; he'd never even read the man's work. The department's new computer—with a flawed word-matching paradigm, Hawty maintained—figured in the gathering of evidence; and Frederick Tawpie, then an assistant professor in charge of the "inquiry," cared more for his prospects for advancement than for the facts.

The inquiry proceeded strictly according to rarely invoked rules. Tawpie and the other professors on the departmental affairs committee conveniently forgot their own constant struggle for originality in a publish-or-perish world, and glossed over their own past accidents of similarity. Deals had been struck, alliances cemented. It would have taken a mere raised hand to stop the locomotive heading for Nick, tied to the tracks. He became a target of opportunity in an ideological war that was then raging between increasingly powerful and strident postmodernists who saw ogres of colonialism and capitalism everywhere, and resurgent new traditionalists who promoted the "Western canon" and empiricism as the best grounding for a good education.

Tawpie had ridden the coattails of the former group, now out of vogue and in decline; Una and Dion were still leaders of the latter. Nick, had traveled a middle road, discerning some value even in the most flamboyant absurdities of postmodernist systems…until the betrayal.

Having scaled the icy peak of cynicism, he now looked down with scorn at the pitiful hamlets of theory. *You must have facts, Nick, yes, but also the wisdom to know when they're lying!* as Bluemantle used to shout at him.

Who had brought the initial charge of scholarly misconduct? Nick suspected Tawpie, who had always coveted the top job in the department and had feared that Una would get it one day, as she so richly deserved. She clearly had the superior mind and the deeper soul, along with a more impressive academic record.

The plagiarism allegation, lacking a clearly smoking gun, soon degenerated into a suggestion that Nick *should have* read the earlier critical work; but the damage to his reputation was done. Nick firmly believed that Tawpie had sacrificed him on the altar of his ambition, to prove his power to everyone, especially his power over Una, to demonstrate definitively his skill at conspiracy. By the time the compromise was made for him to resign before being fired, Nick was lower in spirits than he'd ever been. He was fed up with departmental politics, fed up with Frederick Tawpie, fed up with life in general. Vengeful, bitter, directionless, dangerously depressed. Other people go through worse tribulations—much worse—and continue soldiering on. Nick comprehended that fact.

But if you couldn't be self-indulgent with your own misfortune, then it truly was an unjust world. This disgrace was his very own bête noire, and, like a tragic lover in grand opera, he embraced it without reserve. He'd be damned if anyone was going to deprive him of his full measure of self-pity.

Soon thereafter, Tawpie, as a reward for his ignoble career of guile and ass-kissing, made the leap to assistant department head, and recently, to head of the department on the death of the beloved Whitman scholar who'd been at the helm for nearly fifty years. Tawpie delivered a fulsome graveside eulogy that had all the sycophants sniffling, but not Nick, Una, Dion, and a few other departmental subversives, who had long since dubbed Tawpie "the Usurper."

Una saved Nick from his downward trajectory through one of her benevolent tricks. She'd assured a relative of hers that Nick was an expert in genealogy. Reluctantly, Nick went along with the charade, and soon found himself researching and writing a family history, which, to his surprise, won several awards.

More to his surprise, he found in genealogy an outlet for his need to set the record straight—even if it wasn't his own. Having spent his adult life thus far as a scholar, he made the transition without a stumble. In a matter of a couple of years, he attained certification as a professional in the field. He was a CG, a Certified Genealogist. Now he was making a new name for himself, garnering minor acclaim through his frequent articles, but making little money. The business side was not his forte, and he gave it only fitful attention.

"What's that book you're using?" he asked Hawty, with some concern. "Did I buy that? Looks expensive."

"Don't worry; it's my personal copy," she assured him, her eyes on the screen. "I've lent it to the firm. It's a guide to on-line genealogy, already outdated. I bet you've never heard of Rootsfinity.com, the MyAncestors BBS, GenShamus.org—"

"You're right, I haven't. Are you speaking in some kind of code, a peculiar New Orleans patois?" He was ribbing her.

"Joke about it if you want," Hawty replied, "but I'm speaking the language of genealogy's next wave, the Next Big Thing in our specialty. Actually, there's nothing 'next' about it: online genealogy is here now."

Of course, Nick was well aware of the growing importance of the Internet for genealogical research, not to mention communication, but he knew that anything short of unbridled zealotry wouldn't be good enough for Hawty. Like all fundamentalists, she saw only heathens and the saved elect.

"By the way, you have any objections to me reviewing new genealogical computer programs for a trade journal?" she asked.

Early on in her employment, she'd pointed out to Nick the erroneous computer-generated conclusions Tawpie's plagiarism inquiry had reached. Part of her effort to drag him into the Information Age; but he still harbored a suspicion of the soulless microchip, and he had no burning desire to join the ranks of those who bowed down to Almighty Gizmo incarnate in the putty-colored box.

"If it'll bring the firm some cash or publicity, go for it." He walked over to the computer.

Hawty clicked rapidly through Web pages crammed with information. "I thought you'd say that."

Nick watched, fascinated, over her shoulder. Her own tablet computer, mounted on her chair, chimed. She checked it, and her brown face broke into a victorious smile.

"There it is!" she exclaimed. "The Bristol stuff. We can order the microfilms from FHL in Salt Lake City…wait a second"—she scrolled more information onto the screen. "It's a brand new release, but the Plutarch has it, right here in town."

"Good deal," Nick said. "Have we helped Angus and Mrs. Fadge lately?"

Angus Murot and Mrs. Fadge were the volunteers-in-charge at the Plutarch Foundation, a privately endowed historical and genealogical library in a landmark antebellum house of characteristic New Orleans Uptown beauty. Nick served there as the informal-when-he-felt-like-it genealogical advisor. He did just enough gratis work to keep his welcome warm, because it was an excellent place to do research.

"Got a letter from Angus last month," Hawty said. "You've been moving it to the bottom of your pile ever since." She glanced disapprovingly at the unfiled stacks covering his desk. "You know, if you'd been a more systematic scholar, you might have had proof you thought up your own ideas for that Keats article." An old argument she didn't expect to win.

The small anteroom that clients entered by way of the office door was Hawty's domain. Her furniture—which she'd scavenged with admirable economy from storerooms in the building—hugged the walls, to allow her maximum maneuverability. The anteroom was always perfectly, even aggressively, neat. Nick didn't mind the favorable first impression Hawty's efforts created, but he stopped her dictatorial orderliness at the boundaries of *his* room.

"Angus wants to know something about Ontario," Hawty said, "and an ancestor who was a Loyalist during the Revolutionary War."

Nick thought a moment. "Yeah, I remember his question. Do you have any more classes today? No? Great. Find out what you can about this ancestor of his and give Angus a call."

"No problem. I'll hit the Internet and—"

Nick took down two hefty volumes dealing with claims for losses resulting from colonists' loyalty to the English Crown, and later land grants in Canada to families who could prove such loyalty. He plunked them beside the office computer.

"You'd do better to start here, with a little conventional research."

Hawty frowned and contemptuously pushed the books away. "Are you going somewhere? Must be nice to make your own hours."

"I need a jog—of the mind," he answered, heading for the tiny bathroom to change. "Call Detective Bartly, too. NOPD homicide. Tell him I'm working on the problem."

"What problem? Thought you didn't like the police."

"I don't, as a rule, but hey, it's the exceptions that make life interesting. Besides, I owe Bartly a favor; he fixed a ticket for me. And if we get on the list of experts-for-hire, it might mean a lot of business for us down the line. Then we can charge rate-card times three."

Hawty turned back to the computer and deftly manipulated the computer mouse. "What's this detective trying to find out?"

"How 'allégorie' equals 'true faith.'" His voice was partly muffled by clothing passing over his head.

"Now *you're* talking in code," Hawty said.

Nick explained. "That mysterious linguistic equation, including the modified French orthography, was scribbled on a piece of paper in a coat pocket of the heckler, the fat guy I told you about who attacked Nowell at the hotel seminar. He was found floating in the river yesterday morning?"

"I read about that, but I had no idea it was the same dude," Hawty said. "The note must have been about the only thing that wasn't chewed up by the paddle-wheel, so I read. Guess the tourists on the boat got a look at one genuine New Orleans sight: a dead body in the Vieux Carré."

"Bartly is wondering if there's a connection between the two murders, Bluemantle and the heckler."

"Wayne…"

"Therman," Nick said, completing her thought. "Bartly asked me to look into it, see if I can decipher the equation, find any genealogical significance in it. Seems our heckler was pretty much of a dingbat."

"They've decided Bluemantle was murdered, then?" Hawty asked.

"He didn't fall down." There were several thumps from the bathroom as Nick put on his running shoes. "He was pushed, hard, the coroner says. The missing finger wasn't a result of your normal shaving accident, either."

"What about Wayne Therman? Could he have killed Bluemantle?"

"Would have been difficult," Nick said. "He was in police custody."

"Okay, he's off the hook, but dead. So, enlighten me: what do allégorie, true faith, and Bristol have to do with these murders?"

"Not sure. But I had a talk with Nelson Plumlaw this morning."

"The professor at Freret's Architecture School? He's a genealogy buff, right, especially when it comes to Atlantic colonial emigration records?"

"Hawty, you don't miss much, do you? Your memory's almost as good as mine. Nelson told me just enough to make me more confused."

"I think the heckler was snuffed by some crackhead, myself. They'll never catch him." A thought suddenly occurred to Hawty, and she stopped typing. "Don't you come near me in those funky old rags you're wearing, you hear? When's the last time you washed that stuff?...Oh, I'm going for some exercise later, too, *if* I ever finish my work here. I've started swimming therapy twice a week, at the Freret pool. Want to keep my girlish figure from getting to be a big brown beach ball. You ought to join me sometime."

Nick emerged from the bathroom in his gym shorts and tank top. This was his first spring outing without sweats. "Sounds good to me. One of these days I'll take you up on that offer."

Hawty could not hold her laughter.

"What's so funny?" Nick asked, his fragile ego shaken.

"Those…those bony white hairy legs!" was all she could say intelligibly through her mirth. And then, after she'd caught her breath, "Boy, I swear, I've never been so proud of being born black, female, and beautiful."

"Okay, okay, get out your Freret ID."

"Why? Are you going to report me to the dean for making fun of a former faculty member? They never did give you much respect when you were on the payroll, so why should they start now?"

"I'm going to show you a valuable skill genealogists sometimes need: breaking and entering. Our office door will do nicely for a start. Come this way, my young apprentice in crime."

"Oh, goodness, you're going to land *us* instead of the murderer in jail before it's all over!"

Chapter 6

Nick kept to the paved road that snaked through Audubon Park and enclosed the golf course, riding trails, and lagoons. He needed to think, to surrender his body to his mind.

St. Charles Avenue bordered the park; sometimes the photogenic street was part of his route, and on those days he had to stay sharp. Streetcars trundled along the grassy "neutral ground" in the middle of the avenue, and the streetcar drivers, knowing they had technical right-of-way, liked to bear down on unwary joggers and scare the heck out of them with the car's bell. Nor did he want to dodge autos racing across the neutral ground before an onrushing, clanging streetcar, or jog in place at intersections waiting for traffic gunning to beat a light—reckless driving was another hallowed tradition in New Orleans, and it wasn't just the carjackers who were to blame.

In the park, he could let down his guard a bit, as much as one should in a dangerous city like New Orleans.

The mild weather had brought the annual migration of transients from all over the world. There were several clutches of them in the park, sitting in groups, sharing food, cigarettes, joints, conversation, music. They would come for Mardi Gras, the biggest free party in North America, and stay until the cold rains of late November. Where they went during the interval of the few nearly winter-like months, Nick wasn't sure. Farther south—Florida, Mexico, Brazil? He would do the same, he thought, were he in their mismatched shoes.

Nick recognized some of the eternal types that hang out in the Crescent City: aging Woodstockers, bothering a guitar or a harmonica, their minds a 45-rpm record stuck on Jefferson Airplane or Hendrix; tantric contortionists, eyes seeing mystic realms; cursing snail-folk, their ragged worldly possessions in a lump on their shoulders; grifters, sitting alone, ominously observant, gestating the self-justifications of the mass murderer....

After getting thrown off the Freret faculty, he'd wanted to drop out of society, discover what it was like to care about nothing, to have nothing. It was a dream from his wild, idealistic, prodigal undergraduate years. He'd missed the counterculture revolution of the sixties by a decade; but he compensated by developing a certain sympathy for vagabonds and jongleurs, wise fools and mad geniuses, in art and real life. Wasn't it natural, then, for the Romantic era of Byron, Shelley, and Keats to have been his specialty as a teacher of literature?

Una Kern had snatched him from that rootless fate by suggesting genealogical research as therapy for his wounded psyche. It was one of those life-changing lucky moments. He had fallen in love with the many-faceted discipline, even though, as Una had hoped, he had not fallen back in love with her.

Yes, he could have been one of these wanderers he saw lounging under the old spreading oaks. One day they would be statistical shadows, frustrating enigmas for the researcher. Impossible gaps, in genealogical parlance—dead ends, where the tangible trail of a life in the written record stops cold. Nick had a brotherly urge to tell them that each was unique, each important, in ways they couldn't imagine. Though they believed no one missed them now, in the future someone would need them, care about them again, as characters in an unfolding genealogical mystery...like the one that he had come today to ponder: the death of Woodrow Bluemantle, and now, of this kook named Wayne Therman.

In genealogy, apparent coincidences usually aren't. Nick had schooled his mind to see patterns in family history: given names that appear frequently in records might honor parents, siblings, in-laws, or friends; a deed given or received by one branch of a family might suggest a look at nearby land for another branch; birth dates, death dates, marriages, migrations, and disappearances...each small fact adds a clump of clay to the sculpture that is the saga of a family. People do things for reasons. They plan, adapt, act, or fail to act, all for reasons that the genealogist with determination and, especially, imagination can discover.

Bluemantle, Therman? Bluemantle, Therman? Bluemantle, Therman?

His running shoes hitting the pavement drummed this central question into his brain, and the question drew him on to further speculation.

Both men had some relationship with the Society of the *Allégorie*. Both were at the seminar. Both were now dead. Murdered. Coincidence? Nick didn't believe so. Was Gillian somehow "involved," to use Bartly's loaded participle? She too had been at the seminar; more ominously, she had discovered Bluemantle. Nick was, he admitted to himself, biased in her favor. His memory of her graceful body sent him into a dream for a mile and more.

The running was doing its job, allowing his mind to be fluid as his senses dulled and his flesh moved through the humid air.

The newspaper hadn't made much of Bluemantle's murder; the television stations even less. Therman's murder had also been lightly covered, written off as just another victim of the city's rising tidal wave of random violence. Maybe Hawty was right. A fresh outbreak of corruption in NOPD was the lead story; the Public Integrity Division was working overtime. New Orleans residents were jaded when it came to murder; to elicit any reaction greater than a yawn, it needed to be spectacular, involving famous locals whose high-profile misfortunes offer catharsis for the lucky survivors who've made it through another day, dodged another bullet. Bluemantle and his missing finger, Therman and his enigmatic note, didn't cut the mustard.

Detective Bartly had dozens of other murders to solve. There were more than enough conscienceless killers in New Orleans for these two incidents to be wholly unrelated. He had admitted to Nick that the only common threads he saw were the obvious ones: that both of these men had obsessive interest in genealogy—for different reasons—and that this interest had prompted contact or conflict with the Society of the *Allégorie*. A good starting point, possibly, but he had as yet come up with no suspects, and no motives. The weapon used on Therman had not even been determined precisely: a knife, perhaps a sword.

Preston Nowell, when interviewed about both deaths, had pledged the full resources of the Society and had pleaded with Bartly to find the perpetrators, if indeed Bluemantle's death turned out to be murder. It was awful publicity for the Society, he'd complained. He was distraught over Bluemantle's death, but understandably less broken up about Therman's passing.

That morning, Nick's independent track of investigation had taken him to the Architecture School of Freret University. There he had sought a friend's help in seeing the framework—if there was one—below the façade of the recent strange events.

To the thudding rhythm of his stride, he replayed his meeting with Nelson Plumlaw.

Chapter 7

"A mirror image on the water, a doppelganger," Nelson Plumlaw had said that morning to Nick. "Intriguing. Two ships, one French, one English, sailing into colonial New Orleans essentially at the same time, but only one sailing on to fame. And you want me to help you determine which is the real one, which the illusion?"

The two men walked up the broad stone stairs of the massive old building that housed Freret University's Architecture School.

"The two countries were not exactly getting along during the time in question, you know, Nick. An English ship would not have been welcome anywhere near the area. Besides, Bienville's *Code Noir* discouraged Protestants—and banned Jews outright—from settling in the vast expanse of Louisiana. What makes you think this is a case of mistaken identity?"

"Intuition," Nick said.

"I'm not much on intuition, my friend. You know what an empirical rascal I am. You don't make buildings out of intuition, and, in my humble opinion as a non-professional genealogist, you don't make family history out of it, either. For buildings you need numbers, tools, concrete, lumber, and steel; for genealogy, you need sound evidence."

Nelson Plumlaw was a tenured architecture professor at Freret University, who just happened to have a lifelong enthusiasm for genealogy. He was about forty-five, but there was an engaging adolescent playfulness about him that would probably never desert him.

It was nine-thirty; Nelson and Nick were walking through a hangar-like room that housed the drafting tables of about twenty architecture students, all intently hunched over their work. The matte-black ceiling and exposed ductwork contrasted with the soft naturalness of the wood floor. A wall of windows of unusual design gave a restful view of grassy quadrangles and hoary oaks; many panes were flipped open, and wind chimes made soft music of a gentle breeze. In the middle of the room there was a foam-board model of a structure, rising ten feet, so far. The class project, Nelson informed Nick: the fanciful building incorporated design elements from Greek temples, the Pompidou Center, and the Sydney opera house. It could have sprung only from the insatiable minds of students gorging on the world's knowledge, Nick thought. He was reminded how much he missed the fecund energy of the college hothouse.

Nick recited a favorite line of poetry half to himself.

"What are you mumbling about, Herald?"

"That's Roethke. From a poem called 'Cuttings,' about the miraculous regenerative powers of nature, the mind, and humanity. All this creative juice, this urge to grow, Nelson! It's downright invigorating, enough to make *me* want to enroll."

Nelson chuckled. "You literary types, always wearing your emotions on your sleeve. Yet, I've always envied your ability to call up a quotation when you need it. I'm the slave of a thousand reference works. Perhaps that's why I'm in architecture."

They continued toward Nelson's office.

"It's nice in here," said Nick. "Not at all like a hundred-year-old building. It's all in the details, I guess. Architects pay attention to things like doorknobs and windows, furniture arrangement, light, space. And it always seemed to me that architecture students were cooler, weirder, more extroverted than English students. An oral-anal continuum."

"Keep your voice down, please." Nelson grimaced and looked over his shoulder. "Can't you think of another analogy. You're supposed to be so good with words, Mr. Former English Professor."

Nick had momentarily forgotten that Nelson was gay and not especially happy to have the fact broadcast or even hinted at—especially around here. It had been almost a year since Nick had seen him, but he was sure Nelson still kept his sex life strictly off campus. New Orleans, in popular myth a thriving, anarchic fusion of Sodom and Gomorrah on the Mississippi, actually lives by strict rules governing her renowned lewdness. And Freret University, as one of the last loyal courtiers of the old-guard aristocratic families, knew when to bow and scrape and enforce the elaborate decorum that keeps people and their peccadilloes in their places.

"Oh, sorry. Let me put it this way, then," Nick said. "My picture of the architecture student is a guy who spends all year napping in the sun under a tree, and then stays up for three days on coffee and speed to build his amazing final project. These are the people building our bridges!"

They continued their stroll, pausing now and then at a student's board as Nelson admired the design silently, or criticized the work with a sarcastic remark. Some students took his words to heart, others good-humoredly waved him away, as if he were a meddlesome older brother.

"You see, Nick, the reality of architecture is a bit more prosaic than the romantic ideas you have of it. But I don't deny that the two disciplines do indeed attract two distinctly different personalities. I rather like your analogy, actually. Architects are generally extroverts, who live fast and crash hard, who show their meticulous work with a flourish. The writer, or the scholar, on the other hand, is reticent, insecure, secretive, as anxious about his product as a mother with her newborn infant. Of course, generalities seldom pan out. I would say on that continuum, I am somewhere between the two extremes."

Sitting now in Nelson's tidy office, which held more books than standard-issue office furniture, Nick indeed saw nothing extreme about his friend. Nelson sported a spiffy bow tie at the neck of a perfectly pressed French-blue shirt, and red suspenders that secured generously pleated dark-gray gabardines below his epicure's belly. His ruddy, chubby face was smoothly shaved. But his hair contrasted with the generally conservative tone of his clothes: close-cropped on the sides, piled with glistening brown noodles on top. A small declaration of unconventionality.

On a shelf behind Nelson, Nick saw the five exquisite genealogical books the architect had researched, written, laid out, and published. It wasn't that no publishing house had been interested; Nelson simply didn't want to relinquish artistic control to anyone. He had commissioned an old, renowned London bookbindery to make his fine volumes, and collectors reportedly considered them highly desirable. The books dealt with the various lines of his own family, over a period of some six centuries. They had garnered several awards, as well as many accolades from genealogical professionals since he'd first begun to produce them, at the rate of one every two years or so. And they had secured a somewhat unwanted reputation for him as an expert on seventeenth- and eighteenth-century passenger ship migration. Nelson was fond of complaining about the increasing demands on his time from strangers seeking genealogical help of all sorts, but Nick was sure he actually enjoyed his modest fame.

Nelson leaned back in his chair, stretched his arms, and locked his hands behind his head. "Let me ask you this: why hasn't your client…an elderly gentleman, you said?"

"Yeah. From out of town."

"I see. Why hasn't he contacted the Society?"

"Pride, I suppose," Nick said. "You know how these things are. He doesn't want to face the indignity of being turned down if his theory's wrong. He wanted a quiet investigation before he approached the official certifying body, the Society itself. Very upper-crust guy, lots of cash—which largely explains my interest. If you ask me, my client needs another lineage society plaque on his wall like a hole in the head. But, hey, who am I to tell him what to do?"

While Nick spoke, Nelson, like someone who suspects that he is the butt of a joke, studied his visitor closely. At last he appeared to buy Nick's story—which was made out of whole cloth.

"All right, then," Nelson said, aligning three drafting pencils on his desk. "You say this ship entered the struggling French outpost of La Nouvelle-Orléans in—what year was it?"

"Same as the *Allégorie*: 1731."

"Ah, the retrocession. The year the Company of the Indies dumped New Orleans back in the lap of the French government. Well, passenger arrivals aren't centrally indexed for this early period; and the National Archives will be of no help. You'll need to check Filby and Meyer's *Passenger and Immigration Lists Index* for the surname, and Filby's *Bibliography* for any references to the ship. Of course, these show only what's already appeared in print. For the still unpublished material, I suggest the various incarnations of the Louisiana State Museum in Jackson Square and elsewhere, and the Historic New Orleans Collection. You'll want to explore the Notarial Archives, and the public library, downtown, which bills its collection of colonial manuscripts from about 1769, but quite often you'll find earlier material. When the Spanish took over, they inherited some French records, which sometimes appear unexpectedly. You might also swing over to Loyola and check the Spanish Documents Project. But the French *Archives Nationales*, in Paris or La Rochelle or on microfilm, is still your best venue for Company of the Indies records…"

Nick held up his hands to stop the flood of sources he already knew. In fact, he'd spent a very full day Tuesday in a fruitless effort to find this phantom ship—if it was a ship. He didn't want to tell Nelson he had no actual surname to search for, the usual way to begin. All he had was a possible ship's name, *True Faith*, and an equation in a dead man's pocket that might also have figured in the death of Bluemantle.

"There's my problem, Nelson. I've checked around, and there's no sign of my individual's name or of this ship arriving here in 1731. But that doesn't mean there was no such ship, just that maybe that bit of information slipped through the cracks."

"The proverbial impossible gap, eh? Perhaps you're right. I really despise those. But let's remember that not so long ago, startled researchers uncrated thousands of volumes of passenger lists at the Washington National Records Center in Maryland. Filby, I understand, compiles two thousand new references a week. It's my opinion that impossible gaps are rarely impossible after all."

"You just have to exhaust the possible, right?" Nick added.

The computer behind Nelson politely announced, "Darling, you have mail," in what sounded like Marlene Dietrich's pre-recorded voice.

"That tickles me every time she says that." Smiling, Nelson touched some keys and a schematic of a building filled in the screen. "Excellent! I've been waiting for that. Are you still a Luddite, Nick, as in the old days, hoping all the machines will self-destruct? These new computers really *are* remarkable. And this Internet—my word! Amazing!"

"Yeah, well I guess my days atop the pillar are just about over. I may be weakening, but no one's going to make me a cheerleader for high-tech toys."

Nelson chortled as he placed the schematic in a file with a few deft moves of the mouse. He turned again to face Nick.

"Always the radical, eh? Glad to hear it. The world needs people like you."

Nick then explained that his client had a couple of conflicting family traditions. One said that the immigrant ancestor arrived on the *Allégorie*—except he was not listed as having done so, according to the Society's records. The other tradition stated that the ancestor arrived that same date on a ship called the *True Faith*, an English ship. Of course, the man wanted the *Allégorie* tradition to win, Nick said; but he needed certainty.

"It's conceivable, I suppose," Nelson said ruminatively. "These colonial arrival lists are scattered to the winds. To say they are incomplete is a gross understatement. Perhaps some local official rong passenger-list information, or later, years later, .ranscription error, a confusion of the manifests of the two ̣ent ships. This blunder could have been the result of something as simple as a ripped page, an inkblot, or a column of names placed too close to the wrong ship's name. Or perhaps a boozed-up notary or clerk, spelling unfamiliar Anglo-Saxon names with a French twist. And you know of the calendrical confusions: Old Style Julian versus New Style Gregorian, or a new year starting in spring for some, in January for others. The ships might not have arrived on the same day—or even the same year—at all!"

Nelson went on to suggest that the passengers of the *True Faith* could have been English or Irish Catholics, recusants with French-sounding names—a not uncommon situation due to the Norman Conquest and cross-Channel aristocratic and royal marriages. Perhaps they had sought a life among co-religionists in the new French colony on the Mississippi. But he felt sure he would know about such an unusual, though not unprecedented, event.

"So," Nelson said, "if separated from the English ship's name, the passengers' names would not have appeared odd mingled with the *Allégorie*'s passenger list. Stranger things have happened in the annals of record keeping. But you say we have only the testimony of one of the immigrant's great-great-grandsons, who supposedly wrote a monograph, now lost, suggesting that there was some merging? Otherwise, we don't know who walked off the *True Faith*, because no records on this side survived."

"That's about the shape of it," said Nick.

"Well, it's quite convoluted. But anything's possible, considering all the colonial turmoil that was going on. Two different ships, two groups of people, a colossal mistake in record keeping that placed individuals where in fact they were not. Who rightfully belongs to which ship? Hmmm…a corrected passenger list for the famous *Allégorie*. Would deletions be necessary? Additions? Could cause a delicious stink."

Nelson stagily rubbed his hands at the prospect of such a research coup. His love of logic took over. "Obviously, we would need to find the *True Faith* as she *began* her voyage. If you *don't* locate your man on that ship, *and* if individuals from the *True Faith* in fact appear in error on the known list of the *Allégorie*, then you have something solid: there was indeed some sort of merging, and the accuracy of the known list is therefore eminently questionable. When you've proved that, how you convince the Society that they've been in error for nearly two centuries is beyond me. After all, *they* certainly know their own records better than anyone."

Nick had taken the equation "ALLÉGORIE = TRUE FAITH" literally, as a working hypothesis. Could they have been two ships, similar in some essential way, a similarity that now held deadly secrets? He had formulated the scenario of the conflicting family traditions and the faulty records to get Nelson talking about his specialty. There was no one better at it in the city. His ploy was working. It *was* a murder investigation, though, and Nick didn't want Nelson to know any more than necessary.

"An interesting problem," Nelson said. "Almost the inverse of the situation with the *Allégorie*."

"How's that?" Nick asked.

"Well, there's a frustrating impossible gap in the *Allégorie*'s voyage, as well. Your client, I assume, has proof that the *True Faith* left a certain port, but we don't have anything concrete to show that it arrived here. By contrast, we know the *Allégorie* arrived in New Orleans, but we lack primary documentation on its embarkation from the French port, believed to be St.-Félicien-sur-Mer."

"I wasn't aware of that," Nick said.

"Let's get back to this English ship. Frankly I can't imagine what a ship like that was doing here, unless it was something peculiar, an emergency port call, or perhaps it had been captured. Europe was constantly at war, and there was tremendous trade friction in the Southeast at this time among the French, the Spanish, and the English, all jockeying for alliances with the various Indian tribes. This being New Orleans, though, there was some smuggling by the hard-pressed colonists with the Spanish. But France, on paper, guarded her monopoly and tried to keep her arch-foe England and her colonials out. Even in the 1750s, Governor Kerlérec was taken to task for letting in some English merchant ships with much needed flour—the French must have their baguettes, you know. Be that as it may, where does your client say the ship sailed from in 1731?"

"Well, I don't know exactly what British port," Nick said. "That's really why I'm here."

"Oh, this *is* going to be fun for you. Like looking for a needle in the Atlantic. Do I detect the need for a little expense-paid trip to England for research, you sly dog?"

"Could be," Nick said. "I wouldn't argue with that.... Something you mentioned earlier puzzles me: all these years—what, since 1820-something—everyone has just taken the Society's word that their manifest is correct?"

"Oh, certainly not. Eighteen twenty-three was the year of the Society's founding. The documentation, which I and many other researchers have personally reviewed, is beyond reproach. It has been proved with reasonable certainty that the St.-Félicien-sur-Mer records were destroyed in a fire during Napoleonic times. Nevertheless, the departure and arrival are copiously documented through primary testimony by the passengers and crew, Louisiana colonists and officials, and a slew of other contemporary sources. There's even a rare New Orleans broadsheet newspaper of the time. The lineages of the passengers and crew have been exhaustively traced, and they are where they are supposed to be before and after 1731. Which is more than I can say for your research target." Nelson paused; his gaze moved around the room.

Then he found the thread of his thoughts again. "The Society has done really amazing work on the subject. Have you ever been out there? Wonderful place. So well maintained. State-of-the-art facility. There's a special room for their documentary treasures, and they pump out the regular air at night to control mold, mildew, insects, and other ills that manuscripts are heir to. Pump in inert gases, for God's sake, helium or argon. I mean, can you imagine the cost? Absolutely marvelous! You know how I adore technology, as much as you despise it."

Nick said, "For the sake of argument, let's say an English ship named *True Faith* did land in New Orleans on the same day as the *Allégorie*. Where would she have sailed from?"

Nelson crossed his arms and pondered the question. "If it's an English name, one must follow the language, and maybe one's intuition." He winked. "Paying colonists, or 'persons of quality,' as they used to say, from just about any major English port: London, Newcastle, Hull, Liverpool, Plymouth. Since we're talking about possible Catholics, check the Irish ports, too." He snapped his fingers. "Oh, don't forget Bristol—but be aware if you find something there, you may have to tell your client his immigrant ancestor was something less than a person of quality. He may be like our local French Creole blue bloods: most are reluctant to admit descent from colonists before 1727, whom they consider beneath them. It could be a shock."

"I can't help it if the truth hurts," Nick said. "Tell me about Bristol, anyway." *All is not Bristol-fashion, shipshape.* "I'm curious."

Nelson straightened in his chair and cracked his knuckles, as if he were about to give a piano recital. "Well, England was the leader in the shipping to America of indentured servants and of felons condemned to transportation. France tried the convict scheme in Louisiana under John Law and the Company of the West, but that effort was by and large a flop. Bristol was the premier port for such business. And big business it was. You're no doubt familiar with England at this time, through your literary background."

"Sure," Nick said. "In Defoe, Dryden, Pope, Fielding, Sterne, Swift, and retrospectively in Dickens, we see tremendous social upheaval. It was a medieval England, London especially, which faced the first onslaughts of the modern world, the early brutalities of rapid urbanization. The social system wasn't ready. As the population increased, poverty rose. Life and labor were cheap."

"A+ to the literary type!" said Nelson, warming to his subject, cutting in on the dance. "Crime had skyrocketed. The legal system reacted harshly. One could get the death penalty for stealing five shillings of goods from a shop or cutting down a tree. For crimes less severe than murder, treason, rape, witchcraft, highway robbery, arson, and burglary, a convicted criminal might be offered an alternative: transportation, or, as we would call it, exile."

"Any of your ancestors travel that way across?" Nick asked.

"Oh, most certainly. And I'm honored to claim them. That took real guts, and yes, true faith, in one's self, and in God. These convicts were euphemistically called 'His Majesty's Seven-Year Passengers,' seven years being the ordinary term of exile. Being caught back in England before term meant immediate hanging. No reprieve for that. Unless, of course, you could buy your way out of it. England of that day reminds me of our contemporary New Orleans."

"Transportation sounds like a good deal to me," Nick said.

"Doesn't it, though? The unfortunates without the necessary cash for bribes could look forward to public hanging—then perhaps to being drawn and quartered—branding, beheading, amputation, or a slower death by deprivation or one of the myriad diseases on the menu at Newgate, Bridewell, Tyburn, or another city's hellish prison. Most people today know the story of Australia as the destination of transported felons-cum-colonists during the mid- to late-nineteenth century; but America's earlier saga of forced emigration is a secret better kept, and one many would prefer to remain secret."

Nelson stopped here, and looked at his desk. His suddenly preoccupied eyes told Nick that something had occurred to him. But he went on without sharing whatever it was.

"Let me quote some figures," he said, getting up to consult a book. Nick suspected he was trying to hide a look of discovery on his face. *What was it he'd put together?* Nick sensed it was vastly important to the mystery he was investigating. And Bristol seemed to be a crucial clue....

"Yes, here we are," said Nelson, now back in his chair. "Something like 50,000 inmates of the fetid prisons and workhouses of Britain were transported to the English colonies of America, especially Virginia and Maryland. Reprieved felons, prostitutes, orphans, abducted children, political and religious nonconformists, prisoners of war, vagabonds, and just plain old poor folks down on their luck. It was white slavery with a thin veneer of moral justification. You could say America was Britain's first off-shore hazardous waste site."

"Didn't these people jump at the chance to make a new life?"

"Not every lawbreaker turned to crime out of desperation. Why leave England, when there were more and richer pockets to pick than in America? Think of the Mafia or the drug cartels of today; there were plenty of professional criminals, more than ever before in the history of England."

"Fagin and Bill Sikes from *Oliver Twist*."

"Indeed. Another discouragement was the trip itself—so bad that it rivaled the abysmal conditions of the much larger African slave trade. Indentured servant or convict, the transatlantic trip was exceedingly deadly, unless, again, you had sufficient money for bribes; and even then, unscrupulous captains knew many tricks to steal their passengers' valuables and honor. The crossing was normally five weeks; there were enemy ships, storms, leaky vessels, smallpox, lice, and 'jail fever,' which covers about everything else, I suppose. A hundred or two hundred men, women, and children, five weeks chained in the belly of the ship, guns and cannon trained on them to keep down mutinies. The worst captains and crews subjected the men to brutal punishments, and the women to unspeakable humiliations. One in seven died on the trip, twice as many men as women."

"I think I flew that airline once. Talk about rude stewardesses!"

Nelson scarcely heard Nick's remark. He continued.

"After the Transportation Act of 1718, more than a century since the practice had begun, all ships dealing in freighting convicts had a surgeon on board. Someone realized, finally, that the convicts and indentured servants were precious commodities; the object was to get them to the destination alive, if not exactly healthy. The merchants, ship captains, and planters on the other side all profited handsomely. Trading their convicts for cash, tobacco, rum, and sugar, they would also often get paid by the British government for their services. Many a man in the trade became quite wealthy."

"What about the reception on this side?" Nick asked.

"Well, Ben Franklin called them rattlesnakes. But those powerful men on both sides of the ocean who profited from the cheap labor and good commissions tended to be more sanguine about the whole business. Convicts and indentured servants were less expensive to buy than black slaves, and they were treated almost as horribly: they survived meager rations, wore indifferent clothes, lived like domestic animals, were hunted down when they escaped. The difference was, of course, they would eventually be freed. Some were given land, and became good citizens. But xenophobia and nativism set in. Some of the colonial governments, especially Virginia, foreshadowed their later rebellion by defying Parliament and prohibiting some ship captains from unloading their cargo. But Parliament eventually won, and Virginia had no choice. Jamaica and other West Indian colonies, though, were able to stop the flow."

Another piece of e-mail arrived in Nelson's computer.

"Thanks for the information, Nelson. I'll check out those English ports. You're too busy to be chasing my pipe dreams."

"It *is* rather far fetched. Tantamount to saying the *Mayflower* story is a lie." He gave a slight laugh and shook his head, seeming more preoccupied than before. "Some people will do almost anything to get into one of these lineage societies, I suppose. Sad."

"Let's be charitable and say my client's got things fouled up. The *Allégorie* and the *True Faith* probably had nothing to do with each other, outside of my client's delusions." At the door to Nelson's office, Nick turned and said, "Keep those kids in there building the future."

"The future?" said Nelson Plumlaw, his mind apparently on something else. "Oh, yes, most definitely. The future."

Chapter 8

Two bicycles whirred by Nick. He watched them speeding away around the next curve, the riders' butts and legs pumping, encased in latex of shimmering hummingbird hues.

He was back at the St. Charles Avenue entrance of the park. How many times he'd run around the track he didn't know. It was dusk now, and at Audubon Zoo almost a mile away toward the wide river, peacocks screeched with instinctive alarm at the approaching darkness, even though the "albino" alligators were safely confined.

Thanks to Nelson Plumlaw and his encyclopedic knowledge of shipping and settlement practices, Nick was certain Bluemantle's seemingly offhand mention of Bristol had been deliberate and significant.

Nick suddenly noticed, across St. Charles Avenue, Preston Nowell making his way down the steps of Gibbon Hall, the central and largest building of the august granite-faced trio marking the southern boundary of Freret University campus. Yes, even at this distance, in this light, Nick was sure it was Preston Nowell.

Nick had learned some years before from Nelson that the buildings—one of which housed Architecture—were examples of the turn-of-the-century style known as Richardsonian Romanesque. But Gibbon Hall had been given a more descriptive nickname: "the Fortress."

There was someone else beside Nowell, talking his ear off, it seemed to Nick—a student, a girl. A pretty young woman. Nick remembered: young minds, in the flush of discovery, innocent of the defeats, the cynicism, the backstabbing that awaited them. Not all of the streetlights were on; Nowell and the woman soon sank below the level of obscuring old azaleas.

Nick stopped jogging and walked across the grass to the gates of the park, where he took up an unobtrusive watch.

He knew the Fortress well. The Arts & Sciences dean occupied a spacious set of rooms on the main floor; the rest of the hulking edifice was devoted to history and English classrooms, and A & S senior professors' offices. Nick recalled with fondness the dank, low-ceilinged basement classrooms where he'd taught various courses. Obviously the indefatigable Nowell had cobbled together a course definition that incorporated genealogy, and had sold his idea to a dean or department head, probably as part of Freret's public education division, Opportunity College. Not a bad premise, really, genealogy as unifying concept in the study of history, literature, and language.

Nick saw Nowell and the woman clear the azaleas and walk along the sidewalk out of the deeper shadows of the brawny oak trees.

It was Gillian.

Nowell listened to her politely, a strained look of forbearance on his face. A few more yards and they reached Nowell's Range Rover. A streetcar roared by, bound for downtown, and they were lost to Nick's view.

When he could see them again, Nowell had his door open, one leg in the Rover, trying to extricate himself from the conversation. Finally he nodded his head, and Gillian excitedly brought her hands together to her face, doing a little leap of happiness. Nowell had to grab her arm to keep her from straying into the steady stream of cars and SUVs.

Another streetcar, this one heading toward Carrollton, stopped to load riders. It blocked Nick's view again. When it rolled slowly away, Nick saw Nowell craning his long neck to check on traffic, and then pull out onto St. Charles. On the door of the Rover was the Society emblem.

Gillian must have boarded the streetcar, Nick realized. Yes, there she was, making her way to the back of the car, grabbing bench handles, straps, and poles for balance. She finally reached the rear driver's area, used when the streetcar reverses course at the end of the line. She stood there, as if driving the rocking green relic forward by gazing behind, navigating in a mirror.

Nick had never noticed that streetcars at night look like illuminated coffins on wheels.

"Hey, man. You got the time?" a young drifter with stiff long hair and a wild debris-filled beard asked. In the blue gloaming, he sat against an ancient oak and cradled a battered guitar with four strings.

"Yeah," Nick said, "1731."

Across the street, Nelson Plumlaw sat in front of his computer. What he'd read floored him.

Thirty minutes earlier he'd finished serving on the advisory jury for a fifth-year student's project that looked nice, but which, if built, would have collapsed within months. They had let her off gently, he and the other architecture professors; a few kind remarks would tell her what she needed to fix for the next review. The professors knew that one of their primary duties was to prevent suicides of likely providers of future alumni.

Nick's visit that morning had started Nelson thinking. Disturbing thoughts. And after Nick had left his office, he decided to put a question to his friend in London, the manager of the bookbindery, a woman who was thoroughly familiar with English historical texts and records.

Nelson hadn't expected so rapid a response. Twenty-eight pages had arrived while he was judging the student's project. What was it, early morning now in London? The poor woman must have worked all night. And this material, much of it recently released by the British Foreign Office...well, it was curious, to say the least.

On his phone he punched in a number from memory.

"Hello—hello. This is Nelson. Nel-son. You must have driven into some interference. Yes, I can hear you perfectly, now. I'm fine, just fine. It's been quite a while, yes it has. No, no," he said, reassuringly, "that's not why I'm calling. No horrid news of that sort, thank God! I've never been healthier. Listen, I know this is somewhat unexpected, but I'd like to go for a conversational sail. It's important. Sunday good for you?" He listened for a few moments. "Dinner? Splendid idea! I'll meet you there, with a bottle of Beefeater....Certainly I remember where the marina is....I've missed you, too."

Chapter 9

South of City Park there is an oak-entangled neighborhood that became in the twenties substantially what it is today. The streets are named after Homeric figures; the houses are large but restrained in design and materials, consistent with the ethos of Arts-and-Crafts architecture. In New Orleans they're called Bungalow Style. Some of these houses are private residences, others are rental properties, and one, the largest of them all, contains the library and international headquarters of the Society of the Descendants of the Passengers of the *Allégorie*.

Nick knew of the place, but had never had a reason to visit. After the affair at the Grande Marchioness, he understood why he hadn't landed any jobs from hopeful candidates for admission to this hereditary society. Nowell had that business wrapped up, and no scraps were likely to fall to the floor for hungry independent genealogists like Nick.

This Thursday morning, he was just curious. He wanted to see what the impresario of New Orleans genealogy had produced.

The receptionist turned from her computer and greeted him in Spanish-accented English. Guatemala had been her birthplace, he guessed, possibly Honduras; he sensed that her lineage issued from a Mayan matrix. Florita was her name. She sat within an atoll of desks, filing cabinets, and office machines at one end of a narrow, high-ceilinged room girded with wainscoting. There was an air of prosperity and efficiency about the place. Nick could smell fresh paint, and he noticed that every inch of molding gleamed with a recent, thick coat; the carpet seemed to have been installed that very day. This was no fly-by-night outfit.

The fax machine came to obstreperous life behind Florita; tongues of paper slithered out into an already full tray.

"Ay-yi-yi! All right, I hear you," she said, scolding the machine without the full benefit of the English *h*. "That thing, it's going crazy all morning. One of those days, you know?" She shook her head and brought her hands melodramatically to her cheeks. Her dark eyes showed Nick that she was acting for his benefit; she was obviously enjoying the tumult and the company, yet she seemed to be somewhere more pleasant in her mind. Probably in bed with her boyfriend, Nick imagined. Poor guy. There was fire in those black eyes of Florita; life with her would be exciting, exhausting, and surely fatal if her man even thought of cheating on her.

Her jacketed black pantsuit with virginal white accents would have been considered the height of propriety on any other woman; on Florita's lanky but full-breasted bullfighter's body it fairly smoldered with sensuality. Nick peeked over the desk and saw her precariously high heels. *Could she have been the mystery woman at the hotel?* he wondered. Her hair seemed too long for the role, but she could have been wearing it differently that day.

"You are not a member of the Society or a regular library patron, or else I would remember you. You are maybe a family historian?"

"A real live Certified Genealogist, *a su orden, señorita*. I was an acquaintance, something of a colleague, of the late Dr. Bluemantle." Nick gave her a business card, one that contained mostly the truth; he had used bogus ones in his collection to gain access to many a publicly closed or restricted facility.

Nick watched her slip his card in a drawer. "Also, I've been invited here by Mr. Nowell," he said. "Good enough reasons for you, lovely Florita?"

"It's okay, yes," she said, appraising Nick with raised eyebrow. "Dr. Bluemantle, what a sweetheart. I liked him very much. Such a gentleman, but, ah, such a Romeo! He send me red roses. See?" She shook her head and tsked. A dozen blood-red roses in a vase behind her were beginning to curl around the edges. It had been nearly a week since Bluemantle's death.

"Mr. Nowell, he not here right now. You wait with me, yes, if you like, okay? I do not know when he would return. If you like to go into the library, it should be please five dollars."

She resumed her normal activities, about a hundred things simultaneously, as if Nick weren't there.

Had she not understood that he was an invited guest? Or was she demanding the entrance fee simply in a selfish effort to keep him here with her until Nowell's return? He wanted to explore the facility but wasn't crazy about having Nowell policing him while he did.

Nick looked in his old, cracking wallet, and to his horror saw only four ones. There was change in his pants pocket; he could feel it. Maybe a few quarters in his old leather briefcase, which had never looked so dilapidated, it seemed to him. But he decided not to embarrass himself by scrounging and counting it out and coming up short.

Florita was watching him again. Her hand made an impatient gesture that clearly said, *Hand it over, whatever puny sum you have.* So he did.

"I pay the rest for you, yes?" She reached into her purse and pulled out a dollar. She rose from her chair and motioned him forward.

"You are worth a dollar. Because I think you have the hot Latin soul, like me. This dark-brown hair, these thick, strong eyebrows of the philosopher, the kind brown eyes of the priest, the full lips of the passionate lover, the pale and thin face of the dying poet. Yes, I will pay your dollar."

He felt an El Niño of equatorial lust as she, standing close enough to tango, pinned on his visitor's badge.

Over Florita's shoulder, he saw a fax in a memo tray on her desk. A moving-company invoice. He could just make out the address where his old friend's worldly goods had been delivered. A Society envelope with the word "KEYS" written on it lay on top of the fax. With a bit of subtle maneuvering, Nick placed his briefcase over the tray and scraped up the envelope, praying the keys didn't clink.

"You do not forget the favor of a woman, no?" said Florita, ignorant of Nick's crime. "Such a man is worth more than money."

◻

The dimensions of the library surprised him; the street view was deceptive, offering no hint of the vastness and magnificence of the interior. He had never seen so much walnut. Two stories of shelves loaded with books beckoned him.

On the ground floor, in the middle of the splendid facility, were groups of chairs and long tables, where green-shaded lamps provided islands of light. In a commanding position at the far end of the room was a monumental marble grouping, gleaming white, in the emotional, dynamic style of François Rude's *La Marseillaise* on the Arc de Triomphe, all heroic resistance and noble purpose. Nick didn't need to read the pages of the open bronze book at the base to know that this was the moment the passengers of the *Allégorie* sighted their new home.

Then again, maybe the captain was cutting through the mosquitoes. Nick banished that sardonic heresy from his mind.

The captain raised his broadsword in prayerful celebration, women wept or dreamily touched their pregnant bellies, men stared toward the horizon with future struggles in mind, children cavorted, oblivious. Another crew member held aloft the banner with the motto: *En Foi, Invincible.*

In larger-than-life portraits, illustrious members of the Society struck dignified poses wherever there was sufficient wall space. A pair of six-foot-high bronze tablets, in the popular style of the Ten Commandments, hung prominently on one wall and identified this year's "Worthy Shipwrights"—those members who had made substantial donations during life or at death to the "*Allégorie* Foundation." Nameplates almost completely filled both tablets, and the year wasn't half over yet. The message was clear: since you can't take your loot with you, might as well load it into the groaning hull of the *Allégorie* for a few more months of earthly distinction.

Ten or so employees of various hues busied themselves at computer terminals or shelved books from silent carts. All of them looked wholesome and happy. Well paid, Nick didn't doubt. They all wore casual, slightly preppy clothes, blouses and shirts bearing in some form the Society's stylized ship. It seemed that no detail, however small, escaped the attention of Preston Nowell.

A few scattered men and women—all elderly, probably retirees, except for a younger couple exuding moneyed leisure—sat at the tables, surrounded by thick volumes; they scribbled with the desperate concentration of genealogists everywhere racing a facility's closing time. He caught a glimpse of a gray-haired woman hurrying to what was obviously the microfilm room; she carried a stack of small white cardboard boxes containing more reels than she could review in a month.

Within a balustraded enclosure, two young men at their desks engaged in a spirited but hushed discussion of some new group of manuscripts that was being incorporated into the holdings of the library. Nick got the impression that this library ran like clockwork, and that these people genuinely enjoyed working here.

One of these young men noticed Nick wandering about, acting like a tourist. Seeing Nick's visitor's pin, he gave him a quick description of the layout, what was off limits for non-Society members and non-patrons.

"The library has an open-shelf policy, Mr. Herald," the young man said. "So you can select the books you want, rather than fill out those bothersome request forms and have to wait for the staff member to bring them. We do ask that you not reshelve the books. Just deposit them on the carts at the ends of the stacks."

After that polite orientation, Nick was on his own, free to wander at will.

Most of the bottom floor was devoted to general reference, with a wealth of standard resources sometimes lacking in larger facilities. Even some of Nick's humble contributions to genealogical research were here; he mentally saluted the sagacity of the head librarian. A sign informed Nick that a skilled researcher was at his disposal to summon distant data across cyberspace, in case he couldn't operate one of the half-dozen computers in a nook of shelving units. The rest of the building held a seemingly endless collection of books, periodicals, original documents, and personal papers, all relating to the First Families and their ancestors and descendants, for the period stretching from the dawn of written history to last week—there was a weekly newsletter.

The Society, Nick learned from perusing a few books, had its own publishing enterprise, established at least a century ago. He saw the Society's insignia on the spines of hundreds, maybe thousands of well-produced books. Preston Nowell was the present publisher.

Many of these books were family histories, with a heavy sprinkling of "mug books"—local histories featuring engravings or photos of prominent citizens, along with biographies. Nick, as a professional genealogist, looked on such works with healthy skepticism. The author was often an amateur or a hack, working with non-original sources or hearsay evidence; and the mug books printed whatever the paying customer wanted included, usually only the positive aspects of a life.

A family history can be a valuable tool in the investigation of a family line, or a counter-productive exercise in ancestor worship on the part of the family or writer. Most of the publishing houses that make their money primarily from such books are known as vanity presses; and self-published family histories don't get much, or any, peer review prior to publication. Though modern efforts were showing refreshing improvement, Nick had found that most family histories from previous eras were uneven in quality, closer to novels than to professional-grade research. If there were errors in the family mythos, emotional or financial axes to grind, or a disregard for the principles of genealogical evidence, such books might do more harm than good. With the imprimatur of years, a flawed family history or mug book becomes a later "source." Thus are errors transmitted and lies perpetuated.

But publication of a family history is usually a good deal for the *publisher*, who gets his money up front, and therefore urges a lavish production on the all-too-willing writer, whose head is turned by the thought of becoming a genealogical scholar.

With grudging admiration mixed with a little disdain, Nick was beginning to see that the Society of the *Allégorie* had more money-making games than a Louisiana riverboat casino, beginning with the cover charge at the door.

Nick cautioned himself not to point a finger of criticism just yet, on such circumstantial evidence. After all, every library had some family histories, and a few of them, like Nelson Plumlaw's, were masterpieces of scholarship and style. Nick decided to reserve judgment until he'd had a chance to study examples of recent vintage; surely a first-class place like this put out first-class works of genealogy.

He went up one of the iron spiral staircases to the gallery, where more shelves, more books, more acid-free boxes of family records waited in dustless repose. He found himself at the entrance to a hallway; across the gallery, he noticed a similar one leading off the head of the other spiral staircase. Probably offices, Nick supposed, noticing doors along and at the ends of the halls. More sculpture, more paintings on the walls. What was the annual budget of this place? he wondered. Millions, it had to be.

He turned around and rested his elbows on the gallery railing, a more substantial version of the one below, around the librarians' enclosure. From up here, it was an even more dramatic view—he felt as if he were hovering over the deck of the *Allégorie*. In mid-air a few feet below the level of the railing, the captain's marble sword thrust upward, and the banner waved in timeless rigidity. On the far wall, there was a minivan-sized, intricate model of the ship under full sail. Nick hadn't looked back when he entered the main room, so he'd missed it. What a piece of work; must have taken years to put together!

The really rare stuff was in a climate-controlled room at the rear of the gallery. Now facing it, Nick saw a sliding glass door and a study area inside. On closer inspection, he noticed retracted metal doors that probably served to shield the room after hours. There was a keypad to the right of the doorway; a green dot glowed at the top next to a darkened red dot. This was the renowned state-of-the-art facility Nelson Plumlaw had mentioned. To Nick, it suggested a maximum-security prison cell.

According to Nick's guide booklet, scholars and members could study here original letters and testimony of the First Families, certain surviving ship records, family Bibles, and other documents too rare and fragile to leave unprotected. There was only one way in and one way out.

When not in use, the room was emptied of nasty old everyday air, and helium, nitrogen, and argon were pumped in according to a complex protocol to discourage deterioration of the treasures within. Nothing living—not insects, bacteria, or fungi—was supposed to be able to endure in this "anoxic inert atmosphere" of less than 2% oxygen concentration. The Society had even received research grants from the National Archives, which kept the Declaration of Independence and the Constitution under similar conditions, and from the Getty Conservation Institute.

Nowell doesn't miss a trick. Probably has a Washington lobbyist.

A small sign warned, "Rare Documents Room. Authorized Entry Only: Please consult librarian downstairs." When he got close enough the door opened automatically, creating a small climatic event as air rushed out of the pressurized room. He felt on his face just the right levels of humidity and coolness for the preservation of fragile documents—45% relative humidity, and 65 degrees Fahrenheit, according to the booklet. He detected an elusive scent of sea and age—but maybe that was his imagination.

The rest of the library had given Nick a warm, welcoming feeling, like that which he remembered on entering other great libraries; he wasn't sure if it was the staff or the collected knowledge that put him at ease. By contrast, this room was sparely furnished and seemed to Nick as sterile as an operating room. The diffuse but adequate light came from unseen sources. Nick guessed that every inch of the decor and every lighting fixture had been vetted for chemical emissions and ultraviolet rays potentially dangerous to the treasures that were studied here.

One man sat at a table with his back to Nick. Behind a tall ticket-counter desk a strapping young man sat on a stool. There was a register book and a stack of white cloth gloves on the counter. To the right, Nick saw the wired-glass enclosure that held the irreplaceable artifacts. In cases along the walls of the study area, the everyday wardrobes and possessions of Society members through the years were displayed on headless mannequins.

Looking up from the military thriller he was reading, the young man said, "I'm sorry, sir. This room is only for—"

"Yeah, I know," Nick replied. "Society members and library patrons. Just popped in to visit with a friend. I won't touch anything. Promise. What's happening, Coldbread?"

Edward Coldbread was trying to hide behind his hands. At the mention of his name, he flinched as if he'd been stabbed, and hastily covered his notes. He looked up slowly. "You're following me!" he sputtered, pointing a white-gloved hand accusingly at Nick.

The young man at the desk said a few words into a telephone, hung up, and returned to his book, apparently satisfied that Nick was no immediate threat to the precious manuscript collection.

Nick sat down across from Coldbread. On the table were very old handwritten pages, flaking books, and vellum rolls.

Somebody trusts him. Probably not a good idea.

For several years Nick had seen Coldbread frequently at the Plutarch, without a word passing between them. Then, out of the blue, he showed up at his apartment one night, pointing a revolver at him. He accused Nick of trying to horn in on a fortune in gold stolen during the Battle of New Orleans. Coldbread had been searching for it for years. No clue, no matter how unlikely or distant, was beyond the pale for Coldbread; his dogged research had turned him into a passable genealogical scholar. Nick managed to disarm him that night, and they had been uneasy friends and quasi business partners ever since.

"I didn't even know you were in the country," Nick said in his defense. "The last I heard, you were hot on the trail in Australia. Say, you'd make a great butler. Those white gloves are a nice touch."

"Oh, shut up! You know what these are for, as well as I do. Skin oil." His flaccid, bloodless face lost some of its petulance. "My pursuit led nowhere. But the flight was remarkably pleasant. Excellent *foie gras*. Did you uncover anything on our"—he looked around warily—"question?"

A man had just died in southwest Louisiana, supposedly leaving a huge, unexplained bequest in gold to his church. A remnant of the treasure Coldbread had lusted after for so many years? Coldbread often chased after such wisps of speculation.

"What I found out is in your P.O. box as we speak," Nick said. "According to the probate records, if that was the guy, he died with no share of the treasure. He left a grand total of $7,500 to that church, including three gold dollar coins in poor condition. Rumors added a few zeros to the guy's wealth. By the way, you owe me $400."

"I thought you were on retainer."

"Right, but you haven't paid me in two months."

"Well, I'll, er—speak to my bookkeeper. Oh, never mind."

Grumbling, Coldbread withdrew his wallet—with Mickey Mouse embossed on the leather, from Disneyland Paris, he said, with a childlike gleam in his eyes—and paid Nick. Four hundreds. He was the heir to ten-or-so million in his middle years, and as hard as he tried he would never spend it all on his grand passion. He was a smug, fastidious, peevish, paranoid little man, with a face only a mother could love. But he had the antiquarian's wide-eyed fascination with the imagined sights and sounds of the past, combined with something of the professional genealogist's addiction to gathering the obscure facts of family relationships.

Nick had to like the peculiar fellow. Besides, Coldbread had published Nick's last two books, which, for genealogical works, had done fairly well in sales, surprising them both. Coldbread's own works were worthless flights of fancy and self-justification that no reputable house would touch. Which explained why he had his own publishing company.

"I'm onto something here," Coldbread whispered. "A son of one of the Packenham Five might have married a great-granddaughter of an *Allégorie* passenger. If I can find her, I might be able to find her husband's father."

"Which passenger?" Nick asked, innocently enough.

Coldbread shook his head violently. "I refuse."

The Packenham Five, as he'd dubbed them, were five of Lafitte's men within earshot of the dying Sir Edward Packenham, who, Coldbread believed, blabbed the hiding place of a hoard of stolen American gold. If it existed, and if together they found it, Nick and he would split it. Nick had persuaded him that this deal was the least he could do after having tried to murder him. But Nick wasn't holding his breath.

"I might be able to help, but fine," Nick said. "Just remember we have a deal."

"Oh, all right. Now go away, please. I'm busy."

Nick wanted to tell Coldbread what a shit he could be sometimes—well, quite often, actually. But he kept quiet.

Nick walked to the door, which opened with a *whoosh*. He turned back to see Coldbread again absorbed in his studies, his nearly bald head dangling greasy strands perilously close to the manuscript, his lips moving as he read. The young man at the desk took a puffy white surgical cap from a box, walked over to Coldbread, and suggested he put it on.

Off one of the spiral staircases, a long hallway led to a large and impressive paneled door. Busts of past Captain-Directors sat on column pedestals on both sides of the hall, each staring at his counterpart across the colorful naturalistic patterns of an exquisite Savonnerie carpet runner.

The door at the end of the hallway opened an inch, and then more as Gillian Vair emerged; she closed it quickly, carefully, and soundlessly behind her. She entered a code on the numeric keypad beside the door; a green light went out, a red one began flashing.

Gillian started down the hall, a folder under one arm. She stopped in front of one of the marble busts, touched the cold face, and then hurried on, her head lowered.

She was midway down the hall when Nick saw her.

"Hey, I've been trying to get in touch with you," he said, stopping at the entrance to the hall. "Hey, Gillian. Gillian, what's wrong? It's me, Nick."

She seemed not to see him through her tears or hear him even as he held her by her birdlike shoulders and faced her.

He noticed the two rows of marble busts stretching down the hall behind Gillian, and unbidden, Nelson Plumlaw's casual remark about the doppelganger floated into his consciousness. In folklore and in art, he recalled, meeting one's double was an event fraught with danger—and sometimes death.

"Nick? What…what are *you* doing here?" Gillian stammered.

"I was about to ask you the same thing."

"Oh, I work here now," she said, forcing an unconvincing smile. "You know how I told you I was so interested in genealogy?" She tried furtively to wipe the evidence of her tears away.

"Let's go sit down," Nick suggested. "Your color doesn't look so good."

But the rest of her did. She wore a navy cardigan sweater over a cheerful red plaid button-down shirt and camel slacks. Her only concession to library dress code was a scarf that showed dozens of small *Allégorie*s navigating the folded silk.

"Just startled, that's all," she protested, as Nick led her to a study alcove with a table and chairs, among the stacks of books.

"You've been trying to reach me?" She dabbed her eyes and nose with a tissue.

"I certainly didn't call to speak to your machine."

"Sorry. I never check that thing. Anyway, I've been really busy. Started here…what's today?"

"Thursday."

"Yesterday, actually. There's so much to learn."

Nick patted her arm. "I just hope they didn't put you in charge of scheduling anything, somebody who doesn't know what day it is. What's in the office down the hall, with the monumental door?"

"Oh, that's the Captain-Director's office."

"Is that where you were? I heard he wasn't in the building."

She pulled the tied flap folder toward her, avoiding his eyes. "I was in another office. I—I had to get some files."

Nick felt she was lying, but he couldn't be sure. When he'd first noticed her, she was already halfway down the hallway.

"You seem uptight, Gillian. Anything I can do?"

An elevator behind them opened. A man in a wheelchair rolled himself out with effort, nodded and smiled at them, and then rolled toward the Rare Documents Room.

"It's just…just the new job," Gillian said, when the man was gone. "And my family, too. I get sad sometimes when I think about my brother and my father. It's like I have this rat of pain inside, and my soul is a cat. Every now and then the cat nibbles a piece of rat ear, a piece of tail, and saves the rest for later."

"There goes my great idea for the evening. I was about to suggest a sinfully delicious meal, followed by some deliciously good sinning. But I've lost my appetite!"

She loosened up a bit, returning from the dark place where her soul had hidden the rat. "There's nothing I'd rather do tonight than be with you. I'm going to see Daddy this afternoon. Come with me, and then we can play."

Chapter 10

LifePath Estates was the brainchild of a national hospital chain and an international hotel conglomerate. The infirm of any age with the hefty entrance fee, the exorbitant yearly tab, and whatever could be extracted from Medicare and private insurance, could spend pampered convalescent years with resort-hotel amenities and top-notch medical care.

Hugh Montenay had been a resident here since the death of his son nearly two years before. This mild late afternoon he sat in the coppery spring sunlight on a bench, a warm breeze frolicking in his thick salt-and-pepper hair. He was a handsome man with an outdoorsy complexion and a slightly overfed but still-vigorous physique. At sixty-three he looked at least ten years younger. His eyes told a different story, though, of sadness beyond his age.

Now and then he explored the white scar along his left cheek with his left hand; but this seemed only to awaken unpleasant thoughts for him. Soon he would slowly draw his hand away, letting it drop once again into his lap, to rest limply beside his other hand.

"Good afternoon, Mr. Montenay," a stooped, wizened woman said. She had stopped on the gravel path in front of the bench. Her rail-thin husband held the arm that wasn't propped on her cane.

"Isn't it a beautiful view?" she said. "I love to sit there, myself. The pool down the steps, and the fountain, and all the lovely lawn and flowers we have at our disposal…oh, it's simply delightful!"

"Come on, Maude," urged her husband. "He's in one of his moods today. Must'a gotten the wrong kinda candy from his ex-wife."

"Oh, hell!" Mr. Montenay said, with sudden Victorian stage melodrama.

"Well, I think it's nice she sends it," Maude said to her husband, making sure Mr. Montenay heard her, ignoring his outburst.

"But it's the wrong kind, Maude. He doesn't like fruit centers. He likes the creams. I think she does it on purpose."

She patted Mr. Montenay on a knee. "Oh, that's all right, dear. You're just having a bad day. I hope you feel better."

Maude and her husband crunched off down the path and began a careful descent along a handrail. Six wide steps led gradually down to another level of the pleasantly landscaped grounds.

"Daddy?"

Gillian and Nick stood before him now.

"Daddy, this is Nick Herald. He's a good friend. He wanted to meet you."

"How do you do, sir," Nick said, extending his hand. Mr. Montenay kept his hands in his lap and looked reproachfully at his daughter.

"I don't need to be here, Gillian," he said, his dry lips stuck to his teeth in what looked to Nick like a snarl. Mr. Montenay crossed his arms in a pout. His eyes welled up.

The visitors sat on the bench, Gillian between the two men.

"Yes, you do, Daddy. They're good to you out here. You know they are. Look, I brought you some goodies." She bent over her knees to get the gifts from her Limited shopping bag. She presented them with obvious pride. "Here are some new pajamas, all cotton, like you like. And a pair of slippers. A magazine on model shipbuilding. A backgammon game. And our little secret."

She looked around for staff members and then handed him a plastic flask, which he grabbed and stuck in a pocket of his expensive silk robe.

"Here's a box of your stationery, and some nice rollerball pens. They were on special at Rite Aid. A brand new design."

"But K&B has the kind I—"

"Come on, Daddy. I've told you that K&B sold to Rite Aid. Just a different color on the sign, that's all."

K&B's purple oval signs had dotted New Orleans street corners for decades. Mr. Montenay seemed unable to take in the loss of the beloved homegrown drugstore chain. Most other area residents were similarly chagrined.

Gillian turned to Nick, and said in lowered voice: "He used to like building models. And writing letters, especially to Jules, my brother."

"Cigars?" Mr. Montenay asked, looking with disdain at the gifts on the bench beside him.

"Linda sends those. Remember Linda, Jules's wife? You have a picture of her and the grandkids on your TV. I'll call her and ask her to send it a little earlier this time. Don't let them catch you, Daddy."

"Bastards!" said Mr. Montenay.

Nick had interviewed many mentally deteriorating elderly people, trying to squeeze even one drop of genealogical nectar from their silences or jabbering. But this looked like a hopeless case. He was already counting the minutes until he and Gillian would leave.

To Nick, Gillian's father didn't seem to be making an effort, didn't seem to deserve all the love his daughter so obviously had for him. But he tried not to be too hard on the old fellow. He knew from experience that you seldom realize you're being a cranky, selfish asshole at the time, especially not someone as sick as Mr. Montenay. And he had fallen before into the trap of blaming sick friends and family members, as if illness were their deserved punishment for being weak-willed enough to succumb and then to show their suffering.

This was tough on Gillian. Her face wore a look of deflated hope, of old fears turning to resignation. She was the student who knew she didn't know the answers, but sat there staring at her blue book, waiting for some sudden enlightenment, as the other students wrote furiously. It was the way Nick had seen her the night of Bluemantle's death at the hotel.

He put a hand on her shoulder. Mr. Montenay noticed and eyed him with what Nick took to be anger and jealousy.

"What do you do for a living, Dick," Mr. Montenay said, for an instant the normal father of a beautiful woman.

"It's Nick, Daddy, like in Nicholas."

"I'm a professional genealogist. You know, family trees, lineage societies—"

"I *know* what it is!"

"Daddy, now calm down or we'll have to call a nurse. Go on, Nick, please."

Mr. Montenay briefly caressed his scar.

"Well, I was just going to say that genealogy has become very popular, especially for people your age, Mr. Montenay. And it's almost as fun as backgammon. It would be a pleasure to get you started, if you're interested. Gillian, in fact, has just taken a job at the—"

Gillian elbowed Nick and interrupted: "I've just taken a job-aptitude test, Daddy. It showed I'd be good in historical research. We have to go. Goodbye, Daddy. Be sweet."

She got up abruptly, gathered her empty shopping bag and her purse, and kissed her father on the forehead. He weakly returned the kiss on her offered cheek. His eyes filled again and he looked down, shaking his head.

"Goodbye, Mr. Montenay," Nick said, knowing better this time than to offer his hand.

Nick and Gillian began walking away. He took her hand.

"I shouldn't have put you through that," she said. "He's awful with other visitors. And once he gets like this, well, there's no point in staying."

"Why is he here? I'm sure you could arrange care at home for a lot less money, or am I wrong?" he asked. "I haven't had to deal with this yet. My parents are still fairly active and healthy and spending my inheritance in southern California."

"Money isn't a problem. Never has been. Daddy is...well-provided for. No, the problem is, he tried to kill himself after Jules's death. Shot himself in the mouth, but—thank God—he just lost some teeth and a little jaw. He couldn't handle Jules's death. He felt it was somehow his fault. Then I went to pieces for a while, too, under the weight of it all....Oh, you don't want to hear all this."

"Sure I do. I wondered about that scar....Why didn't you want me to tell him about your job at the Society?"

She withdrew her hand and looked away. "He wouldn't be happy that I'd taken such a menial job, after all the schooling he's paid for."

"You have to start somewhere," Nick said, "and the Society's not a bad place to begin, especially if you're aiming at a career in genealogy." But he knew that wasn't it; there was another reason why she didn't want her father to know. He was learning not to expect straight answers from her. It would be futile to ask her why she'd left her Society scarf in the car. She was thinking ahead, way ahead of him.

"Stop!" Mr. Montenay shouted behind them.

His hand out, he walked excitedly toward them, the gravel crunching beneath him. Nick grasped his hand and felt something pressed into his own palm. Looking down, Nick noticed for the first time the man's ring: *En Foi, Invincible*—the ring of the Society of the *Allégorie*.

Mr. Montenay gave Nick a distressing look of expectation, the look of an old dog certain that walk time has arrived. Nick had an odd feeling that Mr. Montenay was entrusting his life to him.

"Oh, Daddy, that was so *good!*" Gillian said brightly, as if to a child who had just performed some adult feat. "Come on, I'll walk once around the path with you. Do you mind, Nick?"

"Take your time. I'll be at the car."

He leaned against his rust-pitted white MGB-GT, a recent replacement for his old BMW, which had finally gone to automotive Valhalla. The crumpled wad Mr. Montenay had passed to him was a page fragment from the box of stationery Gillian had brought. In urgent, large letters Mr. Montenay had scrawled:

ALLÉGORIE = TRUE FAITH.

Chapter 11

Gillian and Nick spent the rest of the afternoon visiting her favorite Uptown gourmet shops for the ingredients to a wonderful dinner at her place. She lived off Broadway—fraternity and sorority row to Freret University—in the bottom story of an unexceptional stucco house. They ate grilled Gulf red snapper on the screened porch by candlelight. A working girl now, she chased him off a bit after midnight.

He put up only a half-hearted fight. He had another stop to make.

◻

Bluemantle knew how to look after Number 1, Nick was thinking, as he drove by the St. Charles address he'd seen on the fax from the moving company. He rounded a corner and parked on one of the narrow car-jammed residential streets that intersect the beloved avenue. He walked back to St. Charles, tripping a few times in the darkness where the sidewalk had lost another battle with the roots of the patient oaks.

Bluemantle's intended domicile was a fifties-vintage condo building with a stylistic nod to Frank Lloyd Wright. The current owner cared enough about it to keep it in perfect repair. The kind of place where the "best" New Orleans families park their elders before the nursing home. It hid behind thriving banana plants and palm trees, fatsia, juniper, Spanish bayonet, and three gaunt Italian cypresses. The dignified building was probably easily missed by tourists gawking from their bus windows for further evidence of New Orleans' bizarreness.

Bluemantle would have loved the place. Nick imagined him riding the streetcar to the end of the line at Carrollton Avenue and South Claiborne—he didn't like driving—and then transferring to a bus which would drop him only a few blocks from the Society library. This residence was quite a perk, where a scholar could do some good work. Write his memoirs, even.

A heavy gate of iron bars squealed twice in different keys as Nick opened and shut it. He entered a small attractive patio with a gurgling fountain somewhere in the shadows. One of the keys he'd removed from Florita's desk worked in the glass lobby door. The secluded stark lobby was mostly glass; the one brick wall contained gray-metal mail bins and the intercom system. Next to this wall was the elevator.

The fourth floor hallway was deserted. A slumbering silence reigned. Nick waited a few moments to make sure no one was stirring and then tiptoed across the thick new carpet toward room 409. He stuck another key in the deadbolt lock above the doorknob and then into the second lock on the knob itself. No problem. But if there was an alarm, his way up would be his way down, in a hurry.

He was in. Easing the door closed, he reached for the small flashlight in his coat pocket. He froze. Jumpy rays from another flashlight lit up the St. Charles end of the spacious, partly furnished condo.

Someone else is here!

The shuffling sound of papers Nick had heard on entering ceased abruptly.

"Who's there?" A woman's voice. "Tell me who it is or I'll—I'll shoot. I have a gun...a big six-shooter."

The beam now bored directly into his eyes. He switched on a room light. "No need for a flashlight duel. I'm Nick Herald. Woodrow Bluemantle, the man moving in here, was my friend. Now it's your turn." He gave his voice the intonation of authority, as if he were here by permission.

Nick began walking the thirty or so feet to the woman. As he got nearer, he saw that she pointed something black and cylindrical at him.

At the windows overlooking the streetcar tracks, she stood awkwardly amid a minor mountain range of moving boxes. Jeans that were a bit too tight for mid-life plumpness, black sweatshirt over substantial bust, short brown no-nonsense hair. She seemed still to be rattled by the appearance of a stranger; but Nick could see from the long anywhere-else-but-here blinks of her blue eyes and the furrows of worry on her comely face that she wished she could escape.

"I'm Carolyn Drathman Bullenger. I knew Dr. Bluemantle, too. And this isn't a gun, as I'm sure you've noticed by now." She threw a thick felt-tip marker into a box.

Nick recognized the name instantly, as he realized he was probably looking at the mystery woman from the hotel. Carolyn Bullenger was the author of one of the few breakout best-sellers of genealogy: a massive seven-hundred-page guide to the Latter-day Saints' Family History Library in Salt Lake City, with enough excruciatingly tedious technical data to please the experts, and enough good-humored sympathy and down-home advice to endear her to bewildered amateurs. She had a string of letters behind her name—MLS, CG, CGL, FASG, FNGS, FUGA—that told of a lifelong enthusiastic devotion to the written record.

"This is an honor," Nick said, meaning it. "I'm a professional genealogist, too. We met once at the NGS Conference in the States a couple of years ago in Valley Forge."

He'd heard her speak at this conference and others, and he believed she richly deserved to be a Certified Genealogical Lecturer. He'd even gotten her autograph on his copy of her famous book. She ran her own genealogical firm and, when her speaking schedule allowed, did work mostly on her own family as the demonstration case for her writings, though she occasionally handled certain lucrative research projects for other individuals and institutions.

"Herald, Herald," she mused aloud, demonstrating that a good genealogist isn't satisfied until she can place a surname where it belongs. Her discomfort was apparently taking a back seat to her insatiable genealogical sixth sense. "Jonathan Nicholas Herald? You write under J. N. Herald, I think. I've read and enjoyed your work."

He was impressed. "Thanks. That means a lot to me, coming from you." Nick waited, not wanting to press her.

"Is Nicholas a line of your family?"

"No, just another given name I can't stand. Actually, the surname was Herzwald. My Jewish half—if a soul can be apportioned according to ethnicity."

"I just read a *fantastic* book on Jewish genealogy, and I think that surname was mentioned several..." She took a deep, penitential breath. "Enough small talk, right? Cut to the chase, Carolyn. I owe you an explanation of why I'm here. When I say I knew Woody, I mean in the extremely intimate Biblical sense, as well, I'm afraid. A long time ago. He cut a dashing figure in those days." She paused and looked at Nick, as if noticing the details of his face for the first time; then she broke off her scrutiny and continued. "He was dynamic, heretical, hypnotic. And I was, well, a party animal, ten years ago. What can I say? This myth about librarians and genealogists being dull crocheters"—she gave a throaty laugh—"let me tell you, that's a load of horse poop!" Her native Texas twang came through loud and clear.

She sat on one of the boxes; it gave slightly, but she didn't notice. Nick sat on another, this one solidly packed.

Nick wondered if Gillian, ten years hence, would give a similar confession filled with regret and shame. Bluemantle had regaled him with a few bawdy bits about his exploits with the younger Carolyn Bullenger. Their debauchery had ended by the time Nick met Bluemantle, about seven years ago.

"He was a good-hearted man, underneath," she said. "He drank to stay angry. Why he ended up in Salt Lake, God only knows. Pure orneriness. But there he was, working for a boiler-room operation that does family trees with little or no research. You know, coats of arms by return mail. Well, I'd gotten married in the meantime." A police cruiser sped by downstairs without a siren. Blue and red flashes filled the room like bloody lightning for a few seconds. "Jonas. Jonas Dilts—he insisted I keep my professional name. He works at the Family History Library. His is a genuine pioneering family of the West; came out in covered wagons. He's Mormon. I converted. Best thing I ever did for my liver. I was a Whiskeypalian." The throaty laugh again. She turned serious. "His wife had died, leaving him two young girls. They're both in college now. Adorable kids, and he's a wonderful man. They love me. I don't want to screw it up. I won't get another chance at a life like this."

"You knew about the memoirs?" Nick asked.

"Yes. Woodrow called me one day last year, drunk as Cooter Brown, to tell me was leaving town, wasn't I glad? He was going to work for the Society of the *Allégorie*. Just a small step up, if you ask me. He also told me he wanted to set the record straight, tell his own story. Frankly, I hadn't been giving him much thought. What's more depressing than holding the bedpan for your former superhero? He was a bad chapter in my life I wanted to put behind me. I certainly have no plans to write *my* memoirs."

"Were you in the Grande Marchioness the day he was killed?"

"Yes. I'm staying at a slightly more reasonable place. I told my husband I was doing some research here—which is true; but I needed to talk to Woodrow. I spent the whole day out at a local stake center doing a book signing and helping in the library."

A stake is the Mormon equivalent of a diocese; each stake center serves as a branch of the Family History Library in Salt Lake City and is open to the general community. In any state, one can thus have access to the church's matchless catalog of microfilmed genealogical records.

"Afterward, around five, I think, I went to his room. I heard voices inside, so I went back to my hotel."

"How many voices?" Nick pressed. "Male or female?"

"Woodrow and another man. But I can't be sure, because there were televisions on loud all over the place. When I found out he was dead...well, I can't tolerate loose ends, in my research or my life. In my hair"—she took a clump in her hand and let if fall—"I have no choice. I couldn't leave New Orleans until I'd settled what I came for, with or without Woodrow's help. I simply had to find out what, if anything, he was going to say about me—and destroy it."

"How did you find out where he was planning to live?"

"I called every major moving company with the story that I was with Child Protection in that state, hunting a deadbeat dad. The dispatchers were only too glad to help. Ninety-nine percent were gals who'd been divorced at least once from some low-life with a beer gut and a birddog he loved better than her."

Typical thoroughness of a great genealogist, Nick thought. "How did you get in?"

"Oh, come on, Nick, don't tell me you've never picked locks in attics, cellars, crypts, cemetery gates, or boarded-up houses to get at some genealogical mother lode." She grabbed a tool lying atop a box; it resembled a small metal flashlight, except that a metal prong with a sharp, wavy tip protruded from the end where the lens should have been. "I had excellent teachers—Woodrow among them, I have to give him that." She handed him the lock pick and showed him how to retract the prong for safe carrying. "Keep it. I have a drawer full of 'em. You'll get the hang of it."

Nick didn't admit that his cat-burglar skills were inferior to hers. Bluemantle had slighted him in that department.

"And have you found the memoirs?" he asked.

Had they ever been here? he wondered. Maybe the killer had taken them from Bluemantle's hotel room. Or was she hiding them in her leather rucksack?

"No. Actually"—she seemed to be debating inwardly making yet another revelation—"I don't think any publisher would touch Woodrow's memoirs with a twenty-foot pole. They'd probably never see the light of day, and if so it would be a vindictive old man's word against everybody he named in them. The whole genealogical community knows he became…aberrational. Somebody's already been through this stuff, anyway. If anybody took them, they don't have much. So I'm not all that worried about the memoirs—if they exist at all. It's some letters I'm really looking for. Some stupid, immature, raunchy letters I wrote when I was in my twenties. Lord, what a bitch in heat I was!"

She explained that Woodrow was aging ungracefully, doing rash things, drinking himself into the grave. What was going to happen when he died? Would the letters surface? How could she deny letters in her own hand?

"That wouldn't go over big in Utah," Nick said.

"No, it wouldn't."

"Is your husband the jealous type?"

"Jonas? Do you mean, could he have killed…oh, that's absurd! Ridiculous! He doesn't know anything about it. Besides, he's Mormon. They—*we* don't do things like that." After a moment's pause, she added, "Do we?"

"Nah, of course not." Nick stood up and ripped open the box he'd been sitting on. "What do you say we find those damn letters, eh, Carolyn?"

"He kept them," she said, when they'd completed their search. She remembered each letter, and they'd found them all.

"I can't believe it. Son of a gun must've still cared."

Holding the stack of letters, she sniffled a bit at first, and then broke down in an earnest, open-floodgate jag of relief. Nick led her to the dusty couch. Carolyn Bullenger was a strong woman; crying didn't come easily to her.

"You're a good guy, Nick Herald. Where were you ten years ago? Oh, I remember." She sat up straight and wiped her face quickly with the heel of her hand. "You were a teacher—a college English professor, I believe. At Freret U, just down the avenue a bit. Well, I guess you know about silly young women and unwise crushes."

Nick, amazed anew at her hard-drive mind, confirmed it and told her of the scandal that forced him from academia. He also spoke of his friendship with Bluemantle, of his visits to Samford University in Birmingham to sit in on his mentor's courses there. The Baptist-affiliated college, tired of turning a blind eye to the eminent scholar's moral lapses, finally, reluctantly booted him out. It was the start of Bluemantle's humiliating decline; yet, conversely, the beginning of Nick's rehabilitation. The parallels and divergences in their lives traced a cautionary tale Nick would never forget. And like the good genealogist Bluemantle had helped him become, he could not accept an impossible gap as final. He had to follow the downward sweep of Bluemantle's life to the reasons for his murder.

Nick felt he'd probably told Carolyn too much, but there was something about her that invited confidence. And hadn't she been thoroughly forthcoming?

"What do you know about the Society of the *Allégorie*?" he asked her.

"Not much, really. I call it a 'society of last resort,' for people who can't get into the biggies: DAR, Colonial Dames, Signers of the Declaration, one of the good Civil War groups, not to mention Founders and Patriots."

"Toughest of all, I've heard," said Nick.

Carolyn nodded and continued. "In general, the Society does okay work, even if they're a little too pushy with the self-promotion. I've never heard their *serious* research impugned, if that's what you mean. I doubt they knew how far Woodrow had sunk."

"Could Woodrow have found out something damaging?"

"About the Society? Maybe. He had an uncanny knack for unmasking fraud and imprecision. He was fearless, and he thrived on controversy. If there was anything happening like that he would have lapped it up. You're familiar with his 'The Five Franklin Farnhams of Fuller County, Tennessee'?"

Bluemantle's classic article, required reading for every professional genealogist, untangled the knot of five men apparently with the same name living in the same county at the same time. None of them, Bluemantle had discovered, was even remotely related, as descendents of all five had asserted for a hundred-and-fifty years.

"Oh, absolutely," Nick said. "Many times."

"Poor Woodrow. Did you notice the absence of any family photos in his stuff? I heard it wasn't easy to find relatives who gave a flip about his death. Finally a cousin in Massachusetts stepped forward."

"Yeah, I know," Nick said. "I was afraid I'd have to take it on myself. All I could've afforded was a pine box. Fortunately, the Society paid for cremation and shipping the remains, and I suppose it would've given him a decent burial here, if it came down to that."

"Just goes to show that genealogists sometimes get along better with the dead than with the living."

"Carolyn, I want you do me a favor."

"Well, if I can. Shoot."

"Call a New Orleans Police detective named Dave Bartly tomorrow."

"Go to the police!? Are you kidding? After I've tried my darndest to keep my name *out* of the papers!"

"You have a fairly bullet-proof alibi, right?"

"'Fairly'?" she said, still not happy with the suggestion. "Well, yes."

"Then, hey, what's the problem? Tell Bartly you went to see Bluemantle, an old friend from way back. No one answered your knocks, so you left. And tell him about the voices from inside the room. You didn't come forward before because you hadn't heard that it was murder; you've been too busy with your research, whatever. Simple as that."

"Why is my visit so important? Did someone see me?" Her eyes narrowed in recollection. "The room-service kid."

"Very good."

"The little prick stared at my boobs so much, I didn't think he saw the rest of me. What about the letters?"

"They're between you and me."

"And Woodrow, wherever he is." She stood up, covering a yawn. "I'm beat." She hugged him. "Thanks, Nick."

Her hand on the doorknob, she looked back. "If you're ever in Salt Lake, you be sure to look me up, you hear. I'll buy you a drink." She shook her head. "Let's make it a cup of coffee. Nobody's god can make me give that up."

Chapter 12

Research always produces results for a genealogist: results he expected, and those he didn't. It was time for Nick to do some of his own.

Friday morning he heard the alarm go off at six forty-five but turned it off and slept until nine. Eventually, he managed to arrive at his Uptown destination without any no-left-turn tickets.

In the cool, quiet dimness of the microfilm reading room at the Plutarch Foundation, Nick found the English ship *True Faith*.

Nelson Plumlaw had been right on the money. The ship had indeed sailed from Bristol. Nick discovered it listed on the microfilm Hawty had tracked down electronically for him. Apparently no one had ever mentioned the ship in a published article, so it did not appear in the passenger-ship indexes genealogists usually consult. Thousands and thousands of ships and their passengers share that fate; and then one day, when an amateur genealogist stumbles upon an immigrant ancestor who took passage on a hitherto unknown vessel, one more ship is raised from the obscurity of the past.

The *True Faith* had made thirteen uneventful round-trip voyages across the Atlantic in the years preceding 1731, ferrying products mostly at first, slaves twice, and then passengers to the colonies. A later notation on the embarkation listing for the 1731 voyage indicated that the ship was lost at sea; and a still later note in a different hand, referring to legal proceedings, prompted Nick to investigate English judicial and governmental records. The Plutarch had extensive holdings of these.

With a few more hours of studying microfilmed pages of Admiralty, Chancery, and Treasury papers, among others, Nick was able to reconstruct the tragedy of the *True Faith*, and the scandal that followed.

The most interesting information came from "Gaol Delivery Rolls" and "Crown Minute Books" for the Oxford Assize Circuit, Gloucestershire County, England. Nick learned that the *True Faith* was a small, swift merchantman of ninety-five tons capacity, which had begun life as a French-built ship of unknown name in 1710. She had been captured by the English and refitted as an armed transport and store ship during the War of the Spanish Succession, and in 1714 the *True Faith* had returned to private trade. On its last known voyage in 1731, the ship was manned by fifteen crewmen, armed with six small cannon, and loaded with a relatively light cargo of fifty-one felons for transportation—thirty-six men, fifteen women—and manufactured goods. These convicts had already endured considerable hardship. Most of them from London and its environs, they had been sentenced originally there and had languished for months in Newgate prison.

Then, according to the records, in the summer of 1730, they were transferred to rotting old ships, called "prison hulks," in the Thames, where they sat for six fetid weeks, their transportation delayed because of one of the periodic flair-ups of resentment in the colonies at the stream of convicts being dumped there. Finally, those unfortunates left from the original group of eighty-four prisoners were placed aboard the *True Faith* at Bristol in May of 1731. The ship finally sailed for Barbados at the end of that month.

The *True Faith* never made it. The destination never had been Barbados, anyway: it had been Maryland. Certain bureaucrats had connived in a new commercial scheme designed to restore the earlier smooth flow of criminals out of Britain. The idea was to change the name of the *True Faith* to the *Wyvern* sometime during the passage; the convicts were to be described as honest, hard-working indentured servants. This deception was revealed by an embarrassed government junior minister in 1732, when the scandal was aired in a Bristol courtroom and subsequently in the newspapers. Those pesky colonials were to be brazenly hoodwinked, their reluctance to accept any more of Britain's riffraff circumvented, and the mother country's transportation backlog was to be thus eased. The captain and ownership syndicate had been promised secretly an ample reward from the government for the risk; the captain was also to receive payment in colonial land, known as a headright grant, depending on how many of the felons he delivered alive.

The scheme failed. The ship was presumed lost, probably in a strong July Atlantic hurricane that had wreaked havoc along the eastern seaboard of America. No one could say for sure what had happened to the ship. The grief of the relatives in England led to an investigation. The saga was played out in Bristol and not London, to keep the scandal as quiet as possible. A vain hope on the government's part. There was a loud popular outcry on both sides of the Atlantic against the duplicity of the government.

Nick rubbed his eyes; even in the pleasant darkness, he could see furniture and walls moving. He felt as if he'd just stepped off a boat, himself. That's what happens to you when you spend hours under the hood of a microfilm reader.

The fly ball of speculation he'd hit to Nelson was coming down fast: it appeared that the *True Faith* never made it to Maryland, much less New Orleans. No, he couldn't see what this ship of convicts had to with the passengers and crew of the *Allégorie*. Hundreds of miles of water separated them. After all this frantic research, he knew a lot more about the *True Faith*, but he was no closer to cracking Mr. Montenay's mysterious equation or to discovering why Bluemantle and Therman had been killed.

Some sleuth he was. Detective Bartly would never fix another ticket for him.

Then he wheeled the film reel to a list of the convicts' names…and that old zing of discovery up the back of his neck and across his shoulder blades hit him full force.

The names…it was downright spooky! The names of those aboard the *True Faith* were remarkably like those who stepped onto the dock in New Orleans from the *Allégorie*, later that same year.

There was almost a one-for-one correspondence of names that even a non-expert in the field could see. Twelve of the English crew, however, including the captain, did not appear to have made the leap of nationalities, time, and distance.

Nick abstracted some of the information by hand, but got tired of that, and loaded film after film on the copying reader. He wanted everything he'd read during the day on paper, verbatim, to back up his story, to prove to Hawty that he wasn't hallucinating.

Most genealogical research facilities have copiers that eat cash by the handful. Here at the Plutarch, he had a plastic card with unlimited credit. As he enjoyed this rare luxury of free copies, Nick grinned like a kid who's found ten dollars on the sidewalk. Genealogy, for those who don't know where the freebies are, can be an expensive pursuit, one quarter at a time.

Now with the palpable sheets of paper in front of him, he could compare the passenger list of the *True Faith* with the list of the *Allégorie*. He had a copy in his ragged leather briefcase, which his parents had given him on the great day he collected his Ph.D. in English. The briefcase had taken nearly as much abuse as his degree had.

On the English ship, there was a pardoned petty thief named John Knowlington; on the *Allégorie*, a man named Jacques Nowelle first saw the port of New Orleans that famous fall day in

1731. The chief mate on the *True Faith* was Peter Windner; on the French ship there was a man named Pierre D'Hiver. There was a man named Edward Juslin, boatswain, who might have become Édouard Joscalun or Joscelyn—the spelling wasn't clear on the microfilm. And the ship's doctor left Bristol as William Montooth, but seemed to have become Guilliame Montenay during the trip.

Nick paged in his lavishly produced Society history—$45, he'd paid!—to the list of past Captain-Directors. *Well, what do you know*: these four surnames—Joscelyn, D'Hiver, Montenay, and Nowell—appeared many times as Captain-Directors. Many other past Captain-Directors shared surnames with other First Families of the Society and likewise called to Nick's mind English surnames aboard the *True Faith*; some Captain-Directors' names were new to Nick, no doubt descendants whose *Allégorie*-cal surnames had been lost through marriage. But these four stood out for their frequency of service.

Nick was certain he'd found something important here: it was as if Poseidon had waved his trident over the doomed *True Faith*, and with a few exceptions, had transformed English felons and sailors to French persons of quality—who later show up on a ship named the *Allégorie* in colonial New Orleans.

If the *True Faith* was to have arrived in Maryland in July, it was well within belief that it could have made it to New Orleans by October, when the *Allégorie* landed. Why the change of the ship's name? And why did the junior minister in court insist that the ship had been lost, if indeed it had sailed on to New Orleans? Did the British government have knowledge of this?

As usual, the more you know in genealogy, the more you want to know. Keats would understand the yearning.

Where was the connection, the demonstrable proof, beyond the surface evidence of these names, for an identification of the two ships? What happened between the time the *True Faith* disappeared in the Atlantic, and the time the *Allégorie* appeared in New Orleans? Was this strange transformation what Bluemantle had meant, when he all but damned Nowell and the Society? Had he already sniffed out something rotten in the past of the Society, begun to chafe under the burden of secrecy and complicity, biting the hand that fed him? The heckler Therman must have stumbled onto something, too. And it all somehow related to the scribbled words of a depressed old man in a nursing home.

"'All is not Bristol fashion, shipshape,'" Nick mumbled to the papers in front of him.

If he could figure this thing out, it would be his ticket to fame and fortune! He would be lionized as the conscience of his profession, a Galileo, a Darwin, an investigative hero. A Bluemantle, perhaps. The boozy old fellow would probably have been the first to slap Nick on the back.

Rewinding a last reel of microfilm, he watched the centuries roll by in a white blur. He thought of an anchor chain. Was he hauling up a chain of evidence, a chain of lies—or a chain of death?

回

"Did you find what you were looking for, Nick?" Mrs. Fadge asked, looking up at him. She was one of the devoted elderly volunteer staffers, almost a fixture around the Plutarch. He thought maybe she'd shrunk another few inches under the attack of osteoporosis; her blue eyes still were bright and huge in perpetual astonishment behind the thick lenses of her glasses.

"As always. Thanks. I put the reels on the cart there."

"Yes, we have been having a lot of rain, haven't we?" There was no point in talking to her; almost completely deaf. "Come, have some coffee and cake. I want to show you the new goodies you suggested we order."

He couldn't refuse; he'd skipped lunch and her last three invitations. She grabbed his hand and dragged him along through gracious rooms stuffed with books and antiques. Scholars have dreams of an idyllic research library like the Plutarch. Most wish to spend the afterlife in such a place. Bluemantle, of course, would have required the addition of a bevy of Playboy bunnies.

"You bought them *all?*" Nick said, amazed. He walked along the shelves of new acquisitions. Mrs. Fadge had caught the shock on his face, and she happily confirmed his question with a contented nod as she served him coffee, sandwiches, pastries, and fresh fruit. Nick had provided a hierarchy of desirability for recently released genealogical works—his own, not by accident, included in the most desirable category. But the Plutarch had acted with typical extravagance. He figured the new hoard of books and maps had cost about six thousand dollars.

"We haven't had a chance to get them into the main collection. We're a little behind in our work. Some of our volunteers have died. No, no, not Angus. He's here somewhere."

And he found Nick later, on the way out.

"Question, Nick." Angus dropped what looked like years of stymied research on a large, exquisite Robert Adam table with neoclassical fluting and carving. "I'm not holding you up, am I?"

"Absolutely not, Angus. Always a pleasure to help a fellow explorer of ancestral catacombs. Like the Masonic brotherhood, I guess. We're members of a time-honored fraternity. Did Hawty call you?"

"Yessiree, she sure did. She's one smart cookie. Be sure and tell her to come on over here whenever she pleases. Or maybe I told her that already," he said, trying to remember. Angus had a solid gold disposition, that not even the loss of a leg in the Pacific battle for New Georgia during World War II could tarnish; but his memory was another story. "You mentioned Masons. Are you…one of us?"

"Oh, no," Nick said. "Just running my mouth, as usual. But now that we're on the subject, Masonic records can be an important source. Maybe some of your male ancestors belonged to the brotherhood; Freemasonry was especially important in the intellectual background of early America. As a Mason, you may have more access than I would. Check it out."

Angus obediently wrote down every idea Nick threw at him.

For Nick, Angus represented the best aspects of those who take up genealogy: a boundless curiosity, a student's humility, a boxer's resolve and resilience, and a blissful ignorance of the difficulties of scaling Himalayas of often unrewarding documentary material. Over the years Angus had spent a small fortune on postage, fees, and scattershot records searches.

He peppered Nick with dozens of questions. Nick attempted to steer him to the proper resources, without spoiling the joy of discovery for him.

A bit over half an hour later, Angus seemed to be running out of steam, but not of things to ask. Nick always found it hard to fathom why Angus, considering the vast amount of advice he'd received, never could get any further along on his various family lines.

"Hey, Angus, if you ever want to throw in the towel and let a professional take over, I'll cut you a brother-in-law deal."

"Heck, no! It's not the findin' that's so much fun, it's the huntin'. Oh, yeah, I almost forgot." He gave Nick a handbill. "Got a special program tomorrow night. That fella's gonna give a presentation. Supposed to be an expert."

"Well, we know about experts, don't we, Angus?"

"You right, there, boy!" He laughed heartily. "Lots of four-dollar words they want a sawbuck for. You come on back tomorrow night, you hear. We'll feed you real good and then set you loose so you can chase some Saturday-night gals."

"Maybe I'll drop by. Happy hunting, Angus."

回

Walking to his car, Nick could still hear Angus's belly laugh ringing in his ears. He was indeed going to return the next evening, and not only for the prospect of good food and interesting women. The scheduled guest speaker was Preston Nowell.

Chapter 13

Saturday, just before 3 P.M., inside LifePath Estates, this conversation was occurring between a lanky light-brown young man and a pregnant white nurse.

"Look here, girl," said the young orderly, as much to the clock on the wall as to the nurse, "I got to get on out here! My woman's waitin' for me. And she don't like to be waitin'. We goin' to a jammin' party. I got to wash my car, get dressed, go to the cash machine, go to the liquor store—"

"Jamal," Toni the nurse said, a supervisory warning in her voice. "Jamal, the clock says you still have ten minutes on your shift. You want me to make a complaint to the head nurse?"

"Oh, all *right!* Give it here."

Jamal was normally hyperactive. Just now, he couldn't stand still even for a moment. Quitting-time anticipation; he'd been on since six that morning. He decided it was best at least to be moving. Arguing was pointless. If he moved fast enough, they wouldn't be able to hang another task on him.

What could he do? He was outranked. She was a nurse, he was a nobody, and he wanted to keep this job. Sometimes, he half-expected these white folks—and they were always the ones in charge, it seemed to him—to end their commands with "boy," as in the bad old days his parents used to tell him about. At least this one was kind of pretty.

But not nearly as pretty as his own ebony goddess, who was waiting for him while he was playing Stepin Fetchit.

Oh, maaaaaaaan! he lamented to himself, going over all the things he had to do in the hope of bringing his night to a successful conclusion.

Toni had Mr. Montenay's package on the counter of the nurses' station, along with personal mail for other residents that needed to be distributed. Jamal grabbed the package, praying that Toni wouldn't stick him with the other mail.

"Now, I believe he's sitting out on—"

"I know where the old fool be," Jamal interrupted. "He done had his pills yet? I don't want to mess with him if he ain't. What's in here?" He shook the kraft-wrapped package. "If it candy, I sure hope it the right flavor. Creamies. He be pissed off for a week when it wrong."

Jamal crunched along the gravel path, looking apprehensively at the rain clouds building. Just his luck: he'd get his car cleaned, and it would pour. Well, at least the crazy old man was where he was supposed to be, sitting on his bench.

"Look, Old Monty," Jamal said impatiently. "I done brought you a present. Don't ask me who it from, 'cause it ain't on here. Looks like somebody decided to give you a bonus this week. Wish somebody do the same for me."

Preferably, his woman, he thought.

Mr. Montenay took the package, a confused look on his face. The candy usually came on Monday or Tuesday; if he liked it he hid it and made it last until the next week. Last week's candy was all wrong and he'd angrily thrown it in the trash.

"You want me to open it for you, Old Monty?" Jamal asked. Poor old guy, Jamal was thinking, his compassion getting the better of him. At least he could leave when his work was done. He watched the old man trying to make sense of the change in his universe: this was Saturday, wasn't it? Jamal and the rest of the weekend staff were here. If the candy's arrived, where's Wayne?...Jamal knew the nurses weren't going to tell Old Monty about his favorite orderly's death. Wayne Therman was one strange white dude, but Jamal missed his over-the-top coworker and shivered every time he thought about what had happened to him.

Mr. Montenay hugged the package, protecting it.

"Okay, then. I done my duty. See you tomorrow. I be outa here like a space shuttle."

Jamal hurried back down the path, noting once again how much he hated his uniform. Pink and fuchsia, a deliberate corporate departure from the usual clinical white or green. He felt like a cross-dresser from the lower French Quarter. There was a suggestion box right next to the time clock; one day when he wasn't in such a hurry—

Someone kicked him in the butt. No, that wasn't it. Something had exploded behind him. Glass fell from windows in the building, but he couldn't hear it. His ears all of a sudden felt full of cotton. Something hit him on the right shoulder blade. He ducked instinctively; he'd learned that defensive maneuver early in the housing projects where he'd grown up. But it didn't sound like a gunshot. More like a cherry bomb in a mailbox or a toilet. The loudest goddamn noise he'd ever heard, that was for sure!

He felt more than he heard things falling from the sky. Small things, lots of them, thudding to the ground. Was it raining already? Turning around, he saw what had hit him on the back: a mangled bloody hand, with a big, deformed gold ring on a stump of a finger.

Jamal looked toward the apparent source of the explosion. He saw the smoking, charred torso of what had been Old Monty on the grass. The backrest of the iron bench was twisted every which way like a black bow.

Eerie paralyzed silence became pandemonium.

Jamal sighed, kicked some gravel, and put his hands on his hips in disgust.

"Shiiiit! How come he have to get hisself blowed up today?"

Chapter 14

Around dusk, with about an hour to kill before the presentation at the Plutarch Foundation, Nick headed for the Folio, a college hangout on the Broadway side of Freret University, only a few blocks from Gillian's apartment.

    He took St. Charles Avenue, his favorite route from the Quarter to the university, savoring as he drove the sights, sounds, and smells of the distinct neighborhoods that are known collectively as Uptown. Balmy air heavy with the fragrance of blooming sweet olive and the aromas of home cooking streamed in through his open window. He knew each landmark house, soaring church, eccentric shop, gracious hotel, and fabulous restaurant along the grand avenue, as if they were his old friends.

    St. Charles had always been for Nick an enchanted tunnel beneath a canopy of reaching oaks and palms with shaggy dreadlocks and green light poles supporting the streetcars' umbilical cords. Like the many residents who preferred to watch Mardi Gras parades roll down St. Charles rather than wild Canal Street, Nick believed the avenue was the best place to witness New

Orleans' talent for scripting events and cultures into its timeless, cloistered magic show.

Turning right on State Street, he drove through the affluent, historic neighborhood where the Plutarch nestled among massive camellias and black wrought and cast iron, then down Freret, the street that cut through the heart of campus. Nick had never been able to keep straight whether the school had been named after the street, or vice versa, or whether both had taken the name of the powerful antebellum mayor.

He gave up trying to remember as his car growled, smoked, and backfired, reminding him that he needed a functioning muffler and other vital parts. His inspection sticker was a fairly good copier forgery. He liked driving junkers—but junkers with character. They were expendable, and he was not their slave. He refused to worry about a scratch here or a rattle there, so that he could devote brainpower to what really mattered to him: human beings, living and dead.

After passing through the unremarkable residential neighborhoods of houses only sixty or seventy-five years old, he drove through the five blocks of institutional clutter that was Freret University. The campus of the small and exclusive liberal-arts school was a long rectangle having St. Charles Avenue at Audubon Park as its southern boundary, and Willow St. as its northern one. Nick was still weaning himself from conventional compass headings; in New Orleans, you had to learn to use the twisting Mississippi, Lake Pontchartrain, Uptown, and the French Quarter as the best clues to direction. New Orleans looked inward; the rest of the world be damned!

He turned onto a narrow street of scraggly trees and shrubs, overflowing dumpsters, and hand-me-down cars; decrepit apartments and abused fraternity houses leaned against one another. Students sat on steps in the shadows of encroaching night, in front of them beer kegs cooling in galvanized tubs. Nick saw the orange glow of many marijuana joints. He parked by the school tennis courts on the dredged, bleached mollusk shells that are commonly used in Louisiana as parking-lot filler. Court lights blazed like the noonday sun on several games in progress—yet another reminder of the fringe benefits from which he'd been banished.

The Folio was packed with students, faculty, and normal working stiffs from the real world. Voices merged into a steady roar. The music was even louder. There was a mist of burned greasy college food floating about, but very little tobacco smoke; these modern kids seemed a bit smarter about what went into their bodies, Nick was thinking as he entered the bar. Sure they would make mistakes, but most would live to tell grandchildren about it. A sign of the promise of this generation, or maybe just further proof of the idiocy of his own? Such momentous questions got him out of bed each morning, just to see how things were turning out.

He scattered a clutch of students milling around in front of the pay phone. Again, Gillian wasn't home. He didn't bother leaving a message, and resigned himself to the probability that he wouldn't see her tonight and feel the warmth of her skin against his.

Searching the dim interior, he finally spotted his friends, Professors Una Kern and Dion Rambus, sitting in a booth near the bar. He'd talked to Una earlier, and set up this rendezvous.

"We were beginning to wonder if we should call the police," Una said, tapping her wristwatch.

She moved over on the bench, and Nick slipped in next to her.

"Okay, so I'm a little late. But not the police, please! I'm already playing cub detective for the force."

Dion said, "We haven't seen or spoken to you in weeks, Nick. Thank God for Hawty."

"We see her on campus often," Una said. "At least we get word through her that you're still alive. What's going on in the exciting world of genealogy?"

"And what's this about your new relationship with the fascist pigs?" Dion had never gotten over the shootings at Kent State in 1970, even though he was in a Connecticut junior high school at the time.

Nick told them about his efforts to aid in the murder investigations, and about his hunch that the Society of the *Allégorie* had a genealogical mystery at its core that seemed to be related to the murders. He trusted them and valued their advice, yet—again following Bartly's instructions—he revealed nothing that hadn't been reported publicly. Nor did he mention that he and Gillian had become more than casual acquaintances. But he could tell Una was reading between his words. After all their false starts and finalities, he couldn't hide anything from her for very long.

She looked great, he noticed, as their conversation flowed with the alcohol. Carefully understated makeup; a fetching rendition of her hair that wove gray heartbreak into dark honey desire; evidence of some firming exercise lately. Were those new glasses covering her remarkable blue eyes? He saw her slight smile as he stared at her spaghetti-strap denim dress. She was positively seductive tonight, very much like the woman he'd been attracted to in their early days together on the Freret faculty. He remembered long-lost details of their lovemaking, and the room became suddenly too warm. Had she done all this fixing-up for him, in expectation of an evening of bibulous camaraderie, and then more?

"Well, that beats my week for excitement," said Dion. He was a tall, thin man, about six-five, with an expressive strawberries-and-cream face that was simultaneously innocent and devilish. His black-and-gray hair frizzed out six-inches in what Nick could only describe as an anachronistic white-man's Afro. He had a pointed beard with symmetrical racing stripes of gray, and a flamboyant mustache. Renaissance through Restoration England was his preferred intellectual stomping ground, and he looked the part, in his black collarless long-sleeve shirt and brocade vest.

"A student fainted during a test," he continued, telling of his "boring" week. "Faking, I'm almost certain. And my son decided to play *baseball* rather than follow my summer study curriculum for him. Chaucer. It would have been fun."

"Oh, Dion!" Una protested. "Give William a chance to be a kid. Get some sunshine, interact with other kids. You were brought up to be a scholar, like a guide dog. Maybe he doesn't want to be another John Stuart Mill. Send him to camp in Colorado or Maine, somewhere he can skin his knee without having heat stroke first."

"What does Rachel think?" Nick asked.

"She sends her apologies. A busy day at the shop." Dion and his wife, Rachel, three years before had bought a famous old bookshop on Maple St., within walking distance of the Folio. "Rachel would have him drudging away in commerce all summer. But I see nothing at all wrong with being a child prodigy. It didn't do me any damage. And as for being a guide dog, I haven't lifted a leg since we've been here, have I?"

Una laughed. "As long as I've known you, I'm still not sure when you're serious." She sipped liberally on her frozen daiquiri. Her drinks usually melted before she finished them, but tonight she was drinking as if she meant it.

"Today's essay question is," Nick said, "What's the truth behind the *Allégorie?* You may open your blue books now. No fainting allowed."

Nick took a meditative sip of his beer; when he spoke again, his tone was less jocular. "Were these two murders symbols of something evil below the glitzy surface of the Society?"

"Why can't you take this Society at face value, Nick?" Una asked. "You're allowing your feverish imagination to run riot. Better watch it, or you'll turn into one of those conspiracy nuts, who write the newspapers all the time and clog up the Web with their bizarre Holocaust denial and Sasquatch sightings."

"God," Dion complained, "if those kooks leave another pastel leaflet under my windshield wiper, I'm going to wire my car to deliver a nasty shock."

Una continued: "I happen to have met Preston Nowell, and I detected no sinister undercurrent. He seemed quite harmless, actually. A very cultivated man."

She adjusted her glasses the way she always did when she'd scored a powerful point in a debate. The glasses started to slip again imperceptibly—her little nose wasn't up to the task of supporting the new designer Italian frames.

"I saw him fencing over at the field house, last week," Dion said. "He's not bad."

Dion was a founding player in the campus Shakespearean company, which consisted of teachers and students. Fencing was an essential skill needed in staging plays of this period.

"I would have challenged him myself, except for this." Dion held up his injured right hand.

"I was going to ask you how that happened," Nick said.

"A minor thing, really," Dion said. "Just a sprain. But the infirmary went overboard out of fear of liability. One of my student actors I was sparring with became a bit too zealous and knocked me down.…Say, I wonder if this Nowell fellow is interested in acting in our productions. We can always use fresh blood—even if it is fake."

"If you ask me," Nick said, "he's got plenty of fake *bloodlines*. Oh, he's a great actor, all right. A few minutes with him, and you'll be convinced you're descended from Charlemagne, Joan of Arc, Louis XIV, and Napoleon."

Nick realized he was sounding a lot like Bluemantle, and he felt instantly depressed. Even though he hadn't seen him for years before last Friday, just knowing that his old mentor was tweaking beards somewhere in the genealogical world had been a heartening idea for Nick.

"What's wrong with popularizing genealogy?" asked Una. "It's not the Eleusinian Mysteries. That's what really bothers you about Mr. Nowell and his Society, isn't it? You really can be an elitist snob, sometimes, unwilling to allow the serfs their little pleasures." She'd become uncharacteristically worked up over the topic; usually she was the one who kept everybody's feet on the ground.

"Well, what about the two murders?" Nick asked, wondering what the hell was eating her. "Both of the victims attended the seminar. Both knew Preston Nowell on a personal basis. And I have reason to believe there's some deception—or a mistake, at best—in the Society's official history. There's smoke; I'm looking for the fire."

"You've told us the police have no real suspects," Una answered. "How can you, a civilian, accuse someone of involvement with murder with absolutely no proof? It's all speculative, circumstantial. Dr. Bluemantle apparently had many enemies. Or, as you suggested, perhaps it was robbery. This other unfortunate victim—well, I understand he was in a bad part of town, at the wrong time."

"They're all bad," Dion said. "All the time."

"You're just jealous of Mr. Nowell's success in genealogy."

Maybe Una had something here. She usually did, when it came to his real feelings. Maybe he *was* chasing a phantom built on professional envy.

"You said he was fencing at the school field house?" he asked Dion, hoping to ease away from this talk of murder and conspiracy, which was obviously casting a pall on their time together. "How does he rate that? I can't even get on the tennis courts anymore."

"He's one of us now," Dion said. "Effectively so, at any rate. And quite chummy with our mutual foe, the esteemed department head, Dr. Frederick Tawpie. Our…*master.*" Dion had to take a big gulp of beer to wash the foul taste of that word away.

"The Usurper," Nick snarled melodramatically. "If I ever decide anyone is worth the effort genuinely to hate, it'll be Tawpie."

Tawpie: the man who had spearheaded the departmental inquiry that had recommended Nick's dismissal, the man who had profited most from Nick's troubles.

"Tawpie and Nowell," Nick said, shaking his head. "And just what exactly are Iago and Macbeth plotting?"

Dion explained: "The Usurper got religion, so to speak: he's now convinced that one of his own ancestors was on that ship with the provocative name."

"Are you kidding me?" Nick slapped his forehead. "Tawpie wants to get in the Society of the *Allégorie*?"

"What's more," said Una, "the Usurper lent his support to a course Nowell is teaching in Opportunity College. Appears to be popular. It's drawn a lot of regular Freret students, I understand."

That explains what Nowell was doing at the school the other night. And Gillian, too. She knew just where to find him to make her pitch for employment at the Society.

Dion grinned, showing the gap between his front teeth. "It didn't hurt that the genealogical evangelist's society made a substantial grant to the English department."

His friend's dome of frizzy hair made Nick think of something a chimney sweep would use. He couldn't help smiling at Dion's outlandish appearance; no wonder his students didn't seem to mind the rigors of his courses. For Dion, teaching wasn't worth doing unless you could make it thrilling every day, memorable every moment. Among other outlandish stunts to make his lessons unforgettable, he had jumped from low windows, dressed up in bizarre costumes, ridden a horse into the classroom, and convened classes outside in raging thunderstorms.

"'Language Ways in Family History: Lexical Evolution in American Life,'" Una said. "A subtitle can do wonders for a course. I have to admit, it *sounds* good."

"But does it have a place in our curriculum?" Dion countered. "The answer is, absolutely not!" He pounded the table with his good hand. "Why, we have undergraduates who are ignorant of Latin and Greek, not to mention Hebrew."

Una rolled her eyes at the absurdity of Dion's stratospheric scholarly standards. "And English," she added.

Dion ranted on, playing up his indignation for his favorite audience. "We have talented professors whose sabbaticals are limited to a laughably inadequate two years. And they're splurging our resources on this, this whim of Tawpie's!—Nick, your glass is empty!" Dion gave a piercing whistle for the waitress. He ordered two more beers.

Una surprised them by pluckily ordering another daiquiri, glancing at Nick for comment. He merely raised perplexed eyebrows at Dion, who now leaned on the table with his chin in a V of his hands, staring at Nick and Una as if they were rare manuscripts he was studying.

They talked awhile about the summer courses Una and Dion had put together. Hers would be "a Victorian hair shirt," according to Dion: the poetry and prose of Matthew Arnold. His would be "typical Restoration superficiality," according to Una: the English comedy of manners.

Eventually Una checked her watch and slurped the remnants of her drink through the straw. "It's been fun. I have to leave, guys." She picked up her purse.

"Wait, Una," Nick pleaded, not budging to let her out. "It's still early. I thought you'd like to join me for a lecture on genealogy. The estimable Preston Nowell, at the Plutarch."

"Well, I—I can't," she said, blushing the color of the drink she'd just drained. Then, regaining her composure, she added, "I can't wait any longer, that is."

"She has a date, Nick," said Dion, winking. "New associate professor. He's a handsome young fellow."

"Oh," Nick said, sliding out of the bench. He understood now why she'd seemed on edge. She'd been waiting to deliver her *coup de grace*, hoping for the chance to show Nick that she, too, had a life. A life beyond him.

As he gave Una a brotherly hug goodbye, he knew he wasn't being fair, generous, noble, or any of the other qualities good friends were supposed to be to each other, but he was jealous and hurt. And it didn't help that the look she was giving him said, *Now you know how it feels.*

Chapter 15

Preston Nowell's presentation at the Plutarch Foundation that night was a shortened version of the one he'd given at the hotel seminar a week before. He'd replaced the crass hype of the shopping-network pitchman with the urbanity of a financial planner advising a patrician client.

The crowd here looked somewhat younger to Nick than the one at the Grande Marchioness, and even richer. Tanned, glittering, sweet-scented men and women—the kind who could appear elegantly casual or casually elegant with equal ease. These were the power-people of New Orleans, or at least a representative sampling. Lots of Plutarch benefactors, Nick was sure. He recognized a few corporate heavyweights, some lawyers and judges, a sprinkling of doctors, an artist or two. Nick cast out lots of charm and business cards hoping to land a trophy genealogical project.

"Mr. Herald—Nick, if I may. So glad you could be here." Nowell grabbed his hand with cocktail-party enthusiasm. Then, more confidentially he asked, "How did I do?"

"You'll have a few takers from this group," Nick said. "I think you really broke through when you compared genealogy to a wealthy estate that should be passed on to their children's children. These people know the estate-tax schedule by heart. You were speaking their language. You're quite a salesman."

If Nowell took offense at the term, he didn't show it.

"Care for some of these? Another drink, perhaps?" Nowell snared some canapés from one passing tray and a glass of wine from another. "I'm ravenous." He paused for serious munching. "It's fortunate that we met tonight. There's something I've been meaning to speak with you about. You're an advisor here at the Plutarch, aren't you?"

The two men had walked out to the porch, into the humid night. Sweet olive and jasmine broadcast heady perfume nearby, somewhere in the darkness of the grounds. The crowd was leaving. Several couples stopped on their way out to tell Nowell they'd already decided to start their family-history project. A son or daughter or secretary would be in touch.

Nick heard the solid thump of expensive car doors slamming on the street.

"Allow me to make a proposition," Nowell said. "How would you like to join the staff of the Society?"

"Well, I—"

"Let me elaborate before you refuse. Woodrow's passing has left us in something of a bind. And I must tell you I was personally devastated; he was rather a difficult man to like, but I respected him and considered myself his friend."

Nick nodded, searching Nowell's face for deception. Either he was a very good liar, or he was being sincere. Was Una right about him, after all?

"At any rate, the position of Honorary Scribe is part ceremony, part public relations, part actual genealogical sleuthing," Nowell was explaining. "And yes, part salesmanship, though I would not ask you to participate in anything that would make you uncomfortable. You would be able to define your own responsibilities. I've seen some of your published work; I believe we have several at the library. I've also made some discreet inquiries. Forgive me for infringing upon your privacy, but I find résumés to be rather misleading, by and large.

"I think you would be ideal for the position, Nick. Two more details about the job: your salary would be $75,000 a year, plus liberal expenses. I'm sure you have a place to live, but we had just purchased a St. Charles Avenue condo for Woodrow. The poor fellow was preparing to move to New Orleans from Salt Lake City. The condo would be at your disposal, should you decide to relocate."

Angus limped out to join the two men. He was very happy with the turnout and tried to pin Nowell down on another appearance. Then he asked Nowell if he would mind looking at a thorny genealogical question he'd run up against in his own research. They excused themselves to Nick and went inside.

Seventy-five grand! Nick knocked back the rest of his wine. *I'm rich! All I have to do is show up and nap in an office....I'd also be closer to discovering the Society's secret, if there is one. Closer to finding out what got Bluemantle killed, and who did it.* Satisfied that he'd dressed up his naked greed in a moral tuxedo, he knew what his answer to Nowell would be.

As the lights inside the Plutarch started to go out, Nowell emerged.

The two men walked out to the street. Nowell went on to explain that Nick could continue with his independent genealogical work while maintaining his position with the Plutarch, if he chose.

"Well, have you decided?" Nowell asked. "I forgot to mention that you'll get to wear a special version of this fabulous ring."

"That's it. The ring tipped the scale. When do I start?"

Both men laughed, best chums. Nick recognized the dynamic of the situation: each man had tacitly agreed to overlook the phoniness of the other. What was Nowell up to? Nick was pretty sure he'd detected, at some indefinite point in their conversation, the forward-looking cunning of the politician, builder, or ship captain. Behind the seemingly adolescent gawkiness of his features, there was a man accustomed to thinking big, deciding with clear-eyed remorselessness. Nick really wanted to dislike this guy, but it wasn't easy.

They had reached the rear of Nowell's Range Rover. He turned off the alarm with his remote, opened the tailgate, and loaded his two bulging briefcases into the back.

"I'm truly gratified that you'll be part of our organization," Nowell said. "A careful scholar like you will take a great deal of weight from my shoulders."

They stepped onto the street on the driver's side of the Rover. Nowell turned, his hand extended to shake.

"Goodnight, Nick. Come by Monday or soon thereafter, and we'll get started."

Behind Nowell, Nick saw the headlights of a speeding car cross the centerline. The car headed straight for them.

He grabbed Nowell's hand, pulled him back, and then shoved the bigger man into the wet grass between the street and the sidewalk.

The car swerved into the Rover near the back left taillights, glanced off wildly, and then sped down the street. It had screeched around a corner and out of sight before Nick could get to his feet.

"You all right?" Nick asked, bending over Nowell, who was sitting on the grass.

Nowell took inventory of himself and attempted to stand.

"My knee. The proverbial 'war injury,' except that in my case, it's quite real. Just help me up, will you."

"Sure. I'll call the police. You need an ambulance?"

"Heavens no, don't do that! It would take the police hours to get here. Don't bother yourself. I'm fine, really. It was just a drunk; he'll come to a bad end soon, carrying on like that. No real harm done; and the truck is well insured, believe me. I'll file an accident report tomorrow. It's my left leg, you see, which should be no problem driving." He was up now, testing the leg for Nick's benefit. It hurt like hell, Nick could see.

They stepped into the street again, walking through the broken plastic and glass. Nick looked both ways warily as Nowell opened his door and hopped in with a grimace of pain.

"You'd better go to the emergency room, Preston."

"Don't worry. I'll be fine. This is becoming a habit with you, rescuing me," he said, giving a strained smile.

"Yeah, seems that way."

Nick watched the Rover head toward St. Charles Avenue. Now he had a new understanding of the term "careful scholar": it's what he'd have to be whenever he was within a mile of Preston Nowell.

◻

On his way home, Nick stopped at a K&B—*whoops, Rite Aid*—on St. Charles for some essentials. The familiar purple, gold, and white color scheme of the dearly departed local drugstore chain, K&B, had been, before its sale to the interloper, as typical of everyday New Orleans as were the Cabildo, St. Louis Cathedral, streetcars, corner oyster bars, flash floods, bleak housing projects, venal politicians, crooked cops, and unsolved murders.

Most New Orleanians simply pretended the new owner and the new corporate colors didn't exist and continued to refer to the stores as K&Bs, in much the same way that the French colonists after 1764 disdained to admit that New Orleans had actually become Spanish property.

New Orleans is a perpetual jazz funeral in which reality, with unaccustomed gaiety twirling fringed umbrellas and boogying to horns and drums, finds itself seduced into becoming the "second line" to the city's solipsistic fantasies.

His MG trailing copious blue smoke, Nick drove downtown, now actually relishing the idea of spending a quiet evening alone among his books.

Chapter 16

Nick trudged up the stairs to his French Quarter apartment, feeling the weight of a half-gallon bottle of tank-car Chianti and a defrosting pizza in the wet paper bag against his chest. These, he decided, would be fit accompaniments for some light research and a late movie on television. Most important, they fitted his deflated finances. A balanced meal, sort of, if you counted fermented grape juice as a fruit and tomato paste as a vegetable. Yesterday a department-store clerk had confiscated his last credit card, and Hawty and Martin's Wine Cellar had claimed the lion's share of Coldbread's belated payment. But next week, he would be in the money! There was always a next week.

He wasn't particularly tired, and he was still more than a little miffed that Una was probably enjoying herself somewhere with another man, touching him, being touched....He foresaw a long, restless night of labored concentration. Vivid flashes of their many episodes of past intimacies blinded him to his surroundings, and he tripped, almost losing the contents of the disintegrating bag to the staircase.

The persistence of sexual memory. A wise primacy built into us all, older than thought, autonomic, a primordial trick to keep us propagating the species. Those synaptic pathways never wither, are forever as immediate as the last moment. Everything about Una came flooding over him: her taste, scent, feel under his lips, her sighs and laughter and moans, the permutations of their embraces....

He took a deep breath and rearranged his load.

Over his wine and pizza he planned to mull over his luck at getting closer to the secrets of the *Allégorie*...and getting paid quite well for it. Maybe that mental cold shower would drive the memory of Una's body from his mind.

After three flights of badly lit stairway smelling of mildew and old trash in cans stationed on each landing, he pushed through the squeaky door of the third floor. On the short dogleg before the long, straight hall that would take him to his apartment, he noticed the carpet was becoming awfully thin. The condo Bluemantle was to occupy certainly was nice, he was thinking. Now that he was upwardly mobile, maybe a mansion on the lake or a nouveau riche pile in some gated community....

Forget it. The Quarter's in your blood. And remember why you're taking the Society job: you're a genealogical gumshoe. So get a grip, and act like one.

Officially, madness rules New Orleans only from Epiphany through Fat Tuesday. All will be forgiven and forgotten on Ash Wednesday, with a smudge on the forehead; and the cycle begins anew. But the Mardi Gras mentality lasts all year in the French

Quarter. Anything goes between what was and what could be. The past marches through everyday life like a never-ending parade, enticing the present to join in an endless round of innovative sin and redoubled contrition.

People who come to New Orleans to unchain their ids for a week in the mild late winter find it hard to leave as spring blooms in their soul. Some stay forever, new slaves of an ageless dream, hoping never to awake. The hardcore lotus-eaters end up in the Quarter.

Nick wouldn't admit to being one of these; but as a student of human nature, several removes of temperament from the stupor of continuous pleasure-seeking, he loved the French Quarter enough to make it his home. He lived on Dauphine, a comfortable distance from the main tourist haunts of Royal and Bourbon. He wouldn't advise a friend to park her nice car here, but otherwise it was a relatively safe block, usually crawling with NOPD uniforms and invisible squads of undercover cops. He could recall only five murders in the immediate neighborhood so far that year—which were duly added to the city's running total on a chalkboard in the window of a nearby bar.

True, you had to make certain concessions to live in the French Quarter. It was noisy, expensive, and dirty, often reeking of indescribably revolting smells; parking was always an adventure, to say the least; the patrol cops were big and cranky; and you could get blown away by a hopped-up fifteen-year-old while reaching for your keys.

But he could handle all that. At least his building was moderately well kept, according to Quarter standards, by the absentee landlords—a family that had lost millions trying to run a small, exclusive hotel in an adjoining building; they were slow to learn that the Quarter, like every good hooker, has no pity for those with romantic notions.

Turning the corner now and glancing forward, Nick saw someone sitting on the carpet, elbows on knees, head down, back to his apartment door.

Startled, he stopped.

Gillian lifted her head and cleared away hair that stuck to her face.

As Nick got closer, he could see she was crying thick streams that showed no sign of running dry.

He knelt down beside her.

"Daddy's dead, Nick."

"Oh, I'm so sorry, kid. He was getting up there, you know. Sometimes it's a blessing for them to go quietly like that—"

"He didn't go quietly. He was murdered. And so was my brother. That bastard Preston Nowell did it, I know he did!" She lost control then.

Nick helped her up and unlocked his door. She knocked over an empty glass that was on the hallway floor. Nick picked it up. Now inside his apartment, he guided her to the couch and cleared the magazines and books littering it.

"Your neighbor made me a couple of drinks," she said, seemingly relieved to be relating details having nothing to do with her father's death. "Maybe more than a couple. Delicious. I don't even know what they were. I think he said he and his roommate have some kind of shop downstairs."

"The guy with the mascara and the bouffant?" Nick asked from the kitchen.

"Uh-huh."

"That was Hurvey."

"Definitely gay. He was very sweet, offered to let me sit in their apartment until you got home. Took my cigarette and flushed it." She wiped her face on the sleeve of her Jazz Fest T-shirt from the year before: The Blues Shuckers, it read, and below, a blue guitar emitted flying oysters, each opening to reveal musical notes.

Nick joined her on the couch and handed her a Ronald McDonald glass with two inches of excellent cognac.

"Drink this. Are you hungry?"

"No, thank you. But I *really* need a cigarette."

"There's an ashtray somewhere around here." He found one under magazines and journals on the coffee table. "Tell me what happened."

She'd been in her sculpture class at Freret when word came that something was wrong. That's why she was in distressed jeans and flip-flops. Nick saw dried clay under her nails.

Detective Bartly was there himself; he took her to the nursing home. She felt he was almost an old friend and was glad to see him. She tried to describe to Nick, between sobs and drags on a cigarette, how horribly disfigured the body of Hugh Montenay was. Of course, there would be an autopsy, an investigation.

Bartly is overworked, Nick thought, as he sipped Chianti from a coffee mug. All of New Orleans' homicide detectives were, he'd read. The recommended maximum caseload was ten, according to the article in the *Times-Picayune*; the superintendent admitted that his homicide detectives handled fifteen last year. And only a forty-nine percent clearance rate—an even worse statistic.

Nick was going to help Bartly improve that percentage. Somehow.

"And that's why I tried to kill him." She drained the rest of the cognac; the crying spasms eased.

"Huh? What? Kill whom? Hey, those drinks Hurvey made for you must have been pretty damn strong."

She put a hand to his cheek. "I tried to kill Nowell, and myself. Tonight. With my car. On State Street in front of the Plutarch. I knew he'd be there. But I saw you, and I pulled away. I didn't want you to get hurt. I *know* he killed my brother and my father. I *know* it! But I don't have any proof."

"Why?" Nick asked.

"They knew something about the Society that would destroy it. Daddy was a Captain-Director, years ago. He got fed up with the way things were, even though he made millions. The Captain-Directors run the Society Endowment. It was $179 million as of last Thursday, according to papers I found in Nowell's office. I copied down lots of figures, outrageous payments to present and retired Captain-Directors. Nobody ever checks up on them. It's been like that for almost two centuries."

Nick whistled. "$179 million?"

She sniffed and nodded. "I remember loud arguments between Daddy and my mother, and with other people in his study, other times. He tried to shield us from the knowledge. Well, Jules—that was my brother—figured it out, I guess, or was close to finding out. You know how lawyers are?"

"To my misfortune," Nick replied, "yes, I do."

"And I don't mean finding out about just the money," Gillian continued. "There's something else. Jules thought he'd make a big splash in the legal world with a book or maybe a suit dealing with the Society's secrets. He never told me exactly what he knew, though—I was too caught up in my own life to care much, anyway. I was more interested in boys and poetry at the time.

"They killed him. Nick, he was too good a skier for that to happen to him. You've got to help me. I want to tear that goddamn place down with my bare hands!" She reached out, as if the Society library were within reach; then she brought clenched fists back to her face. "I'll pay you."

Nick gently lowered her fists. "There's something in Nowell's office that could prove what you suspect, what your father couldn't or wouldn't tell you? That's why you took the job with the Society. And why you were in Nowell's office, that day I saw you at the library. This business about 'really, really' being into genealogy was just a front, to get you in the door."

She let her head loll backward, forward, then upright, working on the remaining tension that the alcohol hadn't banished. "I needed to learn enough to impress Nowell. I even enrolled in his class at Opportunity College. I had to get in, somehow. Because there's a safe, with a book or a manuscript or something. I heard Mother call Daddy a fool once, because he wanted to go public with it. She didn't want to jeopardize his fabulous salary. I don't know what it is, but they're really protective of it, like it's sacred or something. I can get in the office; that's easy. The code is '1-7-3-1.' But I've tried everything I can think of on the safe. And you only get three attempts before the thing shuts down; I'm afraid to go further and set off an alarm....I wanted to do this, on my own, to get even, to destroy that evil Society the way it destroyed my father and my brother."

"Let Bartly handle it, Gillian. We should leave the evidence, if there is any, for him to find. It'll help the case when it goes to court."

"No, no, no! I don't give a goddamn about his investigation, about the law! These people—don't you understand? They're more powerful than the courts and the little politicians who run the government. How do you think they've survived this long? Not by following the rules you and I and everybody else do, that's for sure!"

She closed her eyes; her head sank to his chest. "I'm tired, Nick. So tired."

"Yeah, trying to kill people tends to use up a lot of calories. Come on. Can you walk to the bedroom?"

He helped her to his unmade bed. She fell asleep within a minute. He turned out the lights and closed the bedroom door. Then he went to the kitchen, took his pizza out of the oven and refilled his mug with Chianti—to the top. On his small black-and-white television, he found a typically excellent Kirk Douglas movie he'd never seen.

Chapter 17

"Distinguished Service Cross, Silver Star, Purple Heart, Bronze Star—no, *two* Bronze Stars, unit citations…my dear Preston, it makes me proud to have you as our Captain-Director," said Conrad Joscelyn, walking along the wall where Preston Nowell's military honors were displayed. "Have these really been up here for years? How could I have missed them? I am getting too old and forgetful, I suppose. Anyone for another port?…Oh, my, that was a bad pun, wasn't it? How about you, Arthur?"

"Bring the bottle," Arthur D'Hiver answered, tapping his white cane on the coffee table in the middle of the ensemble of leather wingback chairs. Owlish white brows and lashes tufted his perpetually squinting eyes. He seemed a couple of decades younger than Joscelyn, but more reserved. Preston Nowell attributed this to the man's blindness. D'Hiver, as usual, held his head at a slight listening tilt.

It was late Saturday night. Preston Nowell and the two former Captain-Directors were meeting in his office at Society headquarters.

Nowell started to rise, but Joscelyn from across the room motioned him to sit.

"Please don't trouble yourself, Preston. I certainly know where it is. In spite of the approach of decrepitude, I remember every square inch of this room—except, of course, for your medals and other paraphernalia."

He swept a trembling venous hand around the perimeter of the Captain-Director's office to indicate Nowell's collection of épées, foils, and sabers; there were also a number of fine rifles and shotguns stored vertically in three glass-fronted cabinets. The heads of game animals competed for space on the walls.

"In my day, this room was special to me, too. Indeed, I know all the secret places, for all of our little secrets." Joscelyn chuckled as he opened the doors of the well-disguised bar and took up the bottle.

A man too much in love with his own wittiness, Nowell thought.

Joscelyn walked back to his chair with the slow dignity befitting a former Captain-Director who had just entered his ninetieth year.

D'Hiver spoke next. "We know this is a difficult time for you, Preston." After a few tries with his cane, he found Nowell's bad knee and tapped it lightly to make his point, as was his custom.

Nowell looked down at the red tip; something dark and dried up was on it. He'd missed a few of D'Hiver's words and struggled to redirect his attention to the conversation.

"You've not often been called upon to do such things," D'Hiver was saying. "We old Captain-Directors like to remain in the wings during your time on stage. But we are at war with our enemies. Always have been. I do not intend to lecture you on the horror of battle. *That* you know full well, and my memory is becoming as dim as my sight. You came to us after your war, an enthusiastic young man, interested in genealogy, of impeccable *Allégorie* descent. You promised to fight for the Society as you had done so valiantly for your country. We allowed you to peer into the deepest secrets of the Society. You learned those things that only Captain-Directors can know, which are passed on from generation to generation. We expect you to continue fulfilling your vows to your ancestors."

"I am aware of what I owe both of you," Nowell said. "However, I still maintain that Hugh was a blithering idiot. I ensured that he was taking enough drugs to make an elephant schizophrenic. I had the situation under control. No one would have believed a word he managed to get out. The note he passed to that disturbed orderly, Therman, could have meant anything."

"And everything," Joscelyn said. "Can we take a chance, Preston?" He sipped his port meditatively. "A chance with anyone? We were lucky with Hugh Montenay. My sources in the police department told me about the note. Otherwise, we might never have known, until it was too late. Perhaps Hugh's memory was returning."

"Certainly he'd forgotten how rich we made him!" D'Hiver interjected testily. "Hugh was a gutless ingrate. I never liked him."

Joscelyn gave a nasal drone of agreement. "The Society has made us *all* wealthy beyond our dreams. Preston, we do not intend to meddle in your directorship. We simply feel that you could benefit from our experience, as we benefited from the advice of our elders. You have many profitable years ahead of you. But there is much more than money at stake here."

"I know full well what splendid recompense the Society offers its Captain-Directors, and I have every intention of earning—"

Joscelyn cut Nowell short. "A Captain-Director must act swiftly and decisively. Sentiment has no place in battle. You should have taken care of Wayne Therman long before he began to hurl accusations—harebrained though they were. What if he'd stumbled across something important, or had the intelligence to put certain things together, as Hugh's son did?"

D'Hiver took up the argument: "And while we're on the subject of that orderly, we feel you should be more rigorous in deciding whom you consider for admission. No more riffraff. Ability to pay the initial fees is not enough now; we are interested only in those who have the social and *long-term* financial standing to justify our expenses. Creating an *Allégorie* pedigree is not as simple as it used to be. I remember when the only thing needed was—"

"Yes, yes, Arthur. Let's save our reminiscences for another time, shall we?" Joscelyn wiped his neat white mustache with his ring finger. The soft light of the lamps glinted along the gold frames of his glasses. His cold blue eyes reminded Nowell that beneath his benevolent exterior he was a ruthless man, with a gift for finding weaknesses and using them against his enemies.

"Those medals on the walls," Joscelyn said. "You are justly proud of them, Preston. What if someone were to suggest that you did not deserve them. That you had obtained them under false pretenses. That your whole life and all of your endeavors had been nothing but a play within a play."

"A platoon commander, left for dead in a rice paddy, taken prisoner, indicts his second lieutenant for abandoning him," D'Hiver continued, tapping his emphasis on Nowell's knee. "*We* know it was not true; *we* know the poor man was tortured for five years—a day of that would be an eternity—and finally signed the statement to stay alive, saying anything his captors wanted; *we* know our government never believed it for a moment, after he was released and debriefed, after his complete recantation of everything he'd claimed under duress. It happened in my war, it happens in every war. Which is why, through our connections, we were able to expunge the unfortunate incident from the records."

"I am not on trial here, gentlemen," Nowell said, an edge of anger in his voice. "That matter was laid to rest long ago." It was an uncomfortable subject. He had always wondered: had he indeed deliberately abandoned his hated lieutenant on that horrible, steamy day? The man was a bloody, mangled mess when he last saw him, through a storm of bullets and mortar bursts.

He ached to tell them they didn't need to coerce him. His love for the Society surpassed everything else in his life. There had been no man or woman he cared for as much. In war, patriotism and mission had sustained his young soul. But the Society did more for him now: it gave the past meaning, it gave the future a purpose. No task in the service of the Society was too great to ask of him. And just as in Vietnam during the first days of his initial tour of duty, he'd already stopped counting his kills. He wanted to be a better soldier than he had been. The best, this time.

The two old men sipped their port. Both were exquisitely groomed and carefully dressed in costly, hand-made suits. It was a level of self-assured, quiet style rarely seen today, a relic from an age when a man's wardrobe explained his background at a glance.

"Your dismay is understandable," said Conrad Joscelyn. "Just imagine if this humiliating tale were to resurface, find its way into family histories and official Society records? These days, family histories are more reliable, looked to as serious sources. Who's to say what the judgment of coming generations would be? What seemed so patently obvious to us may not seem so in a century or two."

"Just an illustration, if you will," D'Hiver said, delivering another poke of his cane. "We of the Society should feel the same way when someone threatens to undermine our beloved history, which is all the more at risk for being untrue."

"Our ancestors created a new life in a new world," Joscelyn said. "Our duty to them requires us to fight on their behalf, even if it is a lie we are defending. Is it really so different from your experiences in Vietnam, Preston?"

"I have been thorough, even if I've erred on the side of caution," Nowell said, trying to keep his roiling emotions in check. He hated to lose his temper; doing so always made him feel vulnerable and dirty afterward. "My plan to eliminate the threat of the English records is already in motion. Only a man with Dr. Bluemantle's remarkable combination of skills would be able to make the same discovery. We have a buffer period of some weeks, I believe."

Hiring Bluemantle had been his idea, his fault. A brilliant innovation, to take the Society to new heights of respectability. How was he to know it would go so sour, so quickly? These two would never let him forget that.

"Thorough, yes, but not thorough enough, Preston," Joscelyn said. "We commend you for your efforts thus far. Most of your ideas have been splendid. But here, below decks, you have allowed mutiny to flourish."

"I don't understand."

"Some genealogist you are, my boy!" D'Hiver said, adding a jab of his cane to the jest.

The old bastard was having fun at his expense!

Nowell snatched the cane from D'Hiver and jumped up so violently that he knocked his own heavy chair backward. He stood there, a dark thundercloud looming over the older men, holding the cane like a broadsword poised to sever both of their scrawny necks. The knuckles of his powerful hand were white around the j-curved, rubber-gripped handle.

In another moment he had control of himself again.

He gave the cane back to the searching hands of D'Hiver, righted his chair, and sat down. He took up the bottle and poured himself another glass of port, to the rim of the heavy crystal glass.

"Please excuse me, gentlemen. I've had a rough week. A run-in with a drunk driver aggravated my knee injury. And the police. They keep pestering me with questions about Bluemantle. Twice I've met with them in the conference room....Conrad, kindly explain what you meant by a mutiny flourishing unchecked."

Joscelyn eyed Nowell with sidelong caginess. "We all know that Hugh Montenay had a big mouth," he began. "At first. He was a crusader, who did not like our means or ends. He felt revision of the Society's history, according to his lights, was a better way."

"He had an *ethical* problem," D'Hiver said, making it clear he found such a dilemma a revolting personal habit.

Joscelyn nodded his head. "Yet, Hugh became a good Captain-Director in time. He came to see it our way once again: that even the tiniest hole in the hull of our story would be disastrous. He did, however, speak injudiciously among his family. That was the seed of a poisonous plant. And, alas, when his son came of age and went into law, he took up the muckraking mantle, and, I presume, saw some money to be made, as well. We had to make an extreme example of this bothersome young man, I'm afraid. There was also a *daughter*—"

"Yes, I know the facts of the case," Nowell said, petulantly. If this was the point of the meeting, then everything was all right. "She lives with her mother and poses no threat to us."

"Your information is incorrect, and your conclusion, therefore, is faulty," D'Hiver said, just stopping himself from tapping Nowell's knee. "She is here in New Orleans and visited her father every week, calling herself a friend of the family. She goes by one of her mother's married names: Vair. Pretty thing."

Nowell leaned back in his chair, awareness filling the sails of his mind.

"How would you know if she's pretty or not, you superannuated lecher?" Joscelyn snapped, with the gruffness only an old friend can get away with.

"I can sense the presence of a lovely woman," countered D'Hiver.

Joscelyn stood up, saying, "Pah! You're getting senile faster than I am, Arthur." And then to Nowell, "Yes, Preston, you see now, don't you? She *must* know something she shouldn't. Why would she seek anonymous employment here, after what her father has said against us in the bosom of his family? Why would she disguise her true relationship at the nursing home, knowing as she must that her father is being watched? Hugh must have perverted her mind, just as he did her brother's."

"That family has always caused us problems," D'Hiver said sourly.

"Her knowledge can hurt us," Joscelyn continued, "as surely as a submerged reef could have destroyed the *Allégorie*. She is a danger to us, as is that small-time pedigree mountebank she has befriended."

"This Nick Herald," D'Hiver said, squinting at his glass as if he could see it. "He worries us."

Nowell had not told them he'd just offered Nick the position Bluemantle held. He decided now was not the time to say he believed Nick could more easily be corrupted than Bluemantle. But Gillian's appearance at the Society…was that as ominous as the two old men were suggesting? Perhaps she aspired to being a Captain-Director herself, as was the proud tradition of her family. Nowell rather liked the progressive nature of that idea: the first female Captain-Director, and he enshrined in Society history as her trailblazing mentor, as a champion of diversity. Yes, perhaps innocent actions on her part were being misinterpreted.

Suddenly he was exhausted. He felt like Hamlet in the first two acts of Shakespeare's great tragedy—too many questions to deal with at once.

"You must watch them carefully, Preston," D'Hiver was saying, "and deal with them, if necessary."

"Or we will," said Joscelyn. He now stood before the large carved rendering of the Society's emblem on a panel behind Nowell's substantial desk. He twisted the anchor of the ship and the panel clicked open to reveal a square black metal door with a chrome handle. To the left of the door was an alphanumeric keypad, like those used elsewhere in the building.

A pinpoint red light blinked.

"Is the combination the same?" Joscelyn asked.

"Yes. Of course," Nowell replied, still thinking of all he'd done, all he had to do. Then with some indignation he said, "I would have notified you of any change. I'm aware that, according to the by-laws, a former Captain-Director must also know the combination. Arthur, because of his blindness, is not able to handle it on his own, so you are the one."

Joscelyn carefully, laboriously punched in the code from memory. "The Captain-Director has an awesome responsibility, Preston. He must protect the crew and passengers from the perils of the open sea, where disaster can strike without warning, without pity. He must know many things they cannot know. He must ensure that those who wear the ring of the Society deserve that honor."

Nowell had to restrain himself from telling Joscelyn to just shut up and concentrate on the keys.

After nine monotone beeps, a green pinpoint light glowed. Joscelyn pushed down on the handle. The door opened; a soft blast of trapped air disturbed Joscelyn's hair. This safe shared the inert-gas conservation system with the Rare Documents Room.

Joscelyn removed from the safe a rectangular silver-colored fabric case—a pizza carrier, Nowell had often thought irreverently, back in the happier days of his tenure, before he had bloodied his hands in defense of their ancestry of deceit. The meticulously crafted case, Nowell knew very well, surpassed all existing archival standards and was itself worth a small fortune in development costs. It was, he thought, oddly beautiful in a futuristic way, something temples and churches and mosques would use in the next century to protect their holy texts. With minor difficulty but solemn persistence Joscelyn held the case and its heavy contents close to his chest as he walked back to the other men.

A man who knows how to take care of his back—and his ass, too, Nowell thought. He stared at the shimmering case to hide an unexpected onrush of contempt for these two old men.

Having laid the large bundle on the table, Joscelyn motioned to Nowell to do the honors. Nowell lifted the flap, which was secured by a band of the same material and a small circle of Velcro, and then he eased the large book out. It was bound in tough leather over board, with three parallel straps of metal-studded leather across the spine; gold designs once stamped into the cover had mostly flaked away.

The book showed evidence of much use, past submersions, and arrested rot, possibly of some singeing, too. D'Hiver, with his heightened sense of smell, inhaled deeply of the familiar odor; a religious rapture pried open his usually tightly closed lips.

"Let us all join together in the watchwords of our ancestry," Joscelyn intoned.

"*En Foi, Invincible!*"

"In faith, invincible. This is what it's all about, Preston," D'Hiver said in a hoarse, fervent whisper. "Faith, sacrifice, loyalty, reverence for our heritage of common suffering, and the strength to vanquish our foes." He stamped his cane on the thick carpet with each word of his admonition: "*You must not allow our ship to founder!*"

Nowell, feeling sorry for himself, said: "Easy for you two to say."

Joscelyn sat down again. He slid forward in his chair, making the rich leather creak. "Our hands are not clean, either. Every generation dwells upon its own woes, as if no one else has faced crises. But I assure you, Preston, we have each in our term as Captain-Director had to enforce discipline. Both Arthur and I have rather ugly memories of things that caused us much pain when we were your age."

Nowell found it hard to believe that either of them had been troubled by even the slightest twinge of conscience; but he kept silent.

"There will always be heretics, my dear boy," Joscelyn said.

"Wherever you find them," D'Hiver growled, "burn them!"

"I will do what I have to do, Arthur, Conrad—as I promised to do, as I have always done."

Chapter 18

Nelson Plumlaw rubbed sunscreen on Preston Nowell's broad shoulders and muscular back.

"You smell like a banana in a bowl of coconut shavings," Nelson said.

It was Sunday afternoon, and the two men were sitting on the starboard cushioned bench seat of Nowell's sailboat, *Allégorie Deux*.

"Are you implying that I'm a fruit?" Preston asked, in a playful huff.

"Absolutely," said Nelson. He slapped Nowell on the back. "Keep still, you thing, you."

"Oww! I like that....It's been a wonderful day, hasn't it?" Precisely what Nowell had needed to take his mind off the horrible events of the past dreadful week, to release the tension that had built up inside him to really quite an intolerable level.

"Yes," Nelson replied.

"The wind was just right, the lake wasn't too choppy. I really do believe you would make a good sailor, Nelson."

"I've made some seamen, on occasion."

They laughed at Nelson's wordplay.

"Shall we have a cocktail? I can't wait to break into the Beefeater you brought. It's not too early, do you think?"

"It's five o'clock somewhere," Nelson said, now finished with the application of the lotion. "Why the hell not?! Let's live dangerously. We always have, you and I." To protect his own more sensitive skin from the sun he wore an unbuttoned long-sleeve shirt, sleeves rolled up, shirttail tied around the waist of his shorts. "You always did mix a deadly martini, Preston."

They had furled and secured the sails. After dinner, they would motor back to the marina. Sunset would be late over the vast expanse of Lake Pontchartrain.

Nowell pushed off the cushion to stand up. In the late sunlight, Nelson regarded his friend's bronzed, muscled limbs and the skimpy swimmer's trunks that left very little to the imagination. He took a deep breath and exhaled, admiration evident on his face. "How's the knee, Preston?"

Nowell made his way carefully through the cockpit of the boat, back to the cabin, where the booze was. His left knee was encased in a flexible brace; he tried to keep the leg straight as he descended the four-rung ladder into the teak-lined cabin. Parts of old scars showed under the brace.

"Feeling no pain," he said, raising his voice to be heard. "I picked up a wonderful prescription on the way out here. It's almost too good to be legal."

In the galley corner of the small cabin, he added gin, vermouth, and lemon to the stainless-steel container of ice, and shook it vigorously for a few seconds. "Shaken, not stirred, I hope you notice....So, Agent Bond, are you ready to tell me what this big secret is? You've been so damn coy all day, I can scarcely stand it any longer. As usual, you're such a big tease."

He again peeked in the refrigerator to check the speckled trout bathed in a zesty batter and the crabmeat marinating with artichoke hearts. The lovely smell of melted butter pervaded the cabin. Earlier, Nelson had prepared his famous Creole meunière sauce; Nowell had mixed at home the balsamic vinaigrette salad of greens, apples, hazelnuts, and Roquefort. Now he placed a pot of water for fettuccine on the gentle flame provided by one of the two burners of his new non-pressurized alcohol stove.

"Trout Plumlaw," Nowell called out with cheerful expectation. "Galatoire's, eat your heart out!" All served with fresh crusty bread, a splendid cold French white—a truly memorable meal.

Now content that everything was proceeding nicely, he took up the martinis and turned toward the deck hatch.

"I'm afraid the *Allégorie* is sinking," Nelson declared.

Nowell scurried up the ladder, sloshing the contents of the two stemmed glasses he held.

"That's a terrible joke!" he said, equally miffed and relieved. "You don't say that to the captain of a ship, for God's sake. I rushed out here to see if you were serious." He handed Nelson his depleted martini.

"I am," said Nelson. "Prepare yourself, my friend: I've uncovered the deep, dark secret of your Society."

"What in the world are you talking about?"

"Here, sit. It's time to be outed." Nelson sipped and began: "I know that an English ship called the *True Faith*, bound for Barbados, but actually Maryland, was taken over by desperate transported convicts and part of the crew. That the ship was then ravaged by a hurricane, but rescued by a Spanish warship, which believed it to be a hapless French vessel, and therefore an ally of sorts. This stratagem had been cooked up by two mutinous crewmembers who, strangely enough, spoke excellent French and Spanish.

"I know that this same ship received repairs in Havana, and showed up in New Orleans on the fabled day, a few months later, as the French vessel *l'Allégorie*—a very droll rechristening, if you ask me. This impostor ship, the *Allégorie*, now carried—*voilà*—God-fearing *French* colonists and crew. People of quality. My dear Preston, I know that a massive lie has been constructed to bolster this fraudulent version of history."

Nowell had long since lost his false smile of jaunty dismissal. He looked at his friend for a silent moment. "That's the kookiest story I've ever heard in my life."

Unruffled, Nelson continued: "The two trilingual gents were English spies who had been sent, disguised as crewmen of the *True Faith*, to sniff around the increasingly restive eastern colonies. Afraid of having their cover blown, they acquiesced in the mutiny, even took the lead. They succeeded in getting the captain and the loyal crewmembers set adrift, instead of killed; alas, none of these men survived. But the spies did, their mission now improvised to meet the surprising turn of events. What *cojones*! They sent reports from Louisiana as they could to England. Anyway, that's merely a bare outline. Am I far off?"

Nowell was stunned. He had to force the words past his lips: "How did you find out?" He recalled with dismay his own words to Joscelyn and D'Hiver the night before: *a buffer period of some weeks.*

Nelson looked pleased that Nowell had as much as admitted the deception. "Through friends of friends. It seems that a batch of records has turned up in England. I had heard of the new stuff, but didn't make the connection until Bristol and the two ships came up in a chance conversation the other day. The real issue, though, Preston, is that if *I* know, anyone can. There are people who have some of the facts, but as far as I can tell, no one has put the whole thing together. Well, there *is* a fellow I know who's coming close, but for the wrong reasons. Anyway, I have some thoughts on turning this really quite fascinating story to your advantage." Nelson set his drink down on the cushion behind him and put his hands on Nowell's shoulders. "I do care about you, Preston."

Nowell downed his martini. "I need another drink, after *that*. How about you?"

"Sure." Nelson finished his own drink and handed Nowell his glass.

In the cabin, Nowell felt that he really was sinking. After all he'd done—the years of work, the precautions, the assurances he'd given to Joscelyn and D'Hiver, the violence. And now, these words Nelson had just uttered, like some kind of deadly contagion killing off the things Nowell loved, some plague aboard his ship! He held on to the overhead storage bins on each side of the cabin, his eyes closed, tears seeping out.

It wasn't over yet; there was still a chance. He had never given up, and wasn't about to start now. Bluemantle had taken him by surprise, but he'd handled the situation the best way he could manage at the moment. This unforeseen development was no different. He had to make a decision.

He collected himself; then he picked up the bottle of gin.

"This other person you mentioned, can we persuade him to remain silent? I mean, until we figure something out." Nowell peered out of the cabin. Nelson, now at the rear port corner of the cockpit, seemed mesmerized by the tiny cars on the distant Causeway, astern of them.

"I wouldn't worry too much about him," Nelson replied. "He's a relatively inexperienced genealogist by the name of Nick Herald. Nice enough fellow, but more interested in chasing skirts and lining his pockets than in taking on a lineage society. Former academic. Liberal arts, head in the clouds. Here's what I've been thinking. Can you hear me?"

"Oh yes, I read you loud and clear." Nowell left the cabin and began silently to cross the cockpit. The wheel moved with the current and the rigging whistled in the light breeze. Nelson still sat with his back to the cabin, waiting for his new drink; he rested his forearms on a chrome winch.

"Get the Society a very good PR firm," Nelson said, laying out his plan, "and go public with the story. Paint it as a bold discovery that's surfaced from ongoing Society research. You'll preempt any suspicion, and come off a defender of historical accuracy. Politicians do it all the time: get in front of the bad news, and then reshape it, massage it, control it. You could phrase it this way—"

Nowell hit him just behind the right ear. He felt the skull give way like a coconut.

Nelson Plumlaw fell back on the green cushions, somewhat on his left side, his eyes wide in astonishment, his pupils suddenly almost invisible. Blood began to seep from his nose and right ear. The right pupil then rapidly dilated, eclipsing the green of the iris. A blown pupil. Nowell had seen it plenty of times in Vietnam. If Nelson wasn't dead already, he soon would be.

"I am sorry, Nelson. *God, I am sorry.*"

He dropped the bottle, which was smeared with hair and blood. There were no boats close enough to see what had happened, unless someone was using binoculars.

He had to do something with the body, get the boat cleaned up. No one knew they had been together that day; Nelson was like that, secretive about his relationships. And if anyone found out, Nowell would say he'd dropped Nelson off at the marina. There would be time to move his car before he was reported missing.

The anchor! Maybe that would work. He reached into the cabin for a knife—a heavy-duty serrated one—and began to make his way to the front of the boat, his bad knee slowing him down. Would the fifteen-pound Fortress anchor and few feet of chain keep the body underwater? he wondered. On the rivers and in the paddies of Vietnam, he'd seen hundreds, thousands of bloated corpses floating like corks from the gas of decomposing body tissues. Well, this was all he could think of at the moment. He very much preferred to plan such things beforehand.

At the bow, he unrolled what he believed would be enough chain and nylon rope above it to secure the anchor to Nelson's body. He paused and examined the knife, one of those that could supposedly cut through just about anything. He thought of field dressing big game, which he had observed and done often enough as a gentleman hunter. He did have an ax onboard…yes, perhaps…it would be messy and disgusting, but—

A gut-wrenching scream froze his hands.

Nelson, an animal fear on his uncomprehending bloody face, lurched and thrashed around the cockpit, hitting his demolished skull on the boom.

"Christ!" Nowell said. This was simply too much!

He dropped the anchor on deck and began to scamper back toward the raging man. He lost his footing, almost falling into the lake; then he banged his head against a chrome handrail, drawing blood.

He saw Nelson trip headlong into the cabin. As Nowell crawled across the cabin roof, he heard more anguished howls, and the sounds of things breaking and being flung about. A pot slammed against a wall. Nowell remembered the boiling water for the pasta. Poor Nelson.

Nowell reached the cockpit and lifted the knife to strike as he prepared to step into the cabin.

Nelson's shirt was on fire. He flailed about the cabin, spreading the flames, the styling mousse in his hair flaring up like a tiki torch. His screaming stopped abruptly, and for a moment Nelson just stood there, motionless, aflame, his arms rigid at his side, like a Buddhist monk Nowell had once seen in Saigon, immolating himself in protest on a crowded street. Then Nelson fell.

The cabin was now burning furiously. How long would it be before the smoke attracted attention?

Nowell backed away. His beautiful boat, the rich teak he'd hand rubbed all these years! He didn't have much time, he knew, before the extra plastic bottles of denatured alcohol used as cooking fuel exploded; eventually the diesel for the engine would go, too.

All in all, perhaps this was the best outcome.

He grabbed a small fire extinguisher mounted just inside the cabin and made a few perfunctory sweeps. Then he pulled two life jackets from a cockpit storage bin under the cushions, threw one into the cabin, and put the other one on.

Even as he thought it, he realized what a silly notion it was: pity about the dinner.

He jumped overboard.

Chapter 19

"Yo, Nick! Yo, you got another parking ticket."

Johnny Doe knocked on the office door as he opened it and entered Hawty's anteroom. Seeing she wasn't there, he walked around the corner into the larger book-lined room where Nick's desk was.

"Oh, 'scuse me, man," Johnny said. "Didn't know you had company." A short grubby cigarette bobbed in his mouth with each word. He gave a deep, rattling cough and started to back away from Nick and his visitor.

"That's all right, Johnny," said Nick. "Just give the ticket to him."

"Him? Well, okay, whatever you say, man."

Johnny walked over to Detective Dave Bartly, who was sitting in a chair in front of Nick's desk. Johnny handed the ticket to him.

"He's a cop," Nick said.

Johnny jumped back, as if Bartly had sprouted fangs.

"Yo, I'm clean, man."

"Indeed you are. You've just had a shave, Johnny, haven't you?" Bartly said, having fun playing Sherlock Holmes at the paranoid man's expense. "At a barbershop, I bet you."

He had sniffed Johnny's paradox: a weathered, lantern-jawed face that was oddly smooth and tonsorially fragrant, atop a body that was pure hobo. The man was somewhere in his fifties; his stoop made him appear shorter than he was. He was slight of shoulder, but carried the oversize belly of the gorger and the alcoholic. Probably, he suffered from various common diseases that had not been seen to in his younger years. Johnny favored scrounged clothing of the paramilitary kind. He had no sideburns, but it was impossible to tell much else about the state of his hair because he constantly wore a grungy New Orleans Saints football cap. Nick had always assumed his head was shaved regularly, as well.

"In my job, looks is important," Johnny replied, proudly displaying his smooth chin, which jutted out because of lack of teeth.

"What job is that?"

"Well, I'm a P.I.—private investigator. That's what that means, you know. Just ask Nick, there. He'll tell you."

"That true?" Bartly asked Nick, toying with Johnny.

"Yeah, you could say that. I count on Johnny to do a certain specialized type of snooping. He digs through dumpsters all over town. Be surprised what important genealogical information people throw out as garbage."

"You tell him, Nick!" Johnny laughed-coughed-laughed-coughed. "Part"—cough—"ners!"

"You need a license to be a P.I., Johnny. I'm sure you got one of those, right? You could land in a lot of trouble impersonating a P.I."

"Oh, no, sir. No 'personatin' here. I got my license…now where did I put that thing?" With the shifty sincerity of a man who's been hassled countless times by police, Johnny vigorously patted the dozen or so pouch pockets in his voluminous Army-green parka, which seemed to hold all of his possessions. "It's in here somewhere. Just got it renewed."

"Here, Johnny." Nick handed him a few bills. "Go get a pedicure and a new cigarette. And watch my car. It's a vital piece of automotive history."

Johnny left in a crescendo of coughing.

"Valet parking. This *is* a nice place," Bartly cracked.

"I liked it better when it was a dump, before Hawty domesticated me and it."

"We could use her at the department."

"Forget it. She's mine."

"Johnny Doe?" Bartly asked. "Yeah, I bet. I'm glad to finally meet a live one. Every John Doe I've ever encountered was on a drawer in the morgue, right next to his wife, Jane."

"Or sister. He came with the office. Lives out there, somewhere," Nick said, pointing beyond the windows, to a sickly stand of azaleas in a triangular traffic island. "From bits and pieces he lets slip, I'm guessing he was in Vietnam. Went through some hellish experience. Came back, everything seemed changed; or maybe he realized *he* wasn't the same. So he took off, no inner compass anymore. A lot of people couldn't handle that. They become haters or murderers. But Johnny, or whoever he is, took a gentler course. He went a little cuckoo. Sometimes I think he's saner than I am."

Nick had been to the edge of that cliff himself. He knew Johnny was a part of him, as much a part as the English professor with three degrees and a genealogical certification. In a way, there is a Johnny Doe in all of us, he believed—running from the past, fearing that the demons there will catch up and control our future.

"Murderers," Bartly said. "Now you're talking my language. I'm getting ragged all the way up the line on these cases. I even got called in to see the superintendent. The *superintendent*. Jeez!" He let out a harassed sigh. "We're talking serious shit when the big guy calls you in. Since that bomb went off, the FBI, the ATF, Homeland Security, even Postal Inspectors are trying to get in on the act. And another death yesterday! I can't even go out of town with the wife, without you genealogists producing another body. You say you talked to this Freret architecture professor, Nelson Plumlaw, Wednesday of last week?"

"Right. I knew him from my university days."

"You discuss the details of the cases? You're not supposed to do that. You gave me a consultant's pledge of confidentiality, you know."

"Don't worry, I've been a good little Scout. I didn't want him involved any more than you did. I merely put a hypothetical scenario to him, to learn more about his specialty, which was colonial migration."

"And that line of inquiry was supposed to get us somewhere, huh?" Bartly didn't seem too high on Nick's brand of speculative investigation. "Well, at least you helped me eliminate a suspect. Carolyn Bullenger came in, and we had a nice chat. She's pretty much in the clear. Said to call her in Salt Lake City if I need to ask anything else. So, we're back to Nowell."

"He seems to be the key, the common element in all of these deaths."

"You say he fences," Bartly said. "That's real interesting. Therman was stabbed with some badass toothpick. I'll pass that by the forensic guys. But I don't have any idea *why* Nowell might have killed the four men. Seems to me he had reasons *not* to. He'd just hired Bluemantle, his prize catch. The Therman thing had been going on for a year—old news. The only connection with Montenay is that they were both in charge of the Society, years apart. I'm not even sure they knew each other personally. Ms. Vair didn't give us much to go on. Too upset. And Plumlaw was supposed to be Nowell's longtime friend, probably his former lover."

"I put that together from the newspaper article, which was careful to dance around the issue," Nick said. "I knew about Nelson's, er, preference. But Nowell? That was a shocker."

Bartly rubbed the back of his neck in disappointment. "I actually thought I got the jump on you with that. I interviewed some of Plumlaw's relatives and friends. See, I have been earning my detective's pay."

"Maybe there's more that Nowell is keeping in the closet, so to speak," Nick suggested.

"Could be," Bartly said. "And what secrets are *you* keeping from me. For instance, what's the story with Ms. Vair now working at the Society? I get the feeling you and she are running your own detective agency, with old Johnny Doe doing the dirty work."

Nick ignored the question and asked one of his own: "Does Nowell have alibis?"

"Well, for the first two murders, he was at the Society library; the employees confirm that; and there's a computer system that tracks personnel and indicates he was there when he says he was. The employees could be lying, and the computer could have been tampered with, but it's enough. For Montenay's murder, he wouldn't have to be there. Can he put together a bomb?"

"He was in the military, that's all I know," Nick said. "You'd have to check his service record. But he screwed up with the boat, huh? Can't you nail him on that?"

Bartly stared out the windows. He shook his head; his glasses picked up the daylight, blanking his eyes out momentarily. Nick had fleeting image of Orphan Annie.

"It might have happened the way he tells it. A tragic accident, the loss of a close friend," Bartly said. "He claims something caught on fire in the kitchen—the galley, that is. The Plumlaw guy panicked, refused to jump, and ended up trapped in the cabin. Nowell tried to get to him, but the fire was already too bad. Then there were some explosions. The boat turned over and sank partially. Plumlaw's lungs were full of water, so he was definitely alive when the boat went under. He also had massive trauma to his head."

"Anybody around when it happened."

"We have witnesses in other boats who heard the explosions, saw the smoke, but they were maybe a couple of miles or more away. The boat that finally picked up Nowell ran into the submerged sailboat—which may account for Plumlaw's head trauma. It was getting dark, and the asshole driving it was all excited to be making a rescue. Came in too fast, damaged his own boat pretty bad. The thing is, with water, it contaminates the scene. Not to mention nothing stays where it ought to. So I really don't have a damn thing on Nowell. Oh, yeah: he's got some powerful allies, I'm finding out all of a sudden. They don't like the idea of us questioning him twice before and then putting him through the wringer again yesterday."

Nick walked around the desk. "Well, I do have something that may help us connect Montenay to the others. I was going to wait until I put it all together to tell you…but things have greater urgency than before. I got this from Mr. Montenay. Thursday afternoon, at the nursing home. Gillian and I went to visit him."

Bartly took the note Mr. Montenay had written and slipped to Nick at LifePath Estates. "The same," he said, after examining it closely. "Matches the note the heckler had, I'd say. Now we know where that came from. Hmm: the old man, even from a nursing home, continued to have a strong interest in the Society. He was trying to tell you something, trying to tell anybody who would listen." He paused a moment. "Montenay was killed Saturday."

They looked at each other, the unspoken question between them: if Nick had delivered the note sooner to Bartly or another detective, might Mr. Montenay still be alive?

"Montenay, as you said, was once head of the Society, and Plumlaw was a very good amateur genealogist and historian. These two, like Bluemantle and the heckler—"

"Wayne Therman," Bartly interjected, holding on to the few facts they had. "Who worked out there at the nursing home."

"Yeah. I believe that Montenay and Plumlaw, like Bluemantle and Therman, discovered something that Nowell would kill to suppress."

"I can see you know more than you're telling me," Bartly said. "Let me have it. All of it. Come on."

Nick explained what he'd learned about the ill-fated voyage of the *True Faith*.

Bartly stared at nothing for a moment. "But I thought the Society ship's name was *Allégorie*. What's this other one got to with it, besides being in those two notes?"

"I'm not sure yet. But I have no doubt that Nowell is trying to protect the Society from information the dead men uncovered—or were in the process of uncovering. Family and group honor is a big motive, but there's a lot of money involved, too."

"Honor and money: that's a deadly combination," Bartly said.

"What I've told you is only half the story." Nick saw Bartly's face go skeptical. "Really, I'm leveling with you here, Dave. But I think I know where to look for the other half…at least, that's my working theory."

"The DA doesn't like theory," Bartly said. "He likes incriminating evidence. And so far, we can't provide any."

"Maybe the coroner will come up with something else on Plumlaw," Nick suggested.

"Let's hope so," said the detective. "He was still working on him this morning. With Bluemantle, my partner and I figure an argument turned nasty. After the assailant realized the old guy was dead, he used the straight razor to cut off the finger, maybe to get at that ring. We never found the finger or the ring, and the razor was wiped clean of blood and prints with a towel. Never found that either. Whoever's doing this—if it's one person—is smart, a planner, but a damn good improviser, too. And it looks like he's starting to enjoy it. That's the scary part."

"Give me a little longer," Nick said. "Stall, lie, cry your eyes out, solve some other murders. Whatever it takes to buy me some time. A day or two. I'll get your proof. I may have to break a few minor rules. Anybody going to get upset about that?"

Bartly held up the parking ticket. "Depends on what you mean by minor. My influence only goes so far. Try not to kill anybody, okay? Or get killed."

Chapter 20

"Kick! Kick! Come on, put some effort into it! We're having fun, aren't we?"

The physical therapist walked along Freret University's indoor Olympic-size pool. She blew her shrill whistle to start or end the ten-minute periods of splashing by the eight floating participants. Four other therapists in the water offered encouragement.

Nick sat on a bench of the wooden bleachers, watching. The splashing, the whistles, and shouts of frustration and triumph echoed through the chlorine-pungent natatorium. Hawty swam or treaded water with the aid of foam donuts on her arms and a buoyancy belt. She hadn't seen him. She was enjoying herself. Nick could distinguish her robust laughter in the tumult as she splashed the other swimmers, some of whom were more severely handicapped than she. During the workout periods, Nick saw that she concentrated on the serious business of strengthening her legs, hips, and back. Even after all these years, she hadn't given up hope of walking again.

A few times Nick's eyes burned with tears. Just the chlorine, he tried to convince himself. He looked down at his legs and arms and hands, acutely conscious of a gift and freedom he normally took for granted. He wondered if, in a similar situation, he could find such courage.

After another twenty minutes, the session was over. The young therapists helped the swimmers out of the pool, allowing the more able ones to support themselves on gymnastic parallel bars. Hawty stood grasping the bars, drying herself off, waiting for someone to bring a wheelchair over so she could roll herself into the dressing room.

Nick was proud that others were seeing how independent, how capable Hawty was; he had known that fact since the very first day he met her. In a few minutes, back in her chariot, she emerged from the dressing room in a red-orange-green cotton-and-lace dashiki and matching headband that an African princess would have envied. Her hair, coiled inside the headband, looked like black silk.

"How long have you been here, spying on me like a voyeur, Mr. Leopold Bloom?" she asked.

"Who's your new man, Hawty?" teased a young woman, as she and two other swimmers rolled by in a chorus of *Oooooh*s, *Uh-huh*s, and *Look out now*s.

Hawty waved them on with a good-natured vexation.

"I've been here long enough to be exhausted myself," Nick said. "That was some work-out."

"You're telling me! I'm still kind of shaky. They say it'll get easier. But I'm going to do it before I pass from this earth. I'm going to walk! You mind pushing me over to the UC for a cold drink? My batteries need charging—my body's *and* my chariot's."

"A pleasure," Nick said, taking the handles of her chariot. "Speaking of Leopold Bloom, we can delve into Joyce's use of allegory in *Ulysses*. I want to hear how that paper of yours is coming along for your Modern Lit seminar." He watched in wonder as she unfolded two solar recharging panels and placed them on her work shelf. "And then we can talk about another *Allégorie*."

Thirty minutes later they sat under a shady tree on the quad in front of the University Center.

College, the great leveler. Nick couldn't distinguish the rich kids, whose parents had sent them to Freret because the country-club set styled it "Yale on the Bayou," from the poor kids, who had finagled a scholarship to attend the academically excellent school. Each of them was smart; you had to be to get in. But the frolicking students on the quad seemed blissfully unconcerned that it was costing somebody $25,000 a year for them to exhaust their reserves of decadence. Take your time, Nick wanted to mount a park bench and tell them; it's a mean world out there in the trenches of capitalism.

"You heard about Professor Plumlaw?" Nick said.

"Um-hmm," Hawty replied, finishing a gulp of soda. "It was all over the news last night, and the campus paper did a screaming front page story. The type was bigger than what they used at the end of World War II."

"He died with a secret we need to know."

"What you mean, 'we'? This is beginning to sound very unkosher."

"Well...if you'd rather not be a part of something extremely exciting, something that may immeasurably enhance the reputation of our firm—"

"Something illegal?"

"Just slightly," Nick admitted. "I need you to break into Plumlaw's computer. Quickly and quietly. I don't trust anybody else to do it. The murderer has a lot of influence, but he's juggling too many plates in the air now. He's worried, maybe even scared. We need to mess up his rhythm, force a mistake."

"Another hunch, huh? Are we, by any chance, talking about Preston Nowell, here?"

"What I'm asking you to do will help us answer that question. Can you handle it?"

Hawty proceeded to assault Nick's technologically deficient brain with a numbingly complex survey of the current state of remote computing. Nick could make out only a few terms with any degree of certainty: encryption, firewalls, public/private keys, LANs, proxy servers, bandwidth, Wi-Fi, Blackbeard—

"Blackbeard?" Nick asked with a grin. "How strangely appropriate to our eighteenth-century nautical focus."

"Bluetooth, not Blackbeard!" Hawty retorted. "Sure, I can handle it. I know the guy who designed the campus network; if the machine's still powered up and connected to the wall, it'll be child's play. Are you certain what you're looking for is there?"

"No," Nick confessed.

"Tell me about it while you push me to the LIFT-van stop." Hawty lived in a sorority house nearby.

Nick explained that he thought Nelson had discovered information detailing the transformation of the *True Faith* into the *Allégorie*. He didn't know exactly what that evidence would be, but he had a feeling it had arrived via computer, perhaps even as he sat talking to Nelson for the last time.

"And you think Nowell killed Nelson Plumlaw."

"Yeah. And the others, too. Bartly has next to no physical evidence. He's not even sure what precisely killed Nelson, much less who did it or if it was deliberate. With a motive that suggests a plausible reason for Nowell to do in the victims, the cops could have some leverage to search Society headquarters, maybe question Nowell more pointedly, take the gloves off. So, what I want you—"

"Stop! Stop!" Hawty whispered harshly, slapping his hands away from the handles of her chariot.

"What? Stop talking, stop walking?"

"Stop pushing! Come walk beside me. I don't want him to see me being pushed."

"Who?" asked Nick, bewildered, looking around at the students lounging on the grass or throwing Frisbees. But he obeyed and quickly got in step beside Hawty. She began to guide her chariot with the joystick.

A handsome young man approached on the walkway. He was dark skinned, medium height, youthfully lean, and, like most twenty year olds, full of suppressed energy. He sported a gold nose stud and an earring made, apparently, from a microchip. There was a labyrinthine design—a printed circuit?—cut into his hair. It seemed to Nick that the young man's pants were about to fall down; he had to remind himself that this was the style nowadays.

"Hi, Kedric. This is my boss, Dr. Herald. What are you up to?"

Kedric shook hands with Nick, his eyes on the ground, embarrassed for no reason, still in the grip of the social awkwardness of adolescence. He mumbled something about the computer lab.

"Kedric's the computer whiz I was just telling you about," Hawty said. "He's working on a remote control for my chariot, so when I start walking—and falling—I can call it to come to me."

Nick noticed that Kedric was about to bolt. The emotional ordeal of simultaneously meeting a new adult and receiving the praise of an obviously infatuated older woman was apparently too much for him. He remembered being that way, too, at that age.

"I'll see you later, Hawty," Nick said. "I'm late for an appointment. Nice to meet you Kedric."

He looked back as he walked away; Kedric had stayed after all, and Hawty was explaining something with great animation, commanding the young man's full attention.

Chapter 21

Nowell's latest near brush with death had taken a toll on the staff of the Society library: all looked as if they'd lost a close family member. Some of them shelved books with quivering chins; others were overtaken by sobbing in the middle of their tasks; a few sat at their desks, dazed. Nowell himself, Nick learned from the stoic and somber young man in the Rare Documents Room, was at home, recuperating.

Had they felt this broken up by Bluemantle's death? Preston Nowell hadn't, Nick felt certain.

He found his own way to the room designated as his office; it was spotlessly clean and commendably outfitted with office supplies, still in store wrappers. A fax from Nowell said: "My profuse apologies for missing your first day. Had planned to welcome you personally. Shall return as soon as possible. In meantime, please enjoy our splendid library—and make yourself at home." The fax was dated Tuesday, eight in the morning. It was nine, now.

◻

"What a terreeble spring, Nick Herald," Florita said. "First dear Dr. Bluemantle, then poor Gillian's father, then this very horreeble bad thing with the boat of Mr. Nowell and the death of his friend."

Nick had lewd thoughts about Florita's mouth and his own anatomy each time she trilled an *r*, which happened invariably when she let his last name linger on the back of her tongue. She was drying her eyes with a lace handkerchief. Her midnight hair cascaded down her shoulders like a rainforest waterfall.

"And now, I break up with my boyfriend." She covered her face; it was too much grief to bear.

Nick walked around her desk and sat on her calendar desk pad. He reached for a hand.

"Florita, I realize this is hard on you. These tragedies that end lives are cruel to the living, as well. But you see, I promised Captain-Director Nowell that I would work on an urgent project. I take my responsibilities seriously, and we must all carry on. I hate to let him down, or bother him with minor details of access to the library after hours, or before—I'm an early riser." Florita took great interest in this confidence. "Teach me," Nick urged. "You can do that for me, can't you? Teach me what I need to know? I see you are a caring, giving woman, with a great many things a man would wish to know."

She looked up, a smile of expectation coming to her tear-streaked face. Nick let his ambiguity hang in the air. Did he mean lessons of another sort?...

She squeezed his hands in hers and then let go with a sigh. "Yes, you are right, Nick Herald. We must go on."

In the following five minutes, Nick, struggling with Florita's barrage of Hispano-English, heard how to open the front door with the key she provided, enter her password into the computerized security and personnel systems to deactivate the alarm and gain access to the library itself, turn on and off lights, distribute accumulated faxes to the appropriate trays if he felt like it, fill the Rare Documents Room with breathable air, and bring in the newspaper and feed the stray cats. Other instructions hit him, but didn't stick.

He hoped he remembered an eighth of it all. He hoped Florita didn't see him drop the envelope with Bluemantle's condo keys in it, and slide it with his foot under a chair. He made a great show of finding it.

"What's this?"

"I have been searching for that many days now!" she exulted as she snatched it from his hand. "Gracias, Nick Herald. You are no longer in my debt." She raised her eyebrows, as if to suggest it was indeed a pity that the score was now even.

"What do you say, Florita, we keep the account open, just in case we feel the desire to borrow something else from each other?"

She stood up and nestled between his legs as if she belonged there. Then she brought her lips to within microns of Nick's lips: "A good idea, Nick Herald. Perhaps we will feel the desire soon."

What she did to those *r*'s!...it made him sweat.

Chapter 22

Hugh Montenay's funeral took place in one of the vast cities of tombs bordering I-10 at the end of Canal. This prestigious cemetery dated from the Reconstruction period, when passions ran higher than normal in this hair-trigger city. It looked like the Roman Forum to Nick. Columns, statues, classical temples, ostentation in stone, monumentality in miniature.

The legend was that a planter had not been invited to a ball at a neighboring plantation. In a rage of indignation, he drove his neighbor into bankruptcy through market manipulations, bought the neighbor's land, and then spitefully turned it into the cemetery in which Nick stood on this bright, hot Wednesday, twelve days and three more deaths since Bluemantle's murder.

For Nick, this cemetery and its story said a lot about the character of New Orleans. Here, people have always loved the grand passion and the dramatic gesture. Honor is an obsession, injured pride grounds for retribution. But a medieval fatalism pesters the souls of citizens here and like a malarial mosquito injects a certain fevered surrealism into the blood, a profane infatuation with death. As voluptuous as life can be here, the physical world ultimately is mocked as a mere doubloon snatched from the surging Mardi Gras crowd. To live in New Orleans is to take part enthusiastically in a morality play, to march to a demonic tune in the noisy, bawdy, petty parade that leads one out of this sham of life, ideally to a death with style, the final act accompanied by a jazz band and a raucous street wake, and at last crowned by several tons of marble in a beautiful cemetery.

A good genealogist learns to be a connoisseur of cemeteries, and New Orleans has some of the oldest and most interesting in the country. Since burying below ground isn't done—an old Spanish custom, it is said, and definitely a concession to the soggy soil and frequent flooding—raised tombs and impressive vaults give the city's many cemeteries their distinctive character. New Orleans venerates its dead in a very Latin way. On All Saints' Day families come to picnic in the shade of their ancestors' houses of bones; and their ancestors may return the favor of a visit: coffins sometimes float in the streets during bad floods.

In his new trade, Nick, too, had learned to enjoy cemeteries, as long as he was just passing through.

Mr. Montenay had been Catholic, but Gillian's mother, the former Mrs. Montenay, didn't seem to have much tolerance for any kind of ritual. Away from the small group of mourners under the tent, she instructed the compliant, somewhat abashed priest. From Nick's vantage point, too far away to hear words, Gillian's mother resembled a baseball ump more than a grieving ex-wife: she used hand gestures and body English to declare anything of comfort out of bounds for *this* funeral.

Nick had her pegged. She would spare no tears for Mr. Montenay. Grief was for sentimental weaklings. She was a woman who, when the time came, would die without a second's remorse or regret, not because she had pursued worthy purposes in life, but because she had stomped everyone into the ground with her high heels—and she was damn proud of it. Her hat was yellow, with a small fringe of black veil.

"Thought I'd find you here." Dave Bartly stood next to Nick among the mansions for the dead, out of earshot of the ceremony under the canopy. Bleached vaults lined neat alleys as far as one could see.

"Autopsy on our architecture professor doesn't give us much," Bartly said. "The lake is only fourteen feet deep where the sailboat went down. It was royally messed up by the power yacht that rammed it. So, Plumlaw's injuries are too massive to indicate the exact sequence of events. 'Chain of causes,' we call it. Nowell may be telling the truth. I don't think we could get the grand jury to indict."

"Some detective you are."

"Yeah, well, a confession would always be nice. You got anything for me? You keep telling me this Nowell dude is behind it all. Like I said before, give me some evidence."

"Time, Dave. Just a bit more time," Nick said.

"That's what you told me Monday, two friggin' days ago! I've interrogated Nowell three times, and each time he was perfect. He'll have his lawyer with him, if there's a next time. Everything checked. Sure we found his prints at the hotel, but he had a reason to be there; and the boat thing—well, it looks like an accident. The dude in the river, and this poor bastard, Montenay…nothing, absolutely nothing concrete that points to Nowell. Hell, I may have to put *you* back on the suspect list, if I don't come up with something soon."

Nick laughed that threat off, hoping the detective was just kidding. For a while in uneasy silence they watched the ceremony under the canopy.

"Who's the nice-looking babe next to Gillian?" Bartly asked.

Hmmm. First name basis, eh? "Her sister-in-law. Those are her kids. Can you spot the mother?"

"She's a Mrs. Fleam, I'm told. Yellow hat, right? Wow, she freaks me out. Not exactly overwhelmed by grief, is she?"

Amused, Nick looked at Bartly. "I've been meaning to ask you, Dave: in another life, were you a hippie? I think I saw your incarnation in the Woodstock movie."

"Well, I do play bass in a local band. It's not the kind of music you grew up with. And not for the faint hearted…or the over-the-hill."

"I resemble that remark! I just hope you wear ear protection. The rockers from my generation are partly deaf, if they're alive at all."

"We do. Money's pretty good, which might keep me off the take for a few more years." He grinned. "I'll let you know where our next gig is, if you think you can handle it. My wife sings and plays keyboard. Excuse me. I think I'd better give my card to the poor widow. I want to find out what she knows about explosives. I could dig solving at least one murder this week." He ran a hand through his thick dog-fur hair. "Hear it's supposed to be ninety-five, but we may get some rain. Later, man."

Nick watched the priest finish his condensed performance. The mourners dropped dirt and flowers. Gillian was comforted by her sister-in-law; the kids held their aunt's hands. The group dispersed.

Except for Mrs. Fleam. Nick saw her walking with a superbly dressed white-haired man with gold-rimmed glasses. She was listening, which was probably a rare event for her, Nick thought. He could not see her face, but something the man said made her stop in her tracks, as if she were genuinely disturbed for the first time today—or ever; the man came back for her, put an arm around her waist with avuncular gentleness and propriety. They walked out of sight, between the tall vaults of prominent New Orleans families.

Nick spent the rest of the afternoon collecting information on birth and death dates, places of origin, relationships, military service, otherwise-unrecorded infants, Masonic membership, and other secrets the determined researcher can discover only firsthand on tombstones. He had several projects going, and his notes from here would help fill in many blanks on client pedigree charts.

One visit to a cemetery can speed a family search and save considerable money fruitlessly lavished on postage, public-records fees, phone calls, books, and website memberships. But he knew not to trust cemeteries too much. They were a notorious source of error, because quite often mistakes were made as information passed from grieving family to attending physician to funeral home to stonecutter.

◩

"Say, my friend, you got some smokes?"

Nick looked up from the family vault he had been studying and photographing—surreptitiously, because he had seen a sign at the gate asking visitors to refrain from taking pictures. This was a remote section of the cemetery, old tombs of long extinct families, seldom visited.

The emaciated, scraggly black man with a ragged beard took two more steps toward Nick. He had few teeth, wild bloodshot eyes, and an odor that took Nick's breath away.

Nick felt something wasn't right, here. His instincts screamed DANGER! He had always considered the warnings about visiting the city's cemeteries alone to be just over-cautious advice for the tourists. This was not going to be a pleasant conversation, he could tell.

A pen, his ancient pocket Instamatic, and his fists constituted his arsenal of likely weapons.

"Sorry, no smokes," Nick said, turning to face the man, who had begun to move forward again, warily, but now without the pretense of bumming a cigarette.

He pulled a knife from a pocket of his filthy pants, which were held up by a motorcyclist's bungee cord looped twice around his narrow waist.

The blade flicked upright.

"Tha's okay. I don't smoke them things nohow."

"What do you want?" Nick asked, backing up.

"Your life, my friend. This a cemetery, ain't you noticed? And I be the Bruthah of Death."

He lunged at Nick with the knife but missed and tripped over his own feet.

Nick swung his camera like a sling and landed it on his attacker's face. The Instamatic shattered on one of Bruthah's projecting cheekbones, leaving a deep cut that began to bleed profusely.

"Look what you done!" Bruthah said reproachfully. He cradled his injured cheek and then studied the blood on his hand. "I gonna kill your ass for real, now!"

Remembering his most effective weapon—his feet—Nick took off between vaults and the wrought-iron fences. The Bruthah of Death staggered after him.

Calling up childhood hide-and-seek evasive maneuvers, Nick felt he must have successfully eluded Bruthah. He stopped to listen, resting on an elaborate corn-stalk iron fence.

Then he heard a noise behind him. He turned and would have been a dead man if a leg with a military boot on the end of it had not tripped up his assailant.

The Bruthah recovered quickly, but one S-hook of his bungee-cord belt was loose and it caught on the fence. The cord yanked the Bruthah back hard. Nick took advantage of his attacker's shock and pain to grab the hand that held the knife, slam it into the fence, and punch him in the diaphragm twice. The Bruthah of Death doubled over, holding onto the fence behind him.

Nick stretched the two ends of the bungee cord until he could wrap both of the Bruthah's wrists and secure them to the fence. The Bruthah, obviously pretty spaced out anyway, offered little resistance.

"Hol' up, hol' up, friend! Don't hurt me no more," pleaded the Bruthah of Death, gasping. "I just trying to make some money for rock. For rock, tha's all. You ain't nothin' to me, I got no arg-yu-ment with you. Old white fucker over there gave me a hunred dolla to take you out. Said he gimme a hunred more when I done it. You know how much rock that be?"

"Where? You mean at the funeral, way over there?"

"Yeah, uh-huh. Old white man, like I said. White hair."

"Gold-rimmed glasses?"

"I don't know. I ain't no fuckin' newspaper reporter. Said there be another hunred Sunday in a urn on one of these little houses for the bodies if I do what he say."

"What was the surname?"

"Sir who?"

"The family name. What was the last name on the little house with the urn?"

"Jos—, Jus—, some honky name. I don't know who, I jus know where. Ain't gonna get that C-note now."

Joscelyn, Nick suspected. A former Captain-Director, protecting the flank. Nick had never seen him before today, but he remembered reading that two besides Nowell were still living, now that Hugh Montenay had been murdered.

"My stomach hurt," the Bruthah complained.

"You're in a hazardous business," Nick said. "You dish it out, you got to take it."

Nick began walking away.

"Wait up, friend! You ain't gonna leave me here, is you? I gonna die. Gonna die of thirst. Friend, wait up!"

"It's a cemetery, remember?" Nick said. "You'll have lots of company."

Johnny Doe appeared from between two hulking vaults and fell in step with Nick.

"Thanks, Johnny. What are you doing out here?"

"Free enterprise, man." He opened his coat to reveal fresh flowers stuck in his waistband. "I just take a few from the prettiest bouquets on the graves and go down to the Quarter to sell 'em. Not too many, or else people'll get pissed off. Especially the ghosts." He looked apprehensively over his shoulder. "I do like the Indians used to; they didn't kill all the buffalo, just the ones they needed to eat."

The sky clouded with time-lapse speed, and bullets of rain began to slam into their heads. The lightning and thunder were enough to send braver men scurrying.

"Come on, Johnny!" Nick screamed, running.

In his car, he found a sour towel among the junk in the back and dried himself off a bit. The rain pounded and the wind shook the little MG.

Johnny stood by his door, in the deluge.

Nick cracked his window. "What the hell are you doing out there, Johnny? Get in! I'll give you a lift."

"Nah, man. Thanks, anyway. I like a good storm. It's the sunny days that get me down. Same old, same old, hour after hour, day after day, year after year. They say Heaven's like that. Hell, too." Thunder boomed, but he shouted over it. "You ever notice, the bad things most often happen when there ain't a cloud in the sky! Oh, yeah, I like a good storm! Reminds me I'm alive!"

"Suit yourself. See you."

Nick started the car and began to drive away.

"Johnny Doe," he said to the figure in his rearview mirror, "you're a wise man."

Chapter 23

"Got it, boss!"

Hawty proudly held the diskette for Nick to see. She rolled manually over to the powerful computer she had persuaded Nick to buy; here at the office, she usually preferred the exercise of maneuvering her chair by muscle.

Nick sat at his desk, hard at work on another genealogical mystery—this one not having violent death at its center. He was puzzling out the complicated skein of heirship that had led him to a bank trust department in rural Indiana, where some important family records were held—wills, deeds, promissory notes. The bank was not being very forthcoming. Nick's experience had taught him that just about everybody had something to hide when money was passed across generations. For small-town banks like this one, the issue was often some fraud perpetrated by an unscrupulous officer half a century ago.

It was Thursday, the day after the Montenay funeral.

"Professor Plumlaw's barn was wide open," Hawty said. "Kedric and I rounded up all the cows and took them for a little walk."

"Good girl. Print that for me, will you?"

Hawty shot a squint-eyed look of censure at him. "Do you have any idea how many trees would have to die for that? You just get your lazy butt over here and read it from the screen with me."

"Hey, they're already cut, the paper's already manufactured," Nick said. "No one's going to order whole forests decimated just because I partake of the old-fashioned pleasure of holding pages in my hands. I'd like to be an idealist, but does it have to be so much trouble?"

Hawty's scowl of disapproval deepened. He surrendered.

Together, sitting before the monitor, they scrolled through the reports and testimony of the saga of the *True Faith*. After more than two hundred and fifty years, the ship sailed once again, on the sea of their imaginations.

Nelson Plumlaw's friend in the bookbindery in London was well versed on the latest developments relating to British government archives. A batch of eighteenth-century documents thought lost since the early nineteenth century had been rediscovered, declassified, and released. Few scholars had yet to delve into the material; none of it had been microfilmed. The woman in London was unaware of the local significance of what she was forwarding to Nelson, but mentioned in her cover e-mail that she would be pleased to handle his project if Nelson decided to do a book on the subject.

"I can't even get my book proposals *read*, much less accepted sight unseen!" Nick exclaimed.

Thirty minutes later, he clenched his fists in exultation. "This is it, kid, the missing link, the equal sign in the equation!" He gave Hawty a kiss on the cheek.

"Therman the heckler and Mr. Montenay were right," Hawty said.

Nick scooted his chair back, limbered up his neck and shoulders, and twisted side to side in a modified jogging warm-up. "The *Allégorie* was actually the *True Faith*. Through a brazen deception, the two English spies—"

"Juslin and Windner?"

"Yeah. The two spies aboard convinced their Spanish rescuers and then the French authorities in New Orleans that the ship was full of industrious French colonists, not transported English felons who'd taken over the vessel. New Orleans was a small, struggling frontier town, with big Indian and slave troubles. Able-bodied colonists were desperately needed. A few bribes"—Nick snapped his fingers—"and doors opened for the initially awkward newcomers."

"Corruption is still a New Orleans specialty," Hawty observed. "Someone at the Society has known this for a long time, right?"

"Since the Society's founding in 1823—well, really, since 1731. How else are we to explain all of the Society's vaunted genealogy that so conveniently detours around this story of mutiny and transformation? We're talking about either very bad scholarship—which I seriously doubt—or a colossal, deliberate lie."

"Think of the money involved," Hawty said, now fully understanding the magnitude of their discovery. "The Society has more promotions than a Target store! What about the hundreds of families who are going to find out they aren't who they think they are? Captain-Director Nowell is going to have some very perturbed folks on his hands."

"And one very curious police detective, if I can arrange it the way I want to. About the money, you don't know the half of it."

"I'm not sure I *want* to know. But tell me this: did the mutinous convicts know that Juslin and Windner were spies? I must have missed that part. You scrolled the thing so fast."

"Apparently not," Nick said. "Juslin and Windner acted like disaffected crewmembers, siding with the convicts. I can see those two calculating that their best chance was to go along with the take-over, betraying the doomed captain and the rest of the crew, who went to their deaths not knowing the truth about them, either. The convicts were probably glad to have the two capable men aboard, to help run the ship."

"Especially during that hurricane," Hawty said.

"It probably didn't take long for them to become the leaders. Tricking the Spanish and then the French must have solidified their position within the group. And they lived out their lives in New Orleans, cloaked in deception: English spies masquerading as mutinous English crewmen posing as French crewmen/colonists. According to these records, they let only the doctor in on their true identity, and one of them continued to report to England well into the Spanish period, forty years later. Long after anyone had ceased to care, the British government stuck with the official story that the *True Faith* had sunk in the hurricane. Eventually, the records of the case fell into the bureaucratic swamp and were lost for two and three-quarters centuries."

"Why didn't any of the convicts try to go back to England?" Hawty asked.

"Some may have, I don't know. But getting caught back in the mother country after transportation meant certain death. If any did make it back, they wouldn't have bragged about it."

"Wonder why the doctor went along with the big fiction," Hawty mused aloud, "if that's what happened?"

"Maybe the two spies threatened him, maybe they'd become friends. My guess is he was a young man with nothing back in England to call him home. It was an exciting time, an exotic place, and this was a once-in-a-lifetime chance for an adventurous soul."

Hawty nodded pensively. "Now we've got a pretty good motive for Detective Bartly."

"Indeed we do, Watson." Nick smiled as Hawty rolled her eyes. "To keep the phony tradition alive, would Nowell be willing to commit murder?"

"Four people have died, and for what?" Hawty said. "A fiction, a fabrication. I wouldn't have believed it without this evidence."

"I'm with you there. This is genealogy turned on its head. Here's an organization supposedly devoted to exploring and celebrating the past, instead obscuring and falsifying it. There could be more unexplained deaths from the roster of Society members through the years."

"Others who couldn't stomach the lies," Hawty added.

"I haven't told you about Gillian's brother; he died in a mysterious accident, too—that's number five. Bluemantle and all of the others must have stumbled across some part of the story, and each victim obviously refused to toe the Society line when warned off."

"How long do you think it will take for this information to get out, officially? How can they stop it now?"

Nick shrugged. "Who knows? The information isn't where it should be. Initially, the historians who run across this *True Faith* material won't know there's an American lineage society based on the voyage of the *Allégorie*; they won't give a damn about genealogy or necessarily see any linkage."

"Genealogy's the batty old aunt in the attic for some of these academics," Hawty said. "We don't get the respect we should."

Nick suppressed a grin at her growing allegiance to their discipline. "Unfortunately, that's how it is. And anybody—historian or genealogist—researching the *Allégorie*, a French ship, would have no obvious reason to go to British naval records, right at the start, would they?"

"We'd all be a lot better off," Hawty said, "if the two disciplines cross-pollinated more often."

Nick told her about a similar case of misplaced records. The British ship *Pelham* was on its way back to England from colonial Virginia, when it was taken by the French privateer *Machant*. The next day, though, the *Pelham* was taken back by the British ship *Blakeny*. But in England, the *Pelham*'s mail and other papers ended up in the archives of the High Court of the Admiralty. It wasn't until 1985 that scholars uncovered the correspondence. The intended recipients of the letters never knew the good or bad news in them, but modern genealogical researchers who looked in this unusual place could plug many an impossible gap.

"Someone had to be first to connect the dots," Hawty said. "I hope all that gets us is a book contract."

Nick shook his head. "Bluemantle was first."

"Uh-huh. And look what it got *him*."

"We'll just have to be more circumspect." Nick crossed his arms in speculation. "A book contract…that has me thinking about our odd little friend and publisher Coldbread. There's a guy who would cheat his own brother for such a discovery. But he's not a murderer—and I speak from first-hand knowledge. Even with motive, means, and opportunity, he couldn't pull the trigger."

"Don't tempt him—he's crazy *enough* trying to solve the mystery of that mythical treasure."

"What stops Coldbread or you or me but doesn't stop a Preston Nowell from stepping over the line, from committing the primeval sin of murder?—if we're right about the shady past of the Society. Is it arrogance taken to the ultimate degree? Or is it something infinitely larger that we all resist, some more effectively than others: the active embrace of evil that exists side by side with good, the violation of the commandment 'Thou shalt have no other gods before Me'? Religion, philosophy, science, and art have all wrestled with the same question for millennia. I guess that's why the police worry about the who and the how of a murder, and we lucky genealogists get to work on the why."

"If your sermon on murder is over, Rabbi Herald, can we get down to brass tacks?"

Nick stood up, stretched, and walked to the windowsill. He poured a cup of coffee. "On this find, Bluemantle and Nelson Plumlaw did the digging, and we, my brilliant and beautiful friend, get to pry open the treasure chest and run our hands through the loot. Want a cup?"

With a few strokes of her arms, Hawty deftly moved her chair next to Nick and pivoted to face him. "No thanks. Must be awful. I made it this morning.... What I want to know is, what's in the safe Gillian told you about? In Nowell's office."

"It must be something that can't be challenged, that ties the Bristol-English half with the New Orleans-French half. I suspect it's some kind of contemporary record of what happened. Something incontrovertibly authentic. Something that holds the full, damaging truth." Nick pointed to the computer monitor, still displaying the information that reached Nelson Plumlaw shortly before he died. "Even this could be a trumped-up story, for reasons of state. Some kind of disinformation planted by the government of that day or this. Let's judge it according to the genealogical standard of proof, Hawty. None of this is original or even primary evidence; we're looking at summaries of reports from individuals who weren't on the scene when the events occurred. Provocative, yes, but not quite clear and convincing. We need more." He tasted the coffee. "Ycchhhhh!"

"Told you," Hawty said, as he headed to the bathroom to pour out the cup. "Why would the Society keep something so incriminating?"

Nick walked restlessly around the office. "I had a great-uncle who took a bullet at Belleau Wood in World War I. Kept it on a chain with his pocket watch his whole life, made sure he was buried with it. We human beings do crazy things like that. We have this urge to hold on to the past, to love it, even if it almost killed us."

Hawty said, "Maybe it's the same urge that gets people interested in genealogy. If we don't know what we were, we can't know what we've become?"

"Good point. I'm going to find out what's in that safe," Nick declared. He threw himself into his unstable desk chair, tilted back abruptly, and propped his feet on his littered desk. "Tonight."

"Nosirree! *We're* going to find out. I've graduated from being the gofer of this place. I want more of the action! Besides, any fool who sits in a wobbly old chair that way might just trip over his own shoelaces and break his neck!"

Chapter 24

After midnight, Gillian's Toyota station wagon—significantly dented at the right front—rolled to a stop, across the street and three houses down from the Society library. Old, muscular live oaks blocked most of the white glare from the streetlights. Big houses set back in well-kept lawns were vague darker silhouettes against the indigo stillness. The air was dense and sluggish, with just a memory of coolness; above, slightly luminescent clouds, heavy with trapped dirty-gray moisture, lumbered across the night sky.

"Gillian, you're with me," Nick said authoritatively. "You know the place better than I do. Hawty, stay on this side of the street, so you can keep the building in sight. If you spot anything I should know about, use your chariot phone to call me on this." He held up a tiny cell phone, which he'd borrowed from his neighbors, the gay shopkeepers; the purple-green-and-gold Mardi Gras motif of the phone flaunted attitude even in the dimness.

"Those colors are definitely you, boss," Hawty said.

"And the glitter, too," Gillian chimed in.

Their teasing cut the tension a bit.

"Let it ring twice, then hang up," Nick instructed. In the twitching glow of a buzzing streetlight, he tried unsuccessfully to make out the number from the phone's display. Gillian flipped the phone open, illuminating the display. "Oh," Nick said humbly and dictated the number for Hawty, who made a note of it.

"What if someone else calls?" Gillian asked.

"I'll take a message," Nick said, annoyed that he hadn't considered that possibility, but not willing to give it much thought now.

He and Gillian unloaded the chariot and held it for Hawty as she skillfully pulled herself out of the back seat.

"This thing gets heavier every time I lift it," Nick said.

"Kedric and I added a few new features. You'll be impressed," Hawty replied.

"Yeah, well, come visit me in the hospital tomorrow after my hernia operation and tell me all about it."

Nick and Gillian crossed the quiet street and climbed the steps to the library porch.

He produced a key.

"I worked my magic on Florita," Nick said apologetically.

"Oh, really?" Her voice dripped jealousy and sarcasm. "You're sure about the alarm code? Only a few people are authorized, and I'm not one of them yet."

"We're about to find out."

Nick unlocked the door and they slipped into the darkened lobby. The keypad beside the door gave a shrill cry, demanding privileged data. After what seemed like years to Nick, he succeeded in punching in the correct numbers. The high-pitched noise stopped.

Gillian glanced at Nick with relief written on her face.

He grinned nervously. "Magic, I told you—even if I'm still an apprentice sorcerer."

They approached the log-in computer terminal at the library door. Nick held back, self-doubt of his ability to get the better of all these microchips creeping in.

"Come on, Nick, you can do it; I know you can." They both understood that they couldn't just march right in. When Florita or a replacement wasn't at the desk to log you in, this door wouldn't open without a valid employee code. "They're a little hung up on security, wouldn't you say?"

"You're not joking....I'm okay," Nick assured her.

"Just concentrate on what Florita showed you—about the log-in procedure, I mean." She winked at him. "She hasn't had a chance to show me how....I don't think she likes me, actually. She must have sensed we have the same taste in men. I'm competition."

Nick decided not to elaborate on how easy it was to get to know Florita. "Well, here goes, we're about to steal second." He finally found the correct screen and, holding his breath, punched in Florita's personal ID again.

"'Access authorized.' Good job!" Gillian said. The door made electro-mechanical noises.

"Hold it a second. I think I can turn on some lights from here, too. Goddamn computers. I hate these things. Now, what did Florita tell me?—"

"This is good enough," Gillian said. "Too risky. We're *breaking in*, remember? We'll just use our flashlights. Let's go."

They entered the main reading room. To Nick it looked even more cavernous than during daylight hours, with infinitely more shadows that made him extremely nervous. This on-the-job training as a cat burglar was for the birds.

He had managed to turn on only the three spotlights above the heroic marble grouping; the frozen captain's sword scintillated in brilliant whiteness, piercing a seemingly solid shaft of light from above. The only other illumination came from the lighted signs over exits and fire extinguishers.

They made for the left spiral staircase and climbed to the second level. Then, following the beams of their flashlights, they ran down the hall, past the solemn busts on pedestals, to Nowell's office door.

"I hope he hasn't changed it," Gillian said, suddenly worried, her hand poised to enter the code. "I'm sure he's figured out who I am by now. I'm taking two weeks off, haven't been here since Daddy's death; but he must have seen my name among the family in the obituary. He wasn't at the funeral, thank God. I might have slapped the bastard and scratched his eyeballs out."

"He doesn't know you know the code," Nick said, reminding himself silently not to cross this vengeful woman. "You aren't supposed to, anyway. So even if he were suspicious of your motives, he had no reason to change the code to his own door. Go for it."

"One-seven-three-one." The green light glowed. "Yes! We're on third, now!" she said, grabbing Nick's arm in glee.

In Nowell's office, Nick shut the massive door behind them.

"It's over here, behind the desk," Gillian said, leading the way quickly to the panel with the Society's emblem carved in relief.

"Gentlemanly sports," Nick said, pausing as his flashlight played along the walls bristling with fencing weapons. There were many rifles and shotguns in glass cases, and wherever space allowed, mounted game stared with unblinking eyes. He guessed that each weapon was a valuable classic of its type.

"What?" Gillian asked impatiently.

"That's what they used to call sports like riding, fencing, hunting, and sailing—whether played by gentlemen or not, it didn't seem to matter. This place looks like the prop room for a Douglas Fairbanks movie."

"Douglas who?"

"Never mind. Before your time."

She moved the anchor on the ship, and the panel opened with a tight click that in the oppressive quiet of the windowless room sounded like a gun being cocked. The red light on the keypad blinked in warning at any unauthorized visitor.

"Go ahead, slugger," Gillian said. "Hit it out of the park." Training her flashlight on the keypad, she moved back to give Nick room.

"Three tries, huh? And then—"

"It just shuts down," she answered. "You know, like an ATM machine or a credit-card terminal when you swipe your card wrong. That's what happened during the day, anyway. But at night…I don't know for sure. Maybe there's an alarm on the fourth wrong try."

Nick took out a piece of paper with three sets of numbers printed on it. "Here goes. 3-6-3-6-4."

The keypad beeped and the word "INCORRECT" crawled across the display. His face burned with nervousness.

"What was that?" Gillian asked.

"The alphanumeric values for 'En Foi.' This keypad is just like the keys on a telephone. See the three letters on each one, two through nine? Now I'll try 'Invincible.'"

"Wow. I didn't consider letters and words in my password tries, just numbers.…Hawty came up with this, didn't she?" Gillian asked, seeing right through Nick's smug explanation.

"Well, uh, yes—but I helped."

"Do you really think that could be it, Nick? Look how long that code is. It's probably something simpler, like Nowell's name or the ship's…in—in Soundex code. That would be just four characters. He wouldn't want to stand here and type ten keys every time he wants to get in the safe."

Nick liked her idea about the Soundex code, an essential genealogical tool for locating surnames in censuses; but it was too late to change the plan now. His mind was putty, operating at a nearly instinctual level. Figuring the Soundex code, normally something he could work out in his head, would take awhile; he didn't carry around the Soundex table in his pocket. *Stick with your plan!*, an ancestral caveman's voice commanded. Speed was of the essence. They would simply have to come back another night if this second attempt and the third failed.

Nick shrugged and started punching in the ten-number string for 'Invincible.' The keypad began beeping even before he finished: "INCORRECT." His forehead was damp from tension.

"I think we may have to call in a pinch-hitter," Gillian said. "I'm going to find a reference book and figure the Soundex for *Allégorie*"

"Wait." Nick took a deep breath and prepared to punch in his last try: the numerical equivalent of "*True Faith.*"

He showed her the numbers and explained the rationale: "Only the members of the Society's inner circle would know this one."

"Three sets of three," Gillian observed analytically. "A bit shorter, relatively easy to remember. And the part about special knowledge does something for me. What the hell, go ahead and give it a try. What's the worst that can happen, we get arrested? Maybe they'll put us in a cell together."

The phone in Nick's pocket warbled twice and then was silent.

"Oh God!" Gillian exclaimed. "Hurry, Nick! That's Hawty warning us. Someone's coming!"

"Yeah," Nick agreed morosely, "Unfortunately, I don't think it was a wrong number. I wouldn't even mind a telemarketer, at this point."

"Hurry!" Gillian insisted.

He began keying in the numbers faster than he wanted to. *Don't make a mistake, pal, and stop shaking while you're at it. That's right, easy does it. This'll be your last try, one way or the other.*

8-7-8-3-3-2-4-8-4.

One long beep, and the green light glowed.

Gillian slammed the safe handle down and pulled the door open. A puff of strange air hit them as it escaped from the dark cubicle of the safe. She grabbed the heavy glittering case that appeared to be the safe's only contents.

"It's...some kind of a book. Big," she grunted, doing her best to arrange the ungainly package on her hip for fleeing. A spiral notebook fell to the floor.

"Gillian, leave that thing here. It's too heavy to carry. We've got to get out of here."

"No!" she countered with indomitable fierceness. "Whatever this is will prove that they knew, prove that they were hiding the truth, that they had a reason to kill anyone who got too close! It's why we came here and I'm not leaving without it!"

Nick didn't argue further. He picked up the spiral notebook; a quick glance at the handwriting told him he now held the memoirs of Woodrow Bluemantle, his murdered old friend. Nick managed to trade loads with Gillian. Then they ran for the door.

"Where do we go?" Gillian asked, her whispered words raspy with fear.

"The other staircase. If it's Nowell, he'll probably come up the one we did. Closest to his office."

They started running down the dark hall. Gillian tripped on a wrinkle in the rug and careened into one of the pedestals. The bust of former Captain-Director Montenay, just missing his flesh-and-blood daughter, crashed to the floor.

Chapter 25

Preston Nowell stood in the tree-sheltered darkness of the walkway. He couldn't remember such a trying period as the last few days had been. He looked up at the massive building before him; a feeling of contentment and certainty flowed through him. His imagination, aided by alcohol, reshaped the indistinct shadowy outlines of gables and eaves and shake-shingle siding into the *Allégorie* itself, riding proudly on the waves, invincible!

A *noble lie*, he thought, worthy of his great efforts.

He put his hand to his forehead; the gash from the horrible episode on the boat now required no more than a small bandage. What a mess this whole sordid spring had been! Even Vietnam had been preferable to this: at least one could attack a definite enemy with weapons of adequate, usually superior strength; one could know the outcome of the battle by counting the bodies lying around.

But this...well, there were a *few* bodies, but in general it was all so incorporeal that he never knew when he was safe, when some sniper was fixing him in the crosshairs. He had begun to feel he would never slay this many-headed Hydra that threatened the Society.

At the moment, though, he felt entitled to the indulgence he had allowed himself tonight. He was pleasantly drunk, just enough to feel the pressure of his anxiety lessened, as if some restricting piece of headgear—a combat helmet, perhaps—had been removed. Maybe, just maybe, things would get back to normal. There had been enough killing. Joscelyn had told him that Gillian wouldn't be a problem anymore; he had found Mrs. Fleam's price, in cash and threats. She would *make* her daughter come live with her, even if kidnapping was the only way. Otherwise, Joscelyn had explained to her, the consequences for her daughter would be dire.

Nowell fumbled with his keys. Strange...the deadbolt seemed to be malfunctioning; apparently he had relocked it instead of unlocked it.

"Okay, Preston," he said, chuckling, "get it together. We're not *that* drunk, now are we? Tired, most assuredly."

All he wanted to do was sit quietly, alone in his office, his captain's cabin now that his boat was gone, surrounded by his toys, cloaked in the imagery of a counterfeit past.

And why shouldn't it be real? he thought. Are we ever sure about the past? We must to a certain degree invent the real past just as we do the falsified past. History, we call it. It is impressionistic, subjective. Who can be sure he is painting an accurate portrait of a lost culture merely from a few pieces of stone? Facts and figures can be used to prop up any argument. The best liar wins.

Now he was in the lobby. He stared at the alarm keypad. Had he already deactivated it? He decided it must be the alcohol, playing tricks with his short-term memory. Perhaps it was the nasty bump to his head. Not to mention that he continued to be extremely preoccupied with the myriad details of the late cluster of dilemmas.

He switched on a lamp at Florita's desk. On a Post-It he wrote: "Flo: Dropped by late. Have handyman call me about the front door situation, tomorrow. Time to replace, update." An organization on the cutting edge of technology certainly needed the latest in front-door security.

As he glanced through some faxes and letters and phone messages in his tray, his mind turned to the events of the evening. The play at Freret University had been fairly well produced, and the dinner afterward at a new restaurant in the Garden District had been superb. He had even enjoyed being with his cousin, who was his usual companion on such social outings, his costume of heterosexuality. Normally such a bitter spinster, she had actually shown some spark of jollity tonight. She'd even told a very funny dirty joke, for heaven's sake!

Nowell suspected nothing until he heard the crash. He was making his way through the lobby at that moment and stopped cold, wondering if he'd actually heard anything at all.

Yes! Of course! He was sure he'd heard something, and he was sure also that the lobby alarm had *not* been on, that the front door had *not* been bolted as it should have been. There was nothing wrong with his memory or his hearing. His enemy was here. That meddling fool, Herald!

Nowell cursed himself for thinking that he could buy him off, that Herald would at least be within reach every day. Joscelyn and D'Hiver had been right. How humiliating it will be to have to admit it—again.

It must be finished. Completely. Now!

He rapidly entered his code into the computer, yanked at the door until it unlatched, and then ran into the main reading room. He ignored the sharp pain in his protesting knee. Peripherally, he noticed the spotlights; but that might have been anybody's oversight, Florita or one of the others being careless in their haste to leave.

The accidental lighting enhanced the drama of the sculpted scene. Stopping involuntarily, he felt a sudden upwelling of emotion. *What beauty, what sacrifice!* Only he could save the Society now. The only truth that mattered was the meaning the myth had for him and other Society members. The *Allégorie* legend was the anchor of their lives.

Where would Herald be? Nowell listened, motionless, still struggling with the alcohol for control of his senses. Perhaps he was wrong after all, and was merely allowing himself to be spooked by paranoia.

He ascended the left spiral staircase with some difficulty, and finally reaching the gallery, stood vigilant in the shadows.

Nothing. His certainty again wavered.

He walked to the hallway leading to his office and switched on the lights. He saw the shattered bust on the floor. Moving closer to examine it, he noted the bunched-up rug. The green light glowed from his office keypad.

He hurried into his office. The panel behind his desk was open, as was the safe door. The silver case with the book was gone! And so were Bluemantle's memoirs!

Preston Nowell loosed a primal, bloodcurdling howl of rage that echoed throughout the building.

Was Herald alone? No. Gillian Vair was probably with him, guiding him with her knowledge—his employees had mentioned seeing Herald and the girl together. Joscelyn and D'Hiver had not counted on such stubbornness from her. The thought that his two elders could make an error in judgment gave him a moment's pale pleasure.

The intruders must still be in the building, trapped up here on the second level. Surprise was on his side. The back service door had a separate, automatic fire-exit alarm, and that wasn't sounding. They would try to get out the front door, maybe at this very moment, as he stood sweating, calculating. He had to catch them. He had to kill them.

His favorite rifle was his Mark V Weatherby .270 Magnum. He went for it, without a second thought. He opened the glass cabinet, removed the gun, shouldered it quickly to refamiliarize himself with the weight and handling. The crisp scope would only be in the way, tonight. As he took a box of cartridges from a drawer, he had flashing recollections of past great hunts in the Swiss Alps, East Africa, and the American West. It was a sweet-shooting, powerful rifle that had brought down the medium-sized trophies magnificently mounted on these very walls—impala, springbok, ibex, wild boar, antelope. He slid back the bolt and efficiently fed three cartridges down into the receiver and magazine; then he chambered a fourth round with a satisfyingly decisive return of the bolt. He reached for extra cartridges from the box, but hesitated. No: a fine marksman should need no more than two shots to do the job.

He ran down the hall, hunting his human prey.

Chapter 26

Hawty had never felt so helpless, so weak, so downright handicapped, damnit, as much as she detested the word! The frustration of everyday existence lived at arm's length was nothing compared with this crisis: her friends were in mortal danger, and there was hardly anything she could do.

Or was there? She had to try.

She rammed the joystick of her chariot forward, crossed the deserted street, bounced violently and painfully over the lip of the driveway Nowell had entered, and raced up the porch handicapped ramp to the front door of the library. At a less dangerous moment she would have complimented the Society on being proactive for the differently abled. But now the safety of her friends was paramount in her mind. Should she call the police? They wouldn't get here in time.

It was up to her.

She could see that the deadbolt was open, but the doorknob's automatic latch bolt wasn't. That Nowell dude had looked a little drunk to her, a bit unsteady on his feet; he must have forgotten to turn the deadbolt once he'd entered. Good thing! She used her

Freret ID on the old-fashioned latch. Slid it in, sawed in and out, up and down. The technique worked perfectly. She wouldn't laugh at Nick and his unorthodox methods ever again, she vowed to herself and God, if only she could save him and Gillian.

At the computer, she quickly figured out how to employ Florita's ID code, which Nick had shared with her as they planned tonight's heist.

She stealthily opened the door to the big reading room; and though she didn't know exactly how she was going to help her friends, she felt capable of miracles.

Chapter 27

"Your office," Gillian said, barely louder than her rapid breaths.

"No. That's the first place he'll look," Nick countered.

They were crouching behind a unit of bookshelves, to the left of the Rare Documents Room, which was sealed for the night behind its forbidding metal doors. This was as far as they had been able to get, when Nowell bounded up the nearer staircase and into the hall leading to his office, and then moments later, out again. Nick remembered that there was an elevator behind them, somewhere in the dark; but it wouldn't do them much good. Too slow, too noisy. They'd never make it.

They heard Nowell walking rapidly. Nick put a finger to his lips. Their lungs demanded oxygen but they tried to breathe as little as possible. Peering between shelves and books, they saw Nowell stride into their slice of vision. He limped noticeably, but nonetheless was a frightening sight, especially with that damn elephant gun or whatever he was carrying, Nick thought. Their vantage point, and the long shadows the features of his face cast, made him seem gigantic, monstrous, deadly. He was surely heading for Nick's office, across the gallery.

A moment later, they heard sounds echoing from the other hallway: keys jangling, a door opening, the flick of a light switch, silence. Then slow footsteps on carpet and bare floor. Watchful steps punctuated by the squeaking of expensive shoe leather.

Nowell was stalking them. He would flush them like quail eventually, Nick realized through the suffocating net of descending fear, even if it took all night. He had the time and the gun. The only chance was to rush him, giving Gillian a slim hope of escape.

Gillian's right earring fell to the floor with a startling clamor. It rocked into silence as they both stared at it. Nick had never been an expert on women's jewelry, but just now he had a marked preference for pierced over clip.

Gillian had reached an unbearable level of terror. She stopped an urge to scream by jamming her chin and mouth into his shoulder.

"Come out, Nick," Nowell said, moving toward the dark study alcove, his jungle training evident in the toe-heel, well-balanced gait he used. "There's no need to make this more difficult than it has to be." His face was completely in shadow. "You've lost. Take it like a man."

A commando in double-breasted pinstripe. Nick made a mental note to laugh about that incongruity another day, if he survived.

"Okay. I have your word you won't shoot?" Nick shouted, pushing Gillian deeper into the darkness. "Keep this, and keep quiet," he whispered, sliding the case holding the massive book to her.

"Yes, you have my word. Come out into the light. Put your hands on top of your head."

Gillian argued with frantic, silent gestures, but Nick ignored her. He left his hiding place as directed, passing out of the deep shadows into the ambient glow from the spotlights shining on the sculpture grouping downstairs. Nowell followed him with the black hole of the barrel. Nick walked rashly toward the Rare Documents Room, farther than he knew he should; he was trying to turn Nowell away from Gillian's hiding place.

"That'll be far enough, Nick," cautioned Nowell, apparently unrattled. "Who else is back there?"

He's too good at this. "No one," said Nick.

"You're not telling me the truth." He listened, turning his head slowly as if he were an owl, fine-tuning his radar-like hearing, listening for forest rodents. He didn't seem fully satisfied, but was in no position to check just now.

"Hey, you should know," Nick said, talking fast, hoping to distract him, to engage his mind. "Aren't you the expert on lies? Lineages and lies? You and your fellow Captain-Directors down through the years. Turned the Society into an industry, made millions, right? Suckered countless people, for generations, people who were simply curious about their family history."

"It isn't the money. Not really...you can't possibly understand."

To Nick he sounded like an overgrown kid, pleading for an adult's absolution, even though he knew he was beyond punishment.

"No, I don't understand why people like you would kill for genealogy," Nick said, "and faked genealogy at that. I've heard of some defensible reasons to take a life: faith, patriotism, revenge, jealousy. But genealogical delusion? Uh-uh, Preston. You're all just plain bonkers, sick. You're not part of some splendid epic battle in which honor is at stake: you're murdering the past, perverting the very essence of genealogy, which is to bring the past to life, to enhance the lives of the living—"

"Stop it!"

"And even though Bluemantle couldn't expose you, there'll be someone next year, and the year after that, and the year after that—"

"Stop it! Shut up! Shut up!"

"The story of the *True Faith*'s further adventures as the *Allégorie* is now public record."

Nick heard the safety click off.

But Nowell did not fire. He ran his shaking left hand over his brow, calming himself.

He turned slightly, so that the light grazed his damp face. Nick saw not remorse or confusion, but a recognition of defeat, the look of a commanding officer, dutiful strategist to the end, who knows his cause is doomed, no matter how long the battle rages. But he would never give up the flag.

The safety clicked on again.

"I'm going to put you in there," Nowell said decisively.

"What, shooting me here too much of a mess, Preston? Worried someone will hear the shots? You need to be careful. You're already on thin ice. You don't want another awkward episode, like Nelson on the boat, huh, or the poor guy who jumped you at the seminar, or Mr. Montenay? In the Rare Documents Room I'll suffocate in the anoxic atmosphere. How very tidy."

"A tragic, unavoidable incident, I'm afraid," Nowell said. "You broke in to steal some of our priceless collection. Your unsavory reputation will make that highly believable. Somehow you gained access to the room, and you were trapped. It'll look like an accident, a lapse in security, a malfunction of a promising prototype for document conservation. The modified atmosphere is pumped out automatically at 6 A.M., but you'll be dead long before then. Safety projections indicate an individual will lapse into coma within a minute."

"Too many coincidences, Preston. My death will be too close to home to get away with. The others—"

"Yes, yes, I killed them! Is that what you want to hear? I killed them, and a few more, or at least I arranged their deaths, as in Hugh Montenay's case. Not something I enjoy admitting. Please believe me. I really didn't know what the job entailed, when I first took it. You see, it seemed so dignified, so civilized, so thoroughly at odds with the madness in which I'd spent the preceding years of my life…Vietnam."

He was silent a moment. Reliving firefights in the jungle? Nick suspected so.

"You mentioned motives," Nowell said, "but you omitted self-defense. Woodrow, Nelson, the others, and now you. All of you threatened the existence of the Society, pushed us too far. I do not kill for pleasure. People, that is. This"—he looked at the rifle as if it were the embodiment of what he was about to do—"is about survival."

"What a nimble dance of reasoning," Nick said.

"Move three steps to your left." Nowell meant business. "And please don't assume that I would not shoot you. You're right that I would prefer a neater way, but I'll most certainly do it."

His hands still atop his head, Nick took three steps to his left. Nowell then moved to the keypad and began punching in a code. The doors folded over each other, and Nick felt the cool, dry air inside the Rare Documents Room hit his neck.

"Everything in there is a lie, isn't it?" Nick said. Nowell almost answered. "Hey, I'm a dead man, anyway, Preston. I'd like to know before the end. Do that for me, at least. A fellow genealogist."

Nowell took a deep breath, scrutinized his situation, and seemed to feel more at ease.

Nick needed more time, time for Nowell to make a mistake.

"I suppose there's no harm," Nowell began. "Not everything is a lie. Where the outside world and actual facts and events have provided convenient dovetails for our history, we have included them. This even enhances our credibility. Whatever does not contradict the gospel of the *Allégorie* is welcome here. And, of course, much of the succeeding genealogical research, in itself, is of a very high quality indeed. It is simply that the assumptions founded upon the story of the *Allégorie* are, shall we say, flawed. We also have filled in a great many lacunae in the historical records of other events. Where we discovered a problem in the seamless continuity between actual events and our special history, we exercised creative genealogy—"

"You faked what you needed," Nick interrupted. "And now others are using your falsified history."

"As you wish. You know, I find it highly hypocritical and ironic," Nowell said, as if he were addressing an assembly of genealogists studying methodology, "that simply because we give people pleasure in their illusions, and allow them to wear a grand costume of scholarship and distinction, we are guilty of committing some kind of crime. How do we differ from the good folks at the neighborhood church, or at Disney, or at the television networks, I would like to know?"

"The good folks at Disney and the networks don't blow up people in real life, and the churches have been out of the crusade business for a few centuries."

"Yes, I see what you mean," said Nowell, like a polite debater conceding a point to an opponent. "I shall always regret that we never got the chance to work together, Nick. You have a sharp imaginative mind and an aggressive empirical sense that would have served the Society well. You're very much like Woodrow Bluemantle at his best, in that sense."

"He smelled something rotten, didn't he?"

"Early on, I confided to Woodrow a minimum of details regarding our special historical situation, and he always *seemed* supportive. I sent him to London to analyze the newly discovered records. We had heard only rumors until then. He reported back to me that there was nothing threatening in the London material. He lied. He didn't deserve to wear our ring. Even in death."

Nick understood Bluemantle now, better than ever before. At first it was probably the pay and perks that had dazzled him; but he was by nature a warrior for truth, and soon he began plotting one final charge against genealogical charlatanism. He must have known of the dangers; still, he was determined to expose the scam.

"I was serious in my offer of the job to you, though of course you took it only to use us." He sighed in what Nick took to be genuine sorrow. "Now, I must have the book. Where is it?"

That's his Achilles heel, my ticket out of here.

"Before I tell you where it is, tell me why it's so important. Satisfy a dying man's last wish. I know at least what Nelson knew. Why hide the rest from me?"

Nowell nodded. "The book contains the ship doctor's daily journal from the voyage of the *True Faith*, or the *Allégorie*, as we refer to it. This young doctor had grown fond of his shipmates, convicts though most of them were. He also knew of the improvised spying mission of the two surviving crewmen; they had told him. For these, and I suppose, other reasons we shall never know, he remained in New Orleans, acquiesced in the scheme, began a family with one of the female convicts from the ship. The ship itself, by the way, was sold to several of the colony's plutocrats, with the proceeds distributed among the First Families. The *Allégorie* group remained very close, blended in with New Orleans society, and grew with the town. Most of them were quite successful, and many of the lines to this day possess power and wealth.

"For thirty-five years this doctor used the same book to chronicle the lives of the passengers and crew and their descendants. Of course, this information is of priceless value to the Society. It is the foundation of our knowledge of these people and times. In a way, what's in there," Nowell said, pointing the rifle to the Rare Documents Room, "is mere stagecraft."

Nick said, "Awkward, to have in the same book what brought the Society into being, and what could destroy it. A risky thing to keep around. The doctor was William Montooth, a.k.a. Guilliame Montenay, wasn't he?"

Nowell looked surprised. "You've done a fine job of getting to the bottom of our little mystery. I should never have underestimated you, Nick. And as for those incriminating yet obscure public records in England which Woodrow failed to inform me accurately about, if you were to survive you would soon hear that a terrorist bomb unfortunately will destroy them. Our organization is quite capable of defending itself. Have I answered all of your questions? Now, where is the book?"

"It's gone. Someone left with it before you got here."

Nowell shook his head. "I am disappointed in you. I thought you were a man of reason. No matter. I'll find it, and I'll find her. After I've taken care of you. Turn around, please."

Nick looked into the dark reading room where he had sat talking to Coldbread the week before. "Air seems just fine in there."

"The reading room retains a normal breathable atmosphere at all times; the reduced temperature and humidity are constant. We use the gases only in the smaller glass-walled enclosure where the material is actually stored. And that is where, tragically, you'll be trapped. Go in."

Nick decided he wasn't going to die like a roach on its back. The time for a brilliant move was now or never—if only he had one.

From below, a noise made Nowell jerk his head a quarter turn. He backed up a few steps to try to see over the balustrade. The noise was moving now, a low rumbling, apparently rising through the floor they were standing on. The noise filled the dark alcove to the left of the Rare Documents Room, and then suddenly stopped.

The elevator! The doors were opening!

Nowell began firing into the darkness the moment he realized it, fearlessly walking directly toward the elevator as if he were taking a Vietcong machine-gun nest. He cocked the bolt expertly after each of the three shots.

The noise was viscerally jarring to Nick. He heard the bullets slam into the metal and wood of the elevator, invisible in the darkness. For a while after that, he couldn't hear much.

"Bullet holes all over the goddamn place!" Nick shouted. "Gunshots in the night! Even in New Orleans, urban warfare gets reported. How you gonna explain that, Preston?!"

Nowell ignored the questions. He glanced down at the spent shell casings, as if wondering who had been so profligate with his bullets.

Nick's head felt full of singing metal. He couldn't be sure he heard Gillian screaming, and elevator doors opening.

Nowell strained to listen, trying to determine the origin of the sounds. Then, something bulky, waist-high, and shiny shot from the darkness at high speed directly at him.

Hawty's chariot—minus Hawty—hit Nowell's bad knee with all the force of fifty pounds traveling ten miles an hour. The pain crumpled him. He bent double, just stopping himself with his gun arm from falling over the wheelchair.

The rifle was flat on the floor below his hand.

Nick sprang at Nowell, managing at the same time to kick the rifle away, toward the hallway, where the busts impassively stared at each other in their marbleized world of deception.

Nowell's combat instincts activated his hands and elbows, though the damaging blow to his knee had worsened his already impaired agility. It was all Nick could do to get in a partially effective left undercut on the bigger man that temporarily bought him some time. Nowell's strong hands closed around his neck. Nick tried the same thing, but Nowell knew what he was doing, and he was winning this strangling contest. In an instant, Nick couldn't breathe.

They grappled, dragging each other toward the railing.

"The knee, the knee!" Gillian cried. "Use your right leg, Nick! Kick him and stomp down on his foot! Can you hear me?!"

Nick caught a fleeting glimpse of the model of the *Allégorie* over Nowell's head, before his vision became obscured, blurred and watery. He felt that he was sinking, plummeting down through blue-green airless water, following a glinting anchor chain that at times seemed to be men and women connected hands to ankles. He sank for miles and miles, and finally, at the bottom, there was Coldbread and the Packenham Five, guarding a huge, humpbacked trunk attached to the end of the chain. Coldbread opened the trunk, waving Nick forward, and inside was...Bluemantle, who said in a torrent of bubbles, *All is not shipshape, Nick, Bristol fashion. Use your right leg, my boy! Kick the son-of-a-bitch in the knee!*

With a last reserve of awareness, Nick savagely kicked Nowell's left knee and came down hard on his opponent's instep. Nowell screamed in pain, and his grip loosened. Then Nick snapped his forehead into Nowell's face—a trick he suddenly remembered from action movies on late-night television.

Nowell staggered sideways, hitting the railing, blood now flowing into his eyes from the gashed bridge of his nose and a split eyebrow. His mangled glasses clattered to the floor.

Stunned only slightly less than Nowell by the head-butt, Nick watched Gillian, as if in slow-motion, dash from the darkness like a long-jumper, and heave with both arms and all of her strength the silver case, which was as big as she from the waist up. In the arc of flight, the flapped case released the journal her ancestor had faithfully kept.

Nowell, blood obscuring his vision, lunged for the book, using his good leg for spring. He latched onto a corner of the heavy volume, and might have regained his balance if the balustrade had held and stopped him.

It didn't.

Gillian at that moment rammed him with Hawty's wheelchair.

He crashed through the railing, the heavy book augmenting his own momentum, carrying him even farther out toward the center of the downstairs reading room.

Nick heard a sickening sound from down there, as of a shovel plunging into gravelly, wet earth. Then something heavy landed on the floor.

Dizzy, gasping for breath, Nick walked to the splintered gap in the railing and looked down.

Nowell, on his back, was impaled upon the stone sword of the captain of the *Allégorie*. The book was at the base of the sculpture. Blood flowed down the alabaster stone and began to pool around it. As life drained from him, his head fell slowly back, the eyes open, gazing one last time at the model of the *Allégorie* on the far wall.

Nick saw two brown hands, then the top of a black-haired head he recognized. It was Hawty, using the backs of the study chairs to work her way clear of the overhanging gallery above her. She was walking, or almost.

"Thank the Lord, you're okay!" she said, looking up at Nick, her anxiousness giving way to joy. She let go of the chair back…and stood unaided. "Where's Gillian?" she asked, sudden worry chasing away her earlier relief.

Gillian, exhausted and crying, joined Nick. He put his arm around the small of her back, as glad as she was to have the support. They both stared in amazement at their savior down below.

"Now I can tell Kedric he's got about all the bugs out of my remote control," Hawty said. She held up the small black box on a lanyard around her neck, pressed a button, and the wheelchair beside Nick and Gillian scooted a few feet backward, like a crawfish making an escape.

"Hawty, you're standing on your own!" Gillian said, through tears.

Nick knew they were tears of just retribution accomplished, and of happiness for Hawty.

"Well, I'll be," Hawty said, looking down. She seemed puzzled, surprised, detached, as if she were observing someone else performing this simple miracle. Then her legs gave way; she fell.

Nick was running for the stairway when Hawty called out, "I'm okay, I'm okay! Don't worry about me. Nothing broken, I'm well padded. Just got so excited, I started congratulating myself and lost my concentration." Then, looking up at the ghastly sight atop the bloody sculpture, she said, "We should call someone, boss."

Nick remembered the cell phone in his pocket. He called 911 and reported Nowell's death.

"I'm sure he's dead, operator. You'd better track down Detective Dave Bartly, Eighth District....That's right, the Vieux Carré station. He's in homicide. Tell him Nick has the truth behind the *Allégorie*....Never mind, just mention my name, Nick Herald....Yeah, I'll be here."

Chapter 28

Frederick Tawpie opened the door of Napoleon House and stepped inside. A seemingly impenetrable mass of bodies confronted him just a foot within the doorway. Two young women behind him asked to get by; they were dressed appropriately for the ninety-degree heat of the late May afternoon outside.

Tawpie put on his most ingratiating grin.

"Oh, but of course, young ladies. It would be my very great pleasure," he cooed, stepping gallantly aside. "Perhaps if we were to meet again inside, you would allow me to buy you both something cool to drink, or…"

The two lovely women looked at each other, exchanged facial pantomime that suggested gagging, and then merged with the dense crowd.

People treated him like an obnoxious tourist, no matter where he was—perhaps a reaction to the cruise leisurewear he favored. Tawpie sighed, ceased holding in his gut, checked his curly orange hair in the mirror within the arches of the nearby bar, drew his fine monogrammed leather portfolio under his left armpit, and waded into the famous old French Quarter bar and restaurant.

He instantly was caught in several eddies of movement. After a twenty-minute involuntary tour of the dining room and the patio, he found himself once again standing before the bar, where he ordered a mineral water, two lemon slices, please. He stood in the few square inches allotted him, contemplating the lucky possessors of the tables in this front room.

He surveyed the pleasantly dilapidated place: flaking plaster walls, tile floor, dark-wood beams, spartan tables and chairs, martial busts of Napoleon, laconic waiters in white shirts and black bow ties and black tux pants. Beethoven's *Eroica* weaved in and out of the crowd noise.

In a back corner, at a small round table by one of the French windows on the Saint Louis Street wall, he spotted Nick, sitting with an extremely attractive blonde young woman.

Tawpie downed his water, uttered an affected sigh of satisfaction to impress those near him who didn't know it was only water, put his glass on the bar, and entered a current that seemed to be flowing toward Nick.

"Ah, Wallace Stevens, I see," Tawpie said, looking down at the worn paperback on Nick's table. "Old habits die hard, eh, Nick?"

"Thinking and feeling, you mean, Frederick? I still do those things, even off the faculty."

Tawpie's chubby torso inflated momentarily with a deep breath, but he didn't respond. Instead, he massaged his fat chin, apparently seeking a new, less confrontational, way to begin.

"Nick, let's be grownup, put the past behind us," he said. "I've been searching for you all day, with the intention of making you an offer. Two offers, as a matter of fact. Do you and the young lady mind if I sit down? I'm absolutely paralyzed with fatigue." Tawpie found a crippled chair nearby, under the pay phone.

"Why not pull up a chair, Frederick," Nick said snidely, "since you already have? This is Gillian. Gillian, meet Professor Frederick Tawpie, head of the English department at Freret."

Gillian turned to Nick. Her lips formed the words, "the Usurper." Nick nodded.

Tawpie was unaware of this silent exchange. Gingerly he tested the chair before putting his substantial bulk upon it. The chair wobbled wildly.

It was clear to Nick that Tawpie—this devious backstabber who'd had a hand in his dismissal and who'd hijacked the English department from his friend, Una Kern, who really deserved to direct it—wasn't here to renew the old bitterness between them. He wanted something, maybe even needed something, and Nick looked forward to the pleasure of turning him down.

"What an ordeal! Oh, this is much better," Tawpie said, a bit uncertainly, noticing now that two of the chair legs were suspect. He placed his portfolio on the table and adjusted his glasses, which had been jostled somewhere along his odyssey. "Well, I've never been here, but an establishment that plays such wonderful music certainly deserves my patronage."

"I'm sure the management will be relieved to hear that," Nick said.

Tawpie had a tendency to cast himself as a gift to lesser mortals.

"Nick, I know we've had our—well, our slight disagreements in the past. But I assure you I have never held any permanent ill-will toward you; nor have I ever sought to make capital of your bad luck."

Nick decided he wouldn't yet call him an egotistical liar. He wanted to hear the rest. Just for fun. "Decent of you, Frederick. Go on."

"I'm sure you're aware that Preston Nowell's death has put us in something of a bind. We—the English department, that is—we had enlisted Mr. Nowell to teach a genealogy course at Opportunity College. Well, to get right to the point, the course is proving so popular it is oversubscribed for the fall semester, and here we are—"

"With your pants down?" Nick sipped his beer as Tawpie continued.

"That vernacular description is as good as any, I suppose. An embarrassing situation, to be sure. It was my intention merely to cancel the damn thing, but some rather influential alumni had already enrolled, and, well, you know that these things can become quite political." Tawpie chuckled, and his double chin jiggled.

"Oh, yes, Frederick, I completely understand."

"Then I had a brainstorm!" Tawpie searched the air above his head and raised his hands in a saint's attitude of awe, acting out his moment of inspiration.

Nick glanced at Gillian and tried to keep from laughing at Tawpie's legendary self-importance.

"Why not call on our old friend and colleague Nick Herald?" Tawpie continued, again oblivious to the silent ridicule. "Renowned genealogical authority in his own right. Something of a popular hero, too, for exposing the dirty dealings at the Society of the *Allégorie*. Who better to replace the perpetrator of the fraud—whom I never fully trusted, incidentally? I've passed the idea by the dean, and she's quite enthusiastic about it, in fact." He cleared his throat, looked down at his fidgeting hands. "You will, of course, officially not be part of the faculty."

"Oh, of course," Nick said, with feigned graciousness.

"It's perhaps a little too soon for that. But who knows what the future holds?" said Tawpie, shrugging amiably, a mere humble department head kneeling before the inscrutable Mover of Things. "I am authorized to say that we'll be quite flexible when it comes to your fee. So, what do you say?"

"No."

"'No'?" Tawpie parroted in his astonishment. Nick could see the man's notorious temper redden his face.

"Now calm down, Frederick. I'm not trying to be difficult. Prior commitments, that's all. Seriously, I *would* consider your offer, otherwise."

"'Prior commitments'?" Tawpie said, seemingly unable to conceive of a world beyond Freret University.

Gillian said, "He's going to England for the Society of the *Allégorie*." Her voice revealed how proud she was of him. "And he'll be editing Dr. Bluemantle's memoirs."

Bluemantle's nearly complete manuscript, it turned out, contained nothing off-color, but much of interest from the professional experiences of a master of the discipline. A few pages of his friend's beautiful longhand were helping Nick flesh out a valedictory final chapter: Woody's last case, the *Allégorie* fraud.

Tawpie sat back, causing his chair to lurch dangerously. "Well—well, congratulations are in order, then. *I* haven't had a sabbatical for years....England," he said, wistfully. "This professional genealogy is rather a good job, it seems. I look forward to reading Dr. Bluemantle's memoirs. I suppose I should start reading the Society's newsletter, as well. I'm a new member, you know? And that brings me to my second offer. A project of a more personal nature."

"Yes?"

"I, too, had an ancestor on that ship, the *Allégorie*, or the *True Faith*, as you now call it. However, I cannot accept the notion that this fellow was a common criminal. No, no. That's simply unimaginable! Surely my ancestor was a political prisoner, a Scotsman who had valiantly fought the English and had chosen life in the New World instead of execution. This much Mr. Nowell had suggested before his untimely demise. You see, I purchased a Level III Ancestral Search from the Society, and there was much work yet to do."

"Level III?" Nick asked. "Then you're out about twenty-five hundred bucks, Frederick."

"He charged me *four thousand!*" Tawpie erupted. "The scoundrel!"

"Don't worry. The Society's no longer in the profit business. I'll get you most of your money back."

"Now, that *is* generous of you!" Tawpie said, a new opinion of Nick forming in his eyes.

"Tawpie, Tawpie...I've heard that name before," said Gillian, as she sipped her white wine.

"Are you familiar with the history of the Society, Gillian?" asked Frederick.

"I should say so! My father was a Captain-Director, and I'm a certified descendant. Plus, I worked at the Society....Oh, now I remember. Tawpie—wasn't he the one who shot a hole in the captain's dinghy? You know, those poor crewmembers set adrift were never seen again."

"Really?" Frederick said, the pallor of dashed pride giving way to blushing shame. "By no means do I doubt your word, young lady, but there seems to be some confusion here. I'm inclined to question any of Mr. Nowell's findings, or any claims put forward as evidence by the previous regime at the Society; perhaps I am not even related to this"—Tawpie closed his eyes and swallowed hard, as if he'd just sucked down a bad oyster—"this transported-convict person. All the more reason for my offer, Nick. I want you to do a thorough genealogical analysis of my family tree to determine the truth." Tawpie grabbed Nick's forearm on the table. "My family's reputation is at stake," he whined, on the verge of tears.

Nick extricated himself from Tawpie's grip. He shook his head in doubt. "Frederick, I've got a lot on my calendar these days. What with picking up the pieces at the Society—"

"Nick's been appointed interim Captain-Director by the Society's trustees," Gillian reported.

"I was just handy, that's all," Nick said humbly.

Joscelyn and D'Hiver had taken poison, like the good descendants of spies that they were. Local and federal cops were combing Society records to unmask the hired assassins who had done the Captain-Directors' dirty work in recent years; the bomb-maker had already been nabbed and charged in Mr. Montenay's murder. Five employees at the library had been dismissed following indictments for fraud; Florita still heated up the lobby. The Society thought it was time for someone from the outside to come in, calm things down, clean things up.

"I had not heard that," Tawpie said, more in control of his emotions now. "But I have been following the story in the press. I *am* impressed, Nick. You are the ideal person for my purposes, then. Please, take the job. At your convenience, of course."

"The Society may not charge anymore, but I do. It'll be expensive, Frederick."

"Cost is no object. Spare no expense. I must know!" said Tawpie, slapping the portfolio with his hand, making the glasses on the table jump. "Forgive me, but this has been weighing on my mind."

"Okay, I'll do it," Nick said.

"Oh, thank you, Nick. Thank you!" Tawpie said effusively. "Allow me to show you what Mr. Nowell had discovered before he died."

Eager to begin explaining the intricate branching of his family tree, Tawpie removed a thick stack of papers from the portfolio.

"Just leave it with me," Nick said, sliding the papers across the table. "I'll be in touch. See you, Frederick."

Dismissed, Tawpie bade an awkward farewell and fought his way to the front door through the crush of hopefuls searching for somewhere to sit.

Gillian released long-suppressed laughter. "What a nerd!" she said, wiping tears of mirth away. "That wasn't the truth I told him. Really, I have no idea who his ancestor was, and I don't care. I just wanted to hassle him; I know how much you dislike him."

"You got *that* right. But, hey, who knows? Frederick used to laugh at genealogy; now he's addicted. That's healthy: studying your family history is one step away from studying your inner self. Maybe he'll learn something that'll make him a better person."

"I doubt it," Gillian said.

"So do I, but people can surprise you. When are you leaving?"

"Soon. A friend's driving me to the airport." She took his hands in hers. "Hawty said you'd probably be at Napoleon House. 'Your branch office,' she calls it. I just wanted to spend a few minutes with you. I don't think I'll ever come back here. Hurts too much."

"For me, New Orleans lets me forget my pain, and I'm not just referring to the favorite local pastimes, either," Nick said, looking at his empty beer mug. "It's more than merely preoccupation with debauchery and booze. It's a philosophy of life, a belief that every sorrow, sin, and joy deserves a ceremony, that yesterdays are never lost. Take this building, for instance. Legend has it that Napoleon was supposed to come here in 1814, but he died on St. Helena before he could escape. New Orleans is a magnet for history's exiles. Their make-believe empires live on, if only at the bottom of an absinthe bottle."

"A fun town for a genealogist, maybe," Gillian said, "but not good for me at the moment."

"Yeah, I understand. So tell me, what's Atlanta like? Never been there."

"Actually, my sister-in-law lives in a quaint little town outside Atlanta; but I say Atlanta because everybody always asks, 'Where's that?' when I mention the town's name. I can heal there, Nick. It's quiet, safe—at least a lot safer than New Orleans. I love her kids so much; they remind me of my brother and me growing up. And her antique shop is adorable. Did I ever tell you I'm really, really interested—"

"Let me guess: you're really, really interested in antiques, huh?"

"I said that about genealogy, too, didn't I? Funny. That wasn't strictly true when I said it, but in a way it is now, even though I wish I'd never heard of that awful ship. As a child, I used to wonder if the universe would be different if I'd said something in a different way, or stepped back through a door, or didn't crunch an ant. I guess it does matter, everything we do. Try to change one little thing in the past, lie about a few events, and look what happens:

people are killing each other right and left. From now on, it's the tomorrows that count for me. You can have all those yesterdays. And I *really, really* mean *that*. Antiques may be part of the past, but they can't hurt me if I don't look any deeper than the varnish."

"Unless you fall out of one," Nick said, jiggling the chair Tawpie had occupied.

They both laughed. "I'll be careful where I sit." She finished her wine and put out her cigarette in the full ashtray. "I feel better about the future, now that I know evil doesn't always win. Who knows, maybe I'll even have kids of my own one day. And stop smoking."

She looked at Nick for a long moment, waiting for his response. He couldn't give her the one he sensed she wanted.

"All I ask is that you get the town right on the birth certificate," he said, finally. "We genealogists are awfully particular about that kind of thing."

"I'll just do that." She patted his tattered volume of Stevens, its title an evocative phrase from one of the poet's greatest works. "Give me a ring if you ever find… *The Palm at the End of the Mind*."

She reached for his face across the small table. They leaned together. She kissed him lightly, sweetly on the lips.

And then she was gone.

After a long time watching the milling crowd, Nick hailed a passing waiter.

"Half a muffuletta. Bag of Zapp's chips, extra spicy. Another Abita Golden—make that two," he said telegraphically.

A slight elevation of eyebrows and a subtle nod from the young man confirmed the order. The waiters were like that at Napoleon House; they didn't get chummy even with longtime customers.

Nick had decided to spend the evening right where he was. No one waited for him at his apartment, a few blocks away. Here, at least he was surrounded by people, strangers though they were. He didn't want to be alone in his exile tonight.

Tilting his chair back against the graffiti-covered wall, he returned to the poetry of Wallace Stevens.

0-595-25899-9

Made in the USA
Lexington, KY
02 April 2011